PRETEND TO BE MY COWBOY

O'SULLIVAN SISTERS (BOOK 1)

SOPHIA QUINN

FLP

ISBN: 978-1-99-115138-4 (Paperback)
ISBN: 978-1-99-115139-1 (Kindle)

Forever Love Publishing Ltd
www.foreverlovepublishing.com
2022 - USA

The man sitting beside Emma on the packed plane was decked out in a fly fishing vest and sunhat—a fact which puzzled her to no end. Was he planning on going straight from the plane to a fishing boat?

She might have asked him, but he never gave her a chance to get a word in edgewise.

She'd come to realize seconds after their flight left Chicago that the man liked to talk, and he did so loudly.

Even worse, he was completely oblivious to the fact that Emma had stuck ear buds in to deter him from aiming that loud mouth in her direction.

Needless to say, it didn't work. And unfortunately for Emma, she was too polite to do anything but nod and smile when he espoused opinions on the state of local politics or rattled off information about the trip he and his buddies had planned.

The buddies in question were sleeping peacefully behind them. How could she not envy them?

By the time they landed, Emma's cheeks ached from the endless closed-mouth smiles she'd had to offer. As far as flights went, this one had not been her favorite. But when their plane taxied to a stop in the perfectly green and expansive valley in the midst of the majestic Rocky Mountains, she forgot all about fly fishermen and their loud opinions.

Her eyes widened with wonder as she took in the snow-capped peaks, enhanced by the vibrant blue sky beyond.

Beautiful. It's like looking at a painting.

She didn't even mind when the pilot came on to say they'd be delayed on the runway for a while. She could look at this view all day.

"So what about you?" Mr. Fishing Vest said.

"Hmm?" She turned her head slightly to address him, but her eyes stayed fixed on the view. She didn't want to be rude, but she couldn't bring herself to tear her gaze away from the peaks in the distance.

"What brings you to Montana?" he asked.

She blinked, her gaze darting to meet his and her lips parting in surprise that after hours of talking, he'd only now thought to ask her that. "Oh, uh…"

"Business trip?" he offered, because apparently his ability to talk knew no bounds. He even answered his own questions now.

"Er, something like that." Close enough. After all, it wasn't *pleasure* that brought her here. Dealing with her deceased father's inheritance wasn't exactly a dream vacation.

He nodded. "Thought so. I know a thing or two about business trips, and you have that look about you."

Her brows arched. "Do I?"

It was hard not to laugh at that one. She was as far from a business woman as you could get.

Before he could expound on what *that look* was meant to be, the flight attendant came over the speaker.

"Sorry folks, we're going to be delayed for a few minutes more. You are now welcome to switch your phones off flight mode and use any electronic devices while you wait, but please remain seated until the captain turns off the seatbelt sign."

Jumping at the chance, Emma reached for her purse and pulled out her phone, using the excuse to call her sister in Chicago. She smiled brightly, hoping it would reach her voice when Lizzy answered.

"You made it?"

"Hello to you too." Emma giggled.

"Hi. So, you've landed?" Worry tinged Lizzy's voice.

Emma cleared her throat, sensing this was not a good time to tease her little sister. "Yes. We landed about two minutes ago."

"How was the flight?"

Emma stole a quick glance at her seatmate who'd only now decided to pull out a magazine about angling.

Where had that been these past few hours?

"Fine," Emma murmured.

Lizzy's sigh was loud through the phone's speaker. "I still don't think you should have gone on your own. Or at all."

Emma turned back to the window, rolling her eyes and pressing her lips together. She didn't want to have this argument again. "I didn't want to do this remotely, and you have a wedding to plan for, remember?"

"I know. Can you believe it's only six weeks away? There's so much to do." Lizzy's tone grew distant for a second and then Emma heard the blender turn on as her sister made a protein smoothie like she did every day after her power walk. "But I still don't like that you're there on your own."

"I'll be fine," Emma said again. The noises in the background on her sister's end were oddly soothing as she rested her forehead against the plastic of the plane's window. Born only one year apart, they'd always been close, but add to that the fact that they'd been roommates in a small Chicago apartment for the past six years, since Lizzy graduated college, and they were basically joined at the hip.

"The internet, telephones, Zoom calls... those were all invented for a reason, you know." Lizzy's dry tone did nothing to sway Emma's decision. It hadn't when they discussed it the first, second, third and fourth time, it wouldn't now.

As much as Emma hated disagreeing with her sister, she was determined to actually see and explore the ranch left to them by a father they barely knew.

"You've never traveled alone before," Lizzy pointed out.

Emma rolled her eyes again, sinking back in her seat as the seat belt sign dinged off and the people around her rushed to their feet. "I might not be a world traveler, but I'm a grown woman who teaches in inner city Chicago. I think I can handle a short trip to a small town in Montana."

Lizzy let out a snort of laughter. "First of all, you're a kindergarten teacher. Let's not pretend you're breaking up knife fights on a daily basis, okay?"

Emma snickered, shifting just in time to dodge Mr. Fishing Vest's giant carry-on as he tugged it out of the overhead.

"Have you met *him* yet?" Lizzy asked.

"The foreman from the ranch?" Emma said. "No, I told you, we just landed. I haven't even gotten off the plane yet."

"You're not going to stay there long, right?" Lizzy's voice held that anxious note that never failed to make Emma's protective older sister radar go into high alert.

"Lizzy, it's going to be okay. We still have plenty of time until your big day. Trust me. None of those last minute details will get missed."

Lizzy let out a long exhale. "You're right. I know you're right. I just need you here, that's all."

Emma winced. The timing really wasn't great. But was there ever a good time to lose one's father?

"Are you sure we can't just sell the ranch from here?" Lizzy asked. She muffled the phone and shouted something.

She'd be talking to their third roommate, Sarah, who'd been living with them for the last four years. The last and best in a long line of roommates who made it possible for the sisters to afford a place in the city.

Emma wasn't exactly rolling in the dough, and neither was Lizzy with her retail job at Nordstrom, but with a third roommate they made it work.

Emma was grateful for the distraction. The rows of passengers before her were filing out of the plane and it was almost time for her to disembark. Definitely not time to rehash this conversation for the millionth time.

She wasn't sure any amount of explaining would make Lizzy understand why she felt like she had to do this in person.

Heck, Emma wasn't sure *she* understood. Frank O'Sullivan might have been their biological father, but he wasn't a dad to them in any way that counted. He hadn't been a part of their lives since he'd divorced their mom when Emma was three.

Since then, he'd sent birthday and Christmas cards every year, and...that was about it. Which was fine by Emma and Lizzy. They already had a dad. Their mom had remarried when Emma was four and their stepdad, Derek, had been the best father any girl could ask for. Frank O'Sullivan had supported the girls financially, but even their mom had stopped having dealings with him decades ago. All requests for money went through a third party. It was all very civil.

Sterile but civil.

Emma had never really minded the fact that she didn't know much about her real father until she'd found out he was gone.

They'd missed his funeral because they hadn't been notified of his death in time, and that was when she realized that she'd never really known him at all...and she never would.

What little Emma knew about their father she could list on one hand, and it mostly came from the stories her mother had shared about the brief, ill-advised marriage in their early twenties, or some business articles she'd found about him online. All of which was summed up in his impersonal obituary as well. He was from Chicago originally, was a successful businessman, and had bought this Montana property as an investment. Apparently over the years he'd turned it into a lucrative working ranch. That was about all she knew. But as for the real man? What he cared about and who he loved?

That was still just as much a mystery now as it had been when she was a child. And that just seemed horribly sad. She still wasn't sure what she hoped to find at the house he'd left to her and her sister, but some part of her needed this closure.

"Lizzy, I've got to go," Emma said, interrupting another muffled conversation her sister was having with Sarah.

She hoped it was about who was going to pick up toilet paper, because their current supply wouldn't last until Emma got back to make her monthly run to Costco.

"Wait, Emma." Lizzy's voice rang with alarm again. "What if you don't have cell reception in Podunk?"

"The town is called Aspire," Emma reminded her patiently as she tucked the phone between her chin and shoulder so she could bend over and snag her own carry-on from beneath the seat in front of her. "And even if I don't have reception there, I'll find some way to keep you updated."

Lizzy sighed. "Fine. But don't get eaten by a bear."

Emma went to say goodbye but Lizzy wasn't done.

"And if you hear banjo music, run."

"Lizzy—"

"Have you seen *The Hills Have Eyes*?" Lizzy continued, clearly enjoying herself now. "Don't take any chances with the locals."

"You are ridiculous." Emma giggled, scooting to take Mr. Fishing Vest's seat as he and his buddies talked so loudly the airplane seemed to vibrate with it. "From what I saw online, Aspire is more like a setting from a Hallmark movie than a horror flick." Her lips curved up at the thought of it. "It'll probably be some quaint little town with friendly, charming people."

"And you say I'm ridiculous," Lizzy said in a rueful tone. "I'm pretty sure all those romance novels have officially ruined your brain."

7

Emma laughed. "I really gotta run. Love you, little sis."

"Love you more," Lizzy shot back.

Emma ended the call just in time to slide into the aisle and follow the group of vest-clad fishermen to the front of the plane.

As if she wasn't already aware that she wasn't in Chicago anymore, the airport clinched it. She followed the rest of the plane passengers to the baggage claim and stopped to gawk at the giant wooden bear hovering threateningly under a sign that read, 'Welcome to Montana.'

She grinned up at it. Welcome, indeed. If this was how they greeted visitors, she'd hate to see what they did when they said farewell.

It wasn't until she grabbed her bag from the carousel and headed toward the airport doors that a wave of nerves hit her square in the chest.

What am I doing here? Is this really how I want to spend a week of my summer vacation? I mean, sure, the mountains are stunning, but...

A second later, a wave of hot air smacked her in the face as she stepped out onto the sidewalk. It was late July and although the air was warm, it had a fresh, inviting essence to it. With this much space around her, she could breathe it in, uninhibited by towering buildings and elevated trains, which for a moment felt claustrophobic compared to this.

She blinked, surprised by the thought. She'd never been bothered by the hustle and bustle of inner-city Chicago before, but this opposing landscape was so vast and open. With a small smile she inhaled, noting how dry the air was. Her blonde hair went into instant static cling mode.

She stood there with her roll-on bag and checked her phone.

No messages. No call.

She glanced around. No foreman.

What exactly was she supposed to do now? Her interactions with the ranch foreman had been brief and to the point. She'd told him what day she was arriving and when, and he'd said he'd pick her up. Or he'd have someone else pick her up?

She nibbled on her bottom lip as she watched passengers around her head toward the parking lot—groups of friends, a talkative young family—and then there was her. Alone.

In Montana.

"Maybe I should have listened to Lizzy," she murmured aloud.

Emma unlocked her phone to find the email exchange. With a frown, she realized she couldn't remember the foreman's name to search for the email thread.

Wonderful.

After a quick, fruitless scroll through her myriad of emails, she dropped her phone into her bag. It was fine. She was fine. She could do this on her own. And besides, it was good practice. She and Lizzy couldn't keep doing everything together once her sister got married and moved in with Connor.

If a ride never showed, she'd just hail a cab. She looked around the parking lot. They did have cabs here, right?

The crowd was dwindling down to only a few remaining stragglers when a dirty blue pickup truck with a horse and cowboy logo painted on the side whipped around the corner and pulled up to the curb.

Emma straightened, a smile already on her face as the driver got out and spotted her. His gaze fixed on her and—

"Oh, Holy Hotness, Batman," she breathed while trying to keep her fixed smile in place.

Two things were clear. He was the hottest cowboy she'd ever seen—in real life or on the big screen—and she'd been spending way too much time with five and six year old children if that was the best phrase she could come up with in the face of this much sexy.

Lizzy would have an epic quip right now. She'd make some sassy comment that didn't involve cartoon characters. But Lizzy was happily going about her routine in Chicago, and Emma was here, face to face with the living embodiment of every cowboy romance she'd ever read. She blinked as if blinded by his good looks.

His dark brown hair fell back and away from his face in a natural wave that his cowboy hat couldn't hide. He had a chiseled jaw, a long, straight nose and deep, dark eyes. And he was taking long, decisive strides in her direction in fitted jeans and a checkered shirt that did nothing to hide the fact that he was built. Not in a muscleman kind of way, but in the rugged, lean, natural way of a man who spent all his time outside, working with his hands.

Emma's mouth went dry as he approached and her smile felt too big. Especially considering his own mouth was set in a firm line, his brows drawn down—not in a scowl, but in a look that said 'serious.'

Come to think of it, everything about this man said *serious*. And when he reached her side and stuck out a hand, even his voice was low and intense. "You Emma O'Sullivan?"

"Yes?" It came out like a question. Like she wasn't sure who she was.

Smooth, Emma. Real smooth.

She swallowed down the ridiculous surge of nervous desire, and her smile widened as she remembered her manners and shook his outstretched hand. "I'm Emma. I'm so sorry but I've forgotten your name."

"Nash," he said, his grip firm. "Nash Donahue."

Nash Donahue. She repeated the name to herself as he let go of her hand and reached for her bag.

There was something comforting in the way he said his name. So serious, and so confident. He didn't seem much older than her, but the way he introduced himself indicated that he knew exactly who he was and where he fitted in the world.

And as she followed him to his truck, determined *not* to check out his butt in those worn jeans, that nervous tension faded.

He was too hot. And if there was one thing she knew about guys at this level of handsome, it was this—they never, ever fell for women like Emma O'Sullivan. So she really had no reason to swoon or make a fool of herself. This was a business trip, and soon enough she'd be safely back home in Chicago and this Nash Donahue would be nothing more than a pleasant memory she could smile about when her romantic heart wanted to conjure up a sweet, unrealistic dream.

2

N ash was never late.

The fact that he'd been late to the airport left him rattled. He was the guy everyone came to for help because he was dependable. And he'd had Miss O'Sullivan's pickup all arranged. One of his ranch hands was supposed to do it. But then Kit's daughter woke up with a cold and only wanted Daddy, JJ got caught up dealing with that fence on the east meadow that kept coming down, and Nash hadn't realized until too late that he was the last man standing.

So yeah, he'd been rattled as he'd driven to the airport, and quite frankly, dreading the task ahead of him. He had nothing against women, but being alone with a strange woman from out of town?

Not exactly his idea of a good time.

He wasn't much of a talker and women, in his experience, expected conversation. Even his little sister badgered him to talk to her on long car rides, and even with her he came up empty after they'd exhausted local gossip and business at the ranch. That was when Casey took over the conversation and regaled him with stories from her college days or, more lately, plans for her upcoming wedding.

"I'm sorry I was late," he said, hauling the suitcase into the backseat.

"No problem." Emma's voice was so cheerful, like she actually meant that.

He turned to find her reaching for the passenger side door of his truck. "Here, allow me." He opened the door and offered Emma a hand to get in.

He might not be any good making small talk with the ladies, but his mama had raised him to treat every woman with respect.

She slipped her hand into his and paused, looking up at the passenger seat before turning back to him with a smile that made her look like an angel and made him feel like he was being blasted by sunlight.

Beautiful.

He swallowed hard. The woman was so dang pretty. He definitely hadn't been expecting that.

He might have been rattled by being late, but that was nothing compared to the effect this woman was having on him right now.

"I have a question." Her voice was so sweet—soft and melodic like she was a Disney princess about to burst into song. And yes, having Casey for a little sister, he'd watched more animated princess flicks than he cared to remember.

"What's that?" he asked.

Her bright blue eyes twinkled, and he noticed a light spray of freckles on her slightly upturned nose. "Is there any way to get into this thing without humiliating myself?"

A shocked laugh slipped out of him. He had not been expecting that.

Her rueful smile as she eyed her sundress and strappy sandals, and then the admittedly high step up into the cab, had him chuckling again.

"Here, I can help—"

"Oh no, I'm just kidding," she said with a wave of her hand. "Mostly."

But Nash was already settling his hands at her waist and lifting, depositing her onto the seat in one quick move that left her blushing and him...

Well, not blushing. He didn't blush.

But he *did* feel a rush of heat that had nothing to do with the glaring summer sun. Once he was behind the wheel he cranked up the air-conditioning.

She shifted in her seat to face him as he drove out of the parking lot.

"How far is it to Aspire?" she asked.

For no reason he could ever explain, he felt like returning her smile. It was just so friendly. And sweet.

"It's an hour to Aspire," he said. "And your father's ranch is about twenty minutes outside of town."

"Will we get to drive through town?"

"Yes, ma'am."

She laughed, and when he turned to her with a brow arched in question, she said, "Sorry, it's just...you called me ma'am."

He scrubbed the back of his neck as he tried to decipher that. Was it lady code for *I'm offended*? Their mother had beaten it into him and his cousins that ladies were addressed as ma'am and men were sir, and old habits were hard to break. "Uh, sorry, I—"

"Oh no," she said. "Don't apologize. It's just that no one's ever called me that before."

"What do they call you?" he asked. He flinched at the stupid question that slipped out. He should never be allowed to talk to women. Particularly beautiful women with bright, cheerful smiles.

But Emma didn't seem to think it was a weird question. "Mainly Emma," she said. "Although my step dad calls me Emmy and my sister, Lizzy, calls me sis. And my students and their parents usually call me Miss Emma."

"You're a teacher?"

She nodded. "Kindergarten." She sighed wistfully as she looked out the window. "It's the best."

He wasn't entirely sure if she was talking about teaching or the view, but he decided it didn't matter.

She turned back to him with an expectant look. "Will you tell me about Aspire?"

"Sure." And then he went blank. What would a pretty lady from a big city want to know about their tiny ranching town? He tapped his fingers on the steering wheel. Probably not the facts and figures surrounding the cattle industry. He glanced over. Right?

Ah heck. He had no idea what she wanted him to say. And this right here was precisely why he hadn't been on a date in over a year. Well, this and the fact that he was pretty sure he knew and had ruled out every woman in Aspire under the age of sixty. Not to mention, he was perfectly content with his life exactly as it was. He got to spend his days working the land, and had plenty of free time to spend with his family and friends.

He glanced over at the woman beside him. So pretty, but no doubt a heap of trouble as well. She'd expect things he didn't know how to give. No, sir. Give him a beer, some

16

buddies, a pool table, and ESPN any night of the week. That was all he needed to be happy. This right here?

He shifted in his seat as he became aware of her. This was like a test.

He never had been much good at tests.

"Would you say it's quaint?" Her sweet, soft voice interrupted his thoughts and he glanced over to see her watching him with an almost-grin. It was the look of someone about to laugh, ready to smile.

It eased the knotted tension in him faster than the sun melted butter.

"Quaint?" he echoed.

She nodded, tucking some of that long blonde hair behind her ear. "Yeah. Would you say it's charming?"

"Uh…" He wasn't nervous anymore, but he was speechless. He also felt like laughing. She wanted to know if Aspire was charming?

She was charming.

He swallowed down the stupid sentiment before it slipped out.

She leaned forward like she couldn't sit still. The way the sunlight hit her through the windows, she fairly glowed with life beside him. Her skin was tanned olive and her sundress showed off a slim, athletic build. She didn't seem to be wearing much makeup, if any, and her loose hair curled at the edges in a way that was natural and carefree.

"I guess what I'm asking is, would you say Aspire is more *Children of the Corn* or *Sweet Home Alabama*?"

He choked on a laugh again. Man, this woman was surprising.

He hadn't known what to expect from Frank O'Sulli-van's daughters in Chicago. Truth be told, Nash and his

17

family hadn't even known Frank *had* daughters in Chicago. Which wasn't all that odd since the man was hardly a chatterbox. His interactions with Nash and the other Donahues had been cut and dry. Business only. If the conversation ever veered into friendly, small-talk, Frank got twitchy and bugged out faster than a spooked stallion. Nash had always thought of him as an impossible mystery to solve.

But since he'd learned of the Chicago girls, Nash supposed some part of him suspected they'd be cold or mercenary or something. Not because they lived in the big city but because in all the years his family had lived next door to Frank's property, he'd never seen them visit.

Emma arched her brows, her eyes dancing with mischievous laughter as she waited for him to respond.

"Truth be told, ma'am, I've never actually seen either of those." He'd just thrown the 'ma'am' in there to watch her smile grow. "But I've heard enough about them to say it's far more like *Sweet Home Alabama*."

Her head fell back against the seat. "I knew it!"

He gave her a sidelong glance. "Why do I feel like there's a story there?"

She rolled her head to the side to look at him. "My sister is a worrywart and she's afraid for my life."

"Ah." To his own surprise he found himself saying, "I'm a little overprotective of my sister too, so I get that."

She agreed with a nod. "It's always been just the two of us, you know? I mean, as far as siblings go. We don't have any cousins so I guess we got really good at taking care of each other."

Just the two of them? He had a hundred questions come up with that casual remark, but he let it slide. She was actually making him enjoy this easy conversation and he wasn't about to destroy it by asking nosy questions about her family.

Besides, she was asking him about his sister a second later, and she listened to his stories about growing up with a girl seven years younger than him with an interest that was flattering. When he told her about Casey's upcoming wedding, she nearly shot out of her seat with excitement.

"My sister's getting married too," she said.

They went back and forth, sharing war stories about being a groomsman and maid of honor for siblings who were as exasperating as they were loveable.

By the time they reached the outskirts of town, Nash realized...he was having fun, which was only mildly alarming. More terrifying was the fact that they'd almost reached the ranch, and he still hadn't learned anything relevant about what she and her sisters planned to do with the ranch now that they owned it.

At some point today, his dad would be grilling him on this topic and he needed to have some sort of answer. He couldn't very well say that he never got a chance to ask because he was having too much fun telling Miss Emma, the kindergarten teacher, about the summer festival in downtown Aspire.

Nope. That would not fly.

His dad wouldn't understand that making this woman light up with another bright smile or let out a peal of laughter had become his new favorite pastime. He didn't even understand this new obsession himself.

It would pass, obviously. It was just attraction. A little crush, perhaps. She'd go back to the city and life would move on. And he'd be left with his well-intentioned family who only had two desires in life—to see him settled and married, preferably with a baby on the way

ASAP, and to buy Frank O'Sullivan's neighboring property.

Well, that second dream was their father's desire. It was his *only* priority at the moment. His father had been waiting years to get his hands on the O'Sullivan spread so they could expand the Donahue empire—his dad's words, not his. And now the time had come. The chance was here.

Assuming, of course, that Frank O'Sullivan's daughters had no interest in the ranch or this town.

"So wait, you have a baseball team?" Emma asked, eyes wide after he'd told her about yet another local tradition at the ballpark.

"It's just a college-level expedition league," he said with a shrug.

"Still, that sounds like so much fun."

He glanced over in surprise because...she was serious. He hadn't realized anyone could get so excited about the local summer festivities that he'd been taking part in, and probably taking for granted, his whole life.

She sank back into her seat with a sigh and turned her attention to the view again. "I don't know how you do it," she said softly.

"Do what?"

She gestured to the green field before her, which was dotted with cattle under the clear blue sky. "I don't know how you drive past this every day and manage to get anything done." She flashed him a smile over her shoulder. "If I lived here I'd probably spend all my time twiddling my thumbs and gawking at the beautiful scenery."

One corner of his mouth hitched up at the image. "I doubt that."

This woman fairly crackled with energy. Not a frantic nervousness, but a life-affirming, peaceful sort of energy.

Like she got up every morning with purpose and went to bed each night knowing she'd done some good in the world.

He found his gaze straying in her direction over and over again with each passing mile. If it wasn't for the fact that wildlife could dart into the road at any moment, he would have been content to sit there and stare at this gorgeous creature who'd just strolled into his life like she belonged there.

Belonged there?

What?

Slow down, buddy.

Get your head on straight.

He tightened his grip on the wheel and stared at the road ahead, determined not to look at her again.

It was a good thing she was only staying in town for a week, because if she lived here…? Well, he might just spend all his time twiddling his thumbs and gawking at *her*.

3

Emma was torn in two. Part of her was anxious to reach her father's house, and another part of her wished this drive could last a lifetime.

She was having fun talking to Nash, that was part of it. Once she'd gotten past the too-hot-to-handle aspect, she found him remarkably easy to talk to. Not to mention, he was a veritable fountain of information about Aspire. The more she learned about the town, the more excited she was to see it with her own eyes.

There was only one topic she hadn't asked Nash about. Her father.

She wasn't sure what was holding her back. Maybe she was afraid of the answers she'd get. Or maybe she just didn't want to admit to this kind, handsome stranger that she barely knew the man. Either way, the closer they got to the house the more she wished they had several more hours to go.

She wasn't ready.

She didn't want to do this on her own. She should have insisted that Lizzy come with her, or even her mom. Heck, it might be weird to show up at her father's house with her step dad, but even that would be preferable to going there alone.

Well... She glanced over at Nash's clean-cut jaw and high cheekbones. Alone with this guy. But she was pretty sure he didn't count as moral support since he was only here as an employee of the ranch.

Ridiculously hot or not, he wasn't her family and he certainly wasn't her boyfriend.

And yet, she wanted nothing more than to stay in this truck with him rather than face whatever legacy her father had left behind. But she couldn't exactly ask Nash to take even more time out of his no doubt busy schedule because she was a chicken who didn't want to face the fact that her father was gone, along with her chance to get to know him.

"You want to stop in town for lunch first?" Nash asked when they reached a junction in the road that would have led them downtown.

Yes! Let's stop for lunch and then a stroll and then maybe dinner and dessert and really just about anything to kill time would do, thanks.

She took a deep breath. "That's all right, thank you, though. I should get this over with."

Get this over with? Nice, Emma. She probably sounded like a heartless witch.

But Nash just flashed her a sympathetic wince.

And just like that, the nice, calming, enjoyable small talk that had so pleasantly distracted her for the majority of their drive came to a grinding halt.

Luckily Nash didn't seem to mind the silence.

When he finally pulled off onto a dirt road that wound through the foothills, Emma was clenching the edge of the seat to keep still. But when the sprawling log cabin came into view, it didn't help.

With a gasp, she pressed her hands and face to the window like an overeager child...or dog. "It's beautiful," she whispered.

"And in good shape, too," Nash said.

Emma sat up straight with a jolt. She hadn't realized he'd heard her. Talking to herself was a bad habit, but she was grateful for it right now because Nash launched into all the facts about the house—when it had been built, the renovations her father had made over the past twenty years, and how he and his family had been taking care of it since Frank left.

"Your family?" She tore her gaze from the giant, multi-level home that overlooked a sweeping valley.

Nash pointed to the far end of the valley. "That ranch over yonder."

Over yonder. Emma made a mental note to tell Lizzy someone had actually used that phrase for real.

"We're so grateful for you and your family's assistance." She turned to smile at Nash and caught a little flinch.

It was over so quickly she wasn't sure if she'd imagined it as he gave her a nod. "It's our pleasure. Neighbors take care of neighbors in these parts."

These parts. It was like living in one of her western romance novels.

Her stomach quivered with amusement, but she kept her laughter in check. He wasn't trying to be funny and she'd rather die than come across as some rude, ignorant city girl.

"That must be nice." And she meant it. Neighbors looking out for each other was a beautiful thing.

Her gaze shifted back to the house.

Her father's home.

"Did he ever live here full-time?" The moment the words slipped out, she wished she could call them back because Nash was squinting at her in confusion.

Probably because she'd just let it slip that she didn't even know where her father had lived for most of his life.

Nope. Nothing weird about that.

"Yeah, he was here full-time for a while after the main house was renovated." He talked slowly, thoughtfully.

She liked that.

And she had a hunch he could tell her a whole lot more about her father, but they slowed to a stop in the curved driveway in front of the house.

Maybe she was moving slower than normal in her hesitation to step inside this large, and totally foreign new home, but Nash beat her to the truck's door and opened it for her.

She unbuckled her seat belt, a swarm of butterflies massacring her insides at the thought of him lifting her down the way he'd lifted her up. Her imagination got the better of her and for a moment she wondered what her life would be like if he took the opportunity to hold her close.

To set her down and then lean in, and…

"Need a hand?" He helped her down, all right. But it was a very perfunctory, almost businesslike lift and drop. Nothing at all like the romantic daydreams she'd just spun in her head.

A wry smile tugged at her lips as she glanced up at him. "Thanks."

What had she thought? One truck ride and he'd be smitten by her charms?

Ha! Hardly.

It wasn't like she was so very repugnant to men, just...the men she found attractive. The only guys who ever asked her out were the kind who looked at her and saw a future she had no interest in sharing.

Maybe it was because she was a teacher, or maybe because she was usually described as 'cute' or 'sweet'— sometimes even adorable—but never hot. Never beautiful.

Definitely not sexy.

So the guys who were attracted all seemed to share one misguided notion about who she was. And that was that— she was their mother. Or the next best thing.

Yes, she liked to bake, and of course she adored children. But did that really mean she wasn't fit for romance?

Was it asking for too much that she meet a guy who looked at her like she was gorgeous? Would it be so bad to feel those wonderfully delicious romantic feelings for a guy who actually liked her back?

"After you." Nash gestured toward the house, and it was only then that she realized she'd been standing there for too long, inhaling his delicious, manly-man scent of leather and grass and soap.

Pushing her shoulders back, she led the way up the steps and through the unlocked door. She stopped inside and held her breath.

Why was she holding her breath? She couldn't say. The empty foyer felt sacred or something. Like she could feel her father's presence if she tried.

She did try, but all she felt was the wind whipping past her into the house.

"The wind picks up something fierce this time of the day," Nash said as he stepped in behind her and shut the door.

"Can I...should I..." She fidgeted with her purse that

she clutched like a blankie. A big part of her wanted to call Lizzy, just to have her voice with her while she went through their father's house. "Can I look around?"

She winced. What a silly question. This was technically her house now. Hers and Lizzy's. But it definitely didn't feel that way. Especially not with the way Nash was making himself at home, slipping off his boots, hanging up his cowboy hat and dropping keys onto a side table with a clatter.

"Of course," Nash said with a small smile. "It's your house. I just live here."

"You do?" She could have kicked herself. Where did she think he lived? The barn?

He gave her another small smile in response. Not much more than an upward tick of one corner of his mouth, but it was enough to soften his features, and—

Oh dear.

Emma looked away with a quick inhale. His features did not need softening. It was bad enough that he was hotter than Hades. She wasn't sure she could handle it if he looked at her with tenderness.

She stepped away from him, hoping to get some distance, but he followed, gesturing toward a door to her right. "I stay in the west wing on the lower level."

She came to a stop at the bottom of a wide, winding staircase that opened to a loft landing which she could tell from here held some killer views of the mountain range to the south.

He pointed upward. "Your father's bedroom and office were up there if you want to check it out."

She nodded but made no move to take a step. Why was this so hard? It shouldn't be. She barely knew the man.

But even as she told herself that, an onslaught of heavy

emotions seemed to pile on top of her. It settled in her chest, and for the life of her she couldn't even make heads or tails of what this was.

Bitterness? Regret? Guilt? Fear?

Maybe all of the above.

Nash moved to her side and lifted his chin toward the stairwell. "Would you like me to take you up there?"

His voice was gentle, his expression kind. And that little show of support gave her the surge of courage she needed to head up the stairs, Nash following just behind.

He filled the heavy silence as they trod up the carpeted steps. "There's another guest area on the lower east side of the house that you can use, if you'd like. Jody, the house-keeper, comes regularly to tidy up the place. She made up a room for you downstairs, but if you'd rather be up here... I know this was where your father and Loretta—"

"Loretta?"She stopped short at the top of the steps.

He joined her on the landing. "Frank's wife."

She stared at him as the words registered. Frank had a wife?

"He remarried?"

Nash nodded, and judging by the way he shuffled in his thick socks and scrubbed the back of his neck, he was just as uncomfortable that he was the one filling her in on this fact as she was.

"I see," she said. Guess the old pops forgot to mention that in his last Christmas card.

Nash cleared his throat and she forced a smile as if that could get rid of these bitter thoughts.

She wasn't bitter. She didn't do bitter. She'd gotten over her father's absence a long time ago. Lizzy too.

She took a deep, calming breath and after a moment her smile actually felt real. "I'm glad he wasn't alone."

Nash nodded, and for a second it looked like he might say something else. When he didn't, she kept moving, poking her head into rooms. There wasn't much to see. The architecture was divine, the furniture lovely...but sparse. And there were no knickknacks, no photos, not even a print on the wall.

"I take it they haven't been living here for a while," she said.

"No," Nash said. "They moved to Bozeman years ago. It's only a couple hours from here but he didn't get back much."

"She must be devastated," Emma murmured.

"Who?"

"Frank's wife." She glanced over at him. "Losing your husband to a car accident. It's just so sudden. She must be heartbroken."

"Uh…" There was that neck scrubbing gesture again as he winced. "Loretta passed away about three years ago."

"Oh." Emma's eyes widened in surprise. "I'm sorry. I didn't know."

His expression was tight, pained. Not for the first time she wondered just how close he'd been to her father and Loretta.

"She got sick," Nash said. "So they eventually moved to the city. Closer to medical care and uh… well, they never came back."

Her chest ached for a man she'd never known. "It must have been too painful for him."

She turned away, heading down the hallway and ducking her head to hide the surge of emotion.

It was ridiculous to be crying over a man she didn't know. Even more idiotic to be this upset about a step-mother she never even knew about.

She took a few deep breaths to calm the tears that threatened to spill, but her hands were shaking when she pushed open a door at the end of the hall.

Her head spun for a second and she caught herself with a hand against the doorframe. This room…

"He had a room for us?" Her voice came out too high and breathless, but the sight of this space with its purple walls, bunk beds and the desk in one corner…it was so clearly meant for daughters. Meant for them.

The air felt too light and she tightened her grip on the door.

"He went to all this trouble," she said with a shake of her head. "And yet he never once invited us out here."

The tears she'd been fighting now stung her eyes and she glanced up to see Nash watching her with concern.

Concern and…confusion.

It wasn't the first time she'd caught him looking at her like that. Like he wasn't sure what to make of her.

"What is it?" she asked.

He rubbed a hand over his mouth, his gaze thoughtful. But before he could speak, her phone rang.

She scrambled for it, hoping it was Lizzy.

It wasn't.

But it was her father's lawyer, the one she was supposed to meet with while she was in town.

After a gregarious welcome that sounded far too cheerful considering the circumstances, they agreed to meet at his office later that afternoon.

When she hung up, she found Nash waiting for her at the top of the stairs. The way he watched her walking toward him made her blush.

He had this intensity that was magnetic and just a little unnerving.

"You set to meet the attorney this afternoon?" he asked.

She nodded. And as she followed him back down the wide staircase, exhaustion settled over her. She supposed being greeted with a one-two punch of surprises could do that to a woman.

Nash glanced over at her, his grin kind of sheepish. "You want to grab a bite to eat before you face the next hurdle?"

She laughed, relieved that he wasn't trying to gloss over how hard this was for her.

It almost made her feel like she could open up to him. Like maybe she had an ally here in Aspire, Montana.

"I'm starving," she admitted.

He walked so close to her when they reached the main floor that his arm brushed against hers, another gentle, subtle show of support. "Well then, luckily for you, your foreman makes a mean omelet."

4

L ord, guide me through this one.
    Nash said a prayer as he followed Emma down the stairs and back out to the truck to fetch her suitcase.

He had no idea what this girl knew about her father— or why she knew so little, for that matter—but it didn't seem like it was his place to tell her.

He was basically a stranger, after all.

"I think I'd be most comfortable staying in the east guest wing," she was saying, her fair hair swishing around her tanned shoulders. "It doesn't feel quite right to invade my father's personal space just yet. You know?"

She glanced over her shoulder at him with those pretty blue eyes and he nearly stumbled the rest of the way down the steps. So genuine. So vulnerable. So kind. Who *was* this woman, and how on earth had she ended up walking into his life?

He nodded at her comment. But no, he had no clue what this woman was going through.

And it wasn't his place to know.

"I'll get it," he said when she started to head for the truck.

She didn't argue, and he busied himself with grabbing her luggage and getting her set up in the east wing guest room. For a man who didn't talk much, he was talking up a storm right now.

"...And you'll find extra towels over there in the linen closet. There's plenty of extra bedding, too, if it gets cold at night." He paused to take a breath, and when he turned to face her, he realized exactly why he was suddenly such a chatty Cathy.

It was guilt, plain and simple. Guilt niggled at his gut and it only grew worse when she gave him that smile of gratitude.

"Thank you, Nash." That soft-spoken gentleness made it a million times worse. "For everything. You've been so gracious and kind to me, and..." She shook her head, sending those loose waves swishing again. "I just don't know how to thank you."

"It's nothing," he muttered.

Her lips parted and it looked like she might protest but he was already walking away, leading her to the kitchen. All the while, his head was swirling with indecision.

Should he have told her about April? He winced at the memory of her tear-filled eyes when she'd seen April's room.

She'd thought that room was for her. For her and her sister in Chicago. So did that mean she didn't know Frank had a daughter with Loretta?

Most likely, since she hadn't even known about Loretta.

Pity and guilt were an unpleasant combination. His heart ached for this woman he hardly knew. No matter

Despite his guilt, and despite this unpleasant jealousy Kit had stirred, he found himself fighting another goofy grin at her enthusiasm. And the fact that she'd aimed that comment at him. Like they'd be the ones going together. He leaned in toward her. "If that's the case, then we'll have to stop there for a late lunch after your appointment today."

Emma clapped her hands together, her smile so wide he could see all her teeth. "I can't wait."

"Me either." He mumbled it under his breath as Emma turned to check something on her phone, but apparently Kit caught it because he was smirking like a devil as he arched his eyebrows at Nash.

Nash shook his head. Now was not the time or place for that conversation.

And besides, there was no conversation to be had. The moment Emma signed off to sell this place, his dad would snatch it up, she would go home, and everyone would be happy.

He cast a sidelong glance in Emma's direction as she typed on her phone.

Yup, everyone would be perfectly happy once she was back in her own world.

Emma glanced up and caught him staring.

"Sorry," she said with a sheepish wince as she tucked the phone back in her purse. "I had to check in with my sister." To Kit, she added, "She worries."

Kit's brows arched. "Your sister?"

Nash could practically see Kit making the connection—he knew April as well as Nash did. She was years younger than them, but everyone knew everyone in Aspire—for better or worse.

Before Kit could mention April's name, Nash cut in.

"We'd better get on the road if we don't want to be late for your appointment."

Emma nodded. "I'm ready."

Nash wondered if Kit could hear the steel in her voice, like she was bracing herself for what was to come next. His heart gave a sharp pang in response.

She was brave, all right. Coming here alone, dealing with her family's business. Not just anyone would step up to the plate like that and face it head-on when she could have just let someone handle it for her.

Kit leaned back, getting ready to stand. "If you're heading into town with Miss Emma here, I'll help JJ finish the fence."

Nash nodded. His men had been working for him long enough that he rarely had to tell them what to do anymore. They saw what needed to be done and made it happen, a fact that made his life as foreman of this property a whole lot easier. "Appreciate that," he said. "But if you need to get back to Chloe—"

"Nah, she's with Aunt Marsha right now and is no doubt being spoiled rotten with too much TV." To Emma, he added a rueful, "Next door neighbor to the rescue yet again. Summer break is challenging with no preschool to keep them occupied, and poor little Chlo-Chlo has a cold too."

"You have a child?" she asked.

Kit held up two fingers. "Twins. Corbin and Chloe. My lovable pigeon pair."

Nash wasn't sure Kit even knew how much his entire demeanor changed when he talked about his children, but he was certain Emma didn't miss it.

Smitten was the only word Nash could think of. And with good reason. Nobody in the world would deny that

Corbin and Chloe were the cutest little preschoolers who'd ever existed.

"How old?" Emma asked. She seemed to forget all about the upcoming appointment as she leaned forward, all eager interest. She peppered Kit with questions once she realized they were about the same age she taught, and next thing Nash knew he was on the outside looking in as his best friend bonded with his newfound crush over the latest Disney movie.

The only question Emma didn't ask, and which Kit didn't offer an explanation for, was what had happened to their mother.

Nash was selfishly grateful. If women didn't fall for Kit's smile, or his looks, or his charming, easy demeanor, they almost certainly got dewy-eyed and soft as molasses when he told the story of how his ex-wife up and left him and the twins when they were only one.

Nash took a glance at the clock over the oven and grunted. "I hate to break up the party, but we'd really better get going if you want to be there on time."

"Oh. Right." Emma pushed her chair back from the counter and started to clear the plates. "Kit, it was such a pleasure meeting you. I hope I get to meet your twins before I leave."

Before I leave. The words were like a splash of cold water and Nash barely heard the rest of Kit and Emma's conversation.

She was leaving. In one week, if he remembered their email exchange correctly.

He glanced over at her as she gathered her belongings to head out. Angelic smile and pretty face withstanding, she had no place here in Aspire—not for the long run.

He couldn't afford to forget that.

41

He shouldn't *want* to forget that.

This intoxicating woman had just caught him off guard, is all. He was smart enough to know that her bright blue eyes and sunshine smiles were an unexpected surprise. All he needed was a good night's sleep and a little logical perspective, then this silly crush would become nothing but a blip in his memory.

5

M r. Billman's office might have been located in the quaintest town Emma had ever seen, but once inside that small stuffy space, it felt like any other lawyer's office anywhere in the world.

The walls were a deep maroon, the furniture heavy, cumbersome oak, and old men stared down at her from portraits on the wall when she entered. The thick carpet muffled her footsteps while Mr. Billman led her to his desk with a warm smile. He hadn't stopped with the small talk since she'd arrived in his lobby a minute ago and she was still ill at ease.

"Please, take a seat." Mr. Billman gestured to the plush chair on the other side of his desk. With his thick black glasses and the silver hair parted down the middle, he reminded her of the guy from those popcorn commercials, Orville Redenbacher.

Nothing about this man was intimidating, so it definitely wasn't his fault that her insides were twisted into knots. She found herself wishing she'd asked Nash to come along for moral support.

But she couldn't have done that, of course. She'd already imposed on the poor man enough as it was. He spent the whole ride into town giving her a lay of the land, and when they drove down Main Street, with its picture-perfect two-story brick buildings and charmingly cheerful signs and storefronts, she'd almost managed to forget why she was here.

For a second, she felt like the heroine in one of those cheesy romance novels her sister always teased her for reading. The kind that were basically Hallmark movies in paperback form.

But that feeling had long since dwindled since Nash had dropped her off at the front door marked Billman & Billman, Esq.

She'd briefly wondered who the second Billman might be. She didn't have a chance to ask, because Mr. Billman wasted no time getting down to business the moment they were seated. "As you know, your father left his property to his daughters…"

She only half listened as he recapped exactly what he'd already told her in their first correspondence.

"Yes, I understand that," she said when he was through. "My sister Lizzy and I have discussed the matter and we would like to sell the property."

"I thought that might be the case," Mr. Billman said with a paternal smile. "We'll just need signatures from all Mr. O'Sullivan's daughters before the property can be put on the market."

"Oh, yes, of course. I'm sorry Lizzy couldn't make it on this trip but I'll arrange for her to sign it remotely and we'll get that back to you as soon as possible."

Mr. Billman stopped fussing with a stack of papers in

front of him, his smile frozen and fading fast. "Er, Miss O'Sullivan—"

"Emma, please," she corrected.

"You do realize you need seven signatures altogether, don't you?"

She blinked. "What do you mean?"

"Emma, this property has been left to *all* your father's children, not just you and Elizabeth."

Emma was hearing things. That was the only explanation.

"*All* his children?" she repeated.

Mr. Billman's smile fell away completely, and her stomach dropped along with it. Dread had her belly churning, and confusion made her head so fuzzy it was hard to speak. "What...uh, what other children?"

His brow furrowed. "You don't know?"

She shook her head, an anxious pit growing in her gut until she was swallowing down a wave of nausea.

Mr. Billman picked up a pen and twisted it between his fingers. "Well, uh, this is awkward."

She leaned forward. This anticipation was killing her. "Mr. Billman, would you please tell me what's going on?"

He cleared his throat. "I thought you were aware, but you and Elizabeth are not Frank O'Sullivan's only children."

Emma's jaw fell open and she gaped at the kindly lawyer. Her heart started to pound erratically as her brain registered his words. "Did he have children with Loretta?"

"One child, yes."

Her mind's eye was filled with images of a purple bedroom with bunk beds and a desk.

Her stomach heaved. She'd assumed it was for her. For Lizzy.

And just like that she remembered Nash's confusion. The way he'd looked like he might protest.

She shut her eyes as humiliation joined the mix of emotions. A near stranger knew her family better than she did. Her father had confided in his foreman and his attorney, but hadn't thought to tell her and Lizzy that they had a sister.

Or...sisters?

Seven signatures, he'd said. Seven. The words cut through her shock. Her brow furrowed and she gave her head a shake to clear it. Resting her hands on the edge of the desk, she gripped the cool wood as if that could ground her and stop the spinning. "So, he had one daughter with Loretta," she said slowly. "But you said we needed *seven* signatures."

"That's correct."

Heat swept through her, making her even more light-headed. She tried to keep impatience out of her voice. "So, who else is there?"

"Well, there's..." He turned his gaze to the stack of papers before him, shuffling through the pages. "Let's see, there's Sierra, you, Elizabeth, Dahlia, Daisy, Rose, and April."

Emma blinked stupidly, completely at a loss for words as Mr. Billman recounted the names and nodded. "Yes, indeed, that makes seven."

"Seven d-daughters?" Her voice came out way too high and tight. Her heart was hammering so loudly she could barely hear herself think.

"Yes," Mr. Billman said. His kindly gaze wasn't without a good deal of pity, which only made her more tense. "And if you want to sell this land, then you are going to need all of them to agree unanimously." He nodded to a separate file. "The will stipulates this very clearly."

"Unanimously?" That word sounded absurdly daunting. "Shouldn't it be majority rules?"

Mr. Billman shook his head. "Frank was very clear. He wanted all of his children to have an option to keep the land and he won't let you sell unless all seven of you want to. If you can't reach a unanimous vote, then the property will continue to be managed by Nash Donahue and the profits each year will be split seven ways."

All of his children. The phrase seemed to hit a snag in her brain and she couldn't move past it.

All of his children. All of them. All *seven* of them.

Mr. Billman's gaze was fixed on her with clear concern.

She took a deep breath. "What kind of profits?"

"The ranch does okay for itself." He shrugged. "It'll be a supplement income."

She rubbed her temples, trying to focus on the logistics rather than the emotions that threatened to drown her. "But split seven ways?"

"With his other investments and the interest running over each year, it'll be enough for each of you to take a luxury vacation every year."

Emma nodded. Money was easy to think about. Facts and figures were almost soothing to focus on in comparison to the bombshell that had just landed in her lap.

A supplemental income. That sounded luxurious in and of itself. Lizzy would be ecstatic at the thought of a five-star vacation. And Emma wouldn't be opposed to supplementing her teaching salary either. She wouldn't spend it on luxury vacations, but if she squirreled the money away, she might be able to afford a place on her own after Lizzy married and moved out.

"And how much is the property worth if we sell?" she asked.

"Uh…" Mr. Billman shuffled more papers around. "I can't give you exact figures, but I'd guesstimate around the ten million mark."

A squeaking sound escaped. "E-excuse me?"

Emma scrambled to work out the math, her brain exploding at the exorbitant figure.

Mr. Billman chuckled. "Exactly. I don't think getting an agreement from your sisters will be a big challenge, Emma. Do you?"

As she continued to stare with wide, unseeing eyes, he put all the paperwork into the folder and held it out to her.

Emma dropped her stare to the folder. "You want *me* to arrange it?"

He nodded with an apologetic shrug. "You're the only daughter to show up, so the responsibility now rests with you, I'm afraid." He pushed the folder in her direction again. "Here are all the details I have, although I'm not sure how up-to-date they are. I tried contacting every sister and managed to reach four of you. And you were the only one willing to come see me."

She found herself staring at the folder in his hands warily, like it might bite. "I don't…I don't know how to do this."

It was a silly thing to say, and it made her sound much younger than her thirty-one years. But for a second, she felt like a child.

A child who'd just been betrayed by her father.

Which was ridiculous. She couldn't be betrayed by a man she barely knew, right?

She took a deep breath and took the folder that was still hovering in mid-air between them. The paperwork couldn't have weighed much but it felt like a million pounds. She eyed it with a shake of her head. "I'm only here for a short time, to see the property and get it ready for sale."

She wasn't even sure why she was protesting. This was her problem now, that was basically what the lawyer was telling her. And yet, some part of her was hoping for a way out of this.

Why did she have to be the one to reach out?

For the first time, she found herself thinking that Lizzy had the right idea. She should've just stayed home and focused on her own life, a relaxing summer vacation—or Lizzy's wedding, at least.

A wave of self-pity hit her hard, not only because she'd drawn the short straw, but because the most exciting plans she had in life were helping to organize her little sister's wedding day.

"I'm sorry, Emma," Mr. Billman said gently. "But you might need to block out a little more time on your calendar, or be prepared to hold onto the land for longer than you thought."

She slumped back in her chair. For a moment she sat there in silence, and Mr. Billman did the same, giving her time to declutter her chaotic thoughts and get her emotions under control.

After a little while, the orderly part of her brain kicked into action. The part of her that had been taking care of Lizzy all these years, the part of her that could organize a wild group of kindergarteners with a single word or a stern look, had her tapping her fingers on the edge of the file.

"Mr. Billman, do you have a pen I could borrow?" She straightened in her seat. "I want to review all this again and take notes so I'm prepared when I talk to my sisters."

6

N ash had never wished so badly to be a fly on the
wall.

He stared up at the stately old brick building that
housed Mr. Billman's office and rocked back on his heels.

Emma had been in there for ages now, and he wished
he had an idea how it was going.

That was bizarre in and of itself. Nash prided himself
on not getting involved in drama—any drama. Certainly
not any of the petty drama that went on in his family, and
definitely not in anyone else's.

But he'd had to stop himself three times now from
following her in there and checking up on her. He hadn't,
though, and he *wouldn't*.

This was Emma's business, not his.

Though his dad wouldn't see it that way.

Patrick Donahue was more invested in the outcome of
the O'Sullivan property than just about anyone.

With a huff of impatience, Nash turned and continued
his pacing down Main Street. He nodded at Anna Swanson, Kit's mother, who was arranging flowers in the store-

front window of the florist shop. She gave him a big wave and a friendly smile. She was retired and only worked there part-time, and Nash wasn't sure he'd seen anyone happier than when Anna was working with flowers.

She and her husband Jonathan were two of the most generous people he'd ever met, volunteering constantly, either at the church or delivering groceries to the elderly. They even took in Kit and the twins when Natalie abandoned them. His best friend still lived with his parents, but the three of them shared the load of the little ones…along with Aunt Marsha, the vibrant elderly woman who Corbin and Chloe adored.

The Swansons were one of those couples that made Aspire the town that it was. Neighbors taking care of neighbors, just like he'd told Emma.

He ducked his head and kept walking. This was why he lived here, and why he'd never had any notions of leaving.

Still didn't, but funny how one afternoon with Emma had left him wondering what else was out there. He took in the familiar cacophony that was Main Street and let out a sigh.

Nope, he was happy here. Aspire might not have a lot to offer a gal who had all the perks of a bustling city like Chicago, but he loved it all the same.

He was so lost in his own thoughts, he nearly missed spotting his Aunt Lisa until he was right in front of her.

"Nash, my boy," she said in that sing-song voice of hers. "I was wondering if you'd ever notice me waving or if you were too busy daydreaming."

"I don't daydream, Aunt Lisa," he said jokingly as he leaned in to give her a hug.

"Oh of course not," she said. She patted his cheek. "I'm sure there's only *very serious* thoughts going on in there."

She'd dropped her voice to sound exceptionally serious and he laughed.

"What are you doing in town?" she asked. "You work so hard on that ranch, I didn't expect to see you until Casey's wedding."

"Yeah, well, even us cowboys need to stock up on groceries now and again," he said. It wasn't a total lie. He'd likely stop for some groceries before heading back. He couldn't exactly offer Emma omelets every meal of the day. But groceries were easier to explain than his real reason for a trip to town.

Not to mention, it wouldn't open him up to a million questions.

His mother wasn't the only Donahue obsessed with seeing him married, although his Aunt Lisa wasn't nearly as vocal about it as some of the others. Namely his mother, but also his Aunt Angela. All three women had married Donahue men. Nash's father was the eldest, followed by Uncle Mace. He'd married Aunt Lisa before Nash was born, and they operated the largest hardware store in the area just outside of town. The couple ran it together and supplied every rancher in the valley.

Then there was Uncle Hansen and Aunt Angela, who ran a boutique motel here in town, because Angela had always wanted to own one.

Between the three brothers, their wives, and their assorted children and grandchildren, the Donahues were the backbone of this town. They had a legacy here. A purpose. And Nash was proud to carry on that tradition.

"You know," his aunt Lisa said slowly as he took one of

her bags from the bakery and walked her to her car. "Speaking of Casey's wedding…"

He shot her a rueful look. "Were we speaking of Casey's wedding? I thought we were talking about groceries."

She laughed. "Fair enough. But if your mother asks, be sure to tell her I tried."

Nash shook his head with a snicker. His mother had enlisted every female in town to try and find out who he was bringing as his date to his sister's wedding. Those who weren't attempting to pry were trying to play matchmaker.

He grimaced at the memory of Janna Elliot's not-so-subtle flirting the other night when he'd gone down to the local pub with JJ and Kit.

Those who weren't trying to pry or play matchmaker were attempting to get invited themselves.

Not that Nash was all that irresistible. He supposed he was attractive enough, but he had none of Kit or JJ's charm or wit. He wasn't half as good looking as either. But there was some pull that came with the Donahue name. They had money, property, and power within the community, which seemed to be a draw for some people, though it likely meant nothing to a city girl from Chicago.

He waved Lisa off and turned back to stalk the lawyer's building some more, but ran into Casey and her fiancé, Ryan, walking out of Mama's Kitchen.

"There's my big bro," Casey shouted out.

She was beaming and waving wildly in her nurse's scrubs, her dark hair pulled back in a low ponytail. She gave him a quick hug and then Ryan, her fiancé who she'd met in college and who now worked as a pharmacist, shook his hand with a warm smile. "What are you doing in town?"

Nash told them the same half-truth he'd told his aunt. "What about you two? Aren't you supposed to be working?"

Casey nudged his arm playfully. "They do let us out for lunch breaks, you know." She gave her fiancé a dreamy smile. "I wasn't about to pass up the chance to have a romantic lunch with my man."

"At Mama's Kitchen," Nash teased with a wink.

She laughed and wrapped her arm around Ryan's waist. "Anywhere's romantic if you're with the right person."

Ryan kissed her forehead, looking like he'd just won first prize at the county fair.

Nash was happy for his little sister, he really was. But he wouldn't be sad to see the day when they grew out of this honeymoon phase. He imagined he'd have to wait until the actual honeymoon came and went, at the very least.

Until then he was stuck with two dopey lovebirds who couldn't go more than two seconds without fawning all over each other.

"So?" Casey asked when she turned to face him again. Gone was the sappy smile and in its place was wide-eyed expectation.

"So...what?"

She smacked his arm. "Who are you bringing as your date?"

His head fell back and Ryan chuckled at his exasperated groan. "Not you too, Casey."

"Hey, I'm just trying to get Mom off my back. She can't even focus on the important stuff because she's so invested in you and who you're going to bring to my wedding. You're running out of days to ask someone, you know?"

Nash looked to the ground, scratching the back of his neck and avoiding eye-contact.

Casey huffed. "I think she believes you're going to get so caught up in the romance of it all that you'll drop to one knee and propose to the lucky lady right then and there."

He shook his head. "Not likely."

"I know. But Mama's got a bee in her bonnet over this whole thing. You know how she gets."

Boy, did he. The Donahue children knew better than anybody how stubborn their mother could be.

"If you don't hurry up and tell her who you're bringing, she'll set you up with someone you don't want to take. It can't be that hard, Nash. Why don't you just ask Susie or Anna-Mae? They're both sweethearts."

"Stop trying to set me up with your friends and let me be." He spotted Emma coming out of the building across the street and snatched the chance to escape. "I gotta run," he said. "Ranch business calls."

Casey started to ask questions but he was already halfway across the street. And he almost stopped right in the center of Main Street traffic when he caught sight of Emma's face.

She was too pale. Shell-shocked.

Aw heck.

He picked up his pace but she didn't seem to notice him until he reached her side.

"Hey," he said. "You okay?"

She stared at him for a full second and then she visibly swallowed. "Yeah. Of course."

He wasn't sure who she was trying to convince, but she certainly wasn't fooling him.

Taking her by the elbow he led her toward his truck. "Let's get you home, huh?"

"Home," she repeated softly. The sarcastic little chuckle that followed sounded so off, so...*wrong* coming from her that it made his heart twist and turn in his chest.

He got her into the truck's cab and made sure she was buckled before heading out of town.

He didn't ask if she still wanted a late lunch at Mama's Kitchen. The answer was written all over her face.

He shouldn't care. That's what he told himself. He shouldn't be so worried about a woman he'd just met. But the longer the silence grew, the more his insides felt like they were caught in a vise.

When they passed the town's limit and got onto the long road that led to the ranch, he glanced at her. "Do you want to talk about it?"

For a second he thought she might not answer.

Then, as if it was ripped from deep inside her, she blurted out, "Seven!"

He gave a start. "What does—"

"Seven daughters," she said, turning to him with wide eyes and flushed cheeks.

He stared at her and then the road in front of him as he tried to make sense of that. "Wait, you mean...Frank had *seven* daughters?"

She didn't answer at first. Her chest heaved as she stared out the window, shaking her head like a malfunctioning robot. And then, all of a sudden, an unexpected tirade exploded out of her.

"All those Christmas and birthday cards! Not once did he say anything! Would it really have been too much to write 'By the way, you have a sister. Oh and another one's just been born and I'm sorry, but I forgot to mention the one I had before I even met your mother.' No, he just shoved some money in a card with a generic *best wishes* and I've been left clueless all this time!" Her delicate hand flew into the air before slapping back onto her thigh. "I mean, wow, *Dad*, good job! Way to spread your seed! How many women has the man been with? He just... walks the earth, leaving a trail of children in his wake! I mean, seven!" She sucked in a breath, then huffed it out again.

Nash didn't dare interrupt her. She was clearly worked up, and although he usually got as far from angry women as he could, the sight of Emma so hurt and unhappy was nearly his undoing.

His fingers itched with the urge to pull the truck over so he could tug her into his arms and hold her tight. His chest ached to wrap her up in a hug and let her cry it out on his shoulder.

But she wasn't crying. Not yet, at least.

Right now she was too angry, and spouting off about things like tracking them down and getting signatures.

"I don't even know how I'm supposed to do this. It's all just been dumped in my lap. I thought I was here for one week to see where my father used to live, sign some paperwork and then I could go back home and get on with my life. But now I find out I have five sisters I didn't even know about and I need every one of them to agree to sell the ranch!" Her voice hitched, stealing the ferocity from her words. "I'm not cut out for this. All I want right now is to go back to my apartment in Chicago and pretend like none of this was happening." She blinked, a wet sheen coating her eyes when she looked at him. "But I can't do that, can I?"

The question was rhetorical, at least he hoped it was.

Licking his bottom lip, he kept his eyes on the road ahead.

They'd just reached the turn off for the property when she turned fully in her seat to face him.

"Did you know?" Her eyes were vibrant, shining with pain and frustration. "Did you know about them?" she asked again, quieter this time, but with no less intensity.

He swallowed. He'd do anything not to hurt this woman, but he couldn't lie. "I knew about April."

A flash of hurt. There and gone in a moment, but he could have sworn he felt it like a dagger to his heart.

"April," she repeated, her brow furrowing. "That was his daughter with Loretta."

He nodded.

"His youngest," she added.

Youngest of seven. The thought was still jarring. He hadn't known Frank well—he wasn't sure anyone in Aspire ever had—but the fact that he had so many children was even a shock to him.

"I didn't know about the others," he said.

She nodded, her composure coming back as she murmured, "Tell me about April."

"To be honest, I don't know much. She was a lot younger than me, so we didn't hang out in the same circles. I think my cousin, Boone, went to school with her for a while."

Emma nodded, threading her fingers together and squeezing until her knuckles turned white.

"Frank and his family liked to keep to themselves. They didn't join many town functions and I don't know if I ever saw them at a festival. In saying that, I think April used to come with her friends sometimes. I'd occasionally see her out riding. You know, just in the distance. But on the whole, they were a very private family. And then they moved to Bozeman when Loretta got sick. I never saw April again."

Emma was quiet for a long moment when he was done. It wasn't until he parked in front of the house that she spoke. "So she lost both of her parents in three years."

He looked over to find her lower lip quivering.

"Poor thing." Her voice came out low and unstable.

His heart just about burst. Here she'd just been dealt the shock of a lifetime and she was crying over someone else's loss.

He got out and went around to her side to help her down. She was quiet. Too quiet.

He might have only known her for half a day but he could sense the small, tight smile she was attempting was for his benefit…

"You've had quite a day," he said as they walked inside. "Do you want to draw a bath, or maybe watch some TV—"

"I'm actually really tired," she said. "I should probably just lie down for a while. And then I need to talk to my sister." Her voice trailed off and she shot him a vulnerable frown. "My sister Lizzy. I guess I have to clarify that now."

He attempted a gentle smile, wishing it was enough to make her feel better, but he doubted it. "Let me know if I can get you anything."

"Thanks, Nash." She started to walk toward her room, but stopped and turned back. "I'm sorry I raised my voice back there. I don't normally get worked up and I definitely didn't mean to lay it all on you like that."

"It's fine," he said.

Truthfully, he felt honored that she'd opened up to him.

But he couldn't exactly tell her that, mainly because it didn't make any sense.

He didn't do drama. He wasn't supposed to be invested in this woman or her life.

All that mattered was the fate of the ranch...right?

"Get some rest," he said, his voice far more gruff than he'd intended.

She nodded and flashed him one last smile that he knew he'd be replaying for the rest of the day. So much for a good night's sleep and logical perspective. He doubted either were on the near horizon.

With a deep breath he headed for the door. What he needed now was to get to work. Get his hands dirty, work up a sweat, and then lose himself to some beers and a game of pool with his buddies.

That was normal. And what he needed right now was normal.

But will normal ever be possible with Miss Emma O'Sullivan living under the same roof?

He shook his head, feeling his resolve to get over this silly crush crumbling right in front of him.

7

E mma's phone sat beside her on the king-sized bed in the guest room. Lizzy had gone quiet on her end, and probably for the best.

They both needed to think. To process.

Emma had tried her best to lie down and rest, like she'd told Nash she was going to, but once alone in her room, her mind had started racing again. The silence after she heard Nash leave the house was unbearable.

And so she'd called Lizzy. It was the call she was dreading least, so best to get it over with, right?

Lizzy's response had been stunned silence followed by a million questions, and now this. A heavy quiet as Lizzy no doubt battled the same jumble of emotions she'd experienced in Mr. Billman's office.

Emma leaned back against the pillows, not exactly relieved now that she'd told Lizzy, but...deflated. Exhausted.

And no closer to knowing what she was supposed to do next. So instead, she studied the room around her, like her father might have left some clues behind in his home.

Some hint as to why he'd kept his secrets, why he hadn't let them know they had far more family than they realized.

One thing was clear. There were no clues to be found in this guest room. It felt more like a hotel room. Clean but sterile. No personal touches. Nothing to make it feel like a home.

Because it wasn't a home. Not her home, at least.

Any connection she'd thought she might have with Frank O'Sullivan because of their shared genetics had been a figment of her imagination. He hadn't loved her and Lizzy from afar, as she'd always hoped. He'd been busy raising another daughter and ignoring four others.

Her head fell back against the wall with a thud.

"Well…" Lizzy sighed. "While this was definitely not the way we'd expected things to go down, it doesn't really change much, does it?"

Emma eyed her phone in disbelief. "Lizzy, we have five other sisters now. That changes everything."

"I know, I know," Lizzy said quickly, and Emma could practically see her sister's picture-perfect features setting into that all-business look she got when she wasn't having other people's drama.

Which was always kind of funny to Emma because Lizzy had no problem embracing her own drama. But clearly right now Lizzy didn't feel like getting dragged into the emotional quagmire that was five new sisters.

Emma couldn't blame her. She wasn't sure what to make of it yet, either.

"I'm just saying that when it comes to whether or not we sell the ranch, you and I are still on the same page, right?"

Emma nodded, even though Lizzy couldn't see her.

"Yeah." She agreed, but felt this weird tug in her chest, so repeated herself for good measure. "Yeah, of course."

"I mean, we have to sell," Lizzy continued. "We don't know anything about running a ranch, and that's a huge chunk of money we'd be getting."

Emma nodded again. That was what she'd been telling herself too.

It had always been the plan, ever since they'd found out about the inheritance. Adding new, unknown, anonymous sisters to the mix didn't change that.

She sat forward, gazing out the large, open window on the far side of the room. Through it she could see the sweeping green land and the blue sky, getting ready to change its colors as sunset approached. A warm breeze blew the scent of wood and wild flowers into the room.

"It's not like you really need the money, though, right?" Emma brushed her finger over her lower lip, still staring at the idyllic picture through her window. "Connor has plenty, doesn't he?"

It was a rhetorical question. Lizzy's fiancé was loaded, and everyone knew it.

Lizzy's laughter on the far end made Emma smile. It sounded so girlish, like they were high school teens swooning over the hottest guys in school. "I know how to pick 'em, right?"

Emma shook her head with a huff of laughter. "I'd say Connor is the one who lucked out by finding you."

"Aww." Her sister's teasing tone lightened the air in Emma's room even more. "But you have to say that. You're my sister."

Emma shrugged. She'd meant what she'd said. Truthfully, she didn't know Connor all that well. Not as well as she'd like, at least. Not for lack of trying, of course. It seemed she and Lizzy were forever trying to match up calendars for her to spend more time with him, but Connor was a busy ad executive, and while he was rich in wealth, he didn't have such luxury with his time.

He seemed nice enough, though, and he made Lizzy happy. That was all that mattered.

A twinge of something unpleasant and toxic had Emma shifting restlessly.

She moved to the edge of the bed, coming to stand as Lizzy chatted away for a few minutes about the latest wedding plans.

It wasn't that she was jealous of Lizzy. Well, she was. But not like that. Mostly she was happy that her sister had found love. And if she was just a little sad for herself because she was thirty-one and still a million miles away from her dream life of a loud, chaotic, child-filled home with a loving, kind man...well, that wasn't Lizzy's fault.

And besides, it wasn't like she wanted what Lizzy had. Connor sounded great, and he was clearly Lizzy's ideal, but he was the opposite of what Emma wished for. He was older, and while he'd been married before, he'd never had kids and didn't seem to want any.

Since kids and a family of her own was all Emma had ever dreamed of, she definitely wasn't envious of what Lizzy had.

She just wished she could find her own version of that happiness.

Lizzy's chatter about the amazingness that was Connor, and how her wedding was going to be the best Chicago has ever seen, ended with a sappy sigh. "I wish I could just fast forward until my wedding day."

Emma smiled as she leaned against the window frame

and looked out. The sight was more soothing than any hot bath or distracting TV show could ever hope to be.

"It'll be here soon enough," she reminded her sister. "And if it was any sooner you'd be freaking out about how much there was left to do."

"You're right, you're right," Lizzy said. "Speaking of, Mom's going with me to the next fitting." She paused. "I love our mother more than anything, but you know she's gonna go behind my back and try to have the seamstress raise the neckline by three inches."

Emma burst out laughing, picturing Lizzy's dress and the plunging neckline. It was a stunning design, but their Mom looked about ready to faint when she first saw it.

"Wow, Lizzy, honey. Is that maybe just a little... revealing?" Her voice had squeaked and Emma had covered her mouth to muffle the laughter.

"Mother! Please! It's not 1901. This dress is the latest fashion, inspired by a Gucci design."

Lizzy laughed as Emma recalled the conversation. "Honestly. You'd think I was trying to walk down the aisle in my birthday suit the way she was going on."

"Well, the good news is, you can redo whatever the seamstress does...and probably do a better job of it," Emma assured her. "You did design the dress yourself."

"I am pretty amazing with my ideas and my sewing machine." She giggled at her own brag, but then her voice became serious. They were talking fashion after all and, according to Lizzy, this was no laughing matter. "Sometimes I wonder if I should have just made the dress myself, but Yolanda is the best seamstress in Chicago and this wedding dress is the most important thing I will ever wear. It needs that professional touch."

Lizzy was adorable.

Emma tipped her head to the side and smiled. "Oh, sis, I miss you already."

She sighed. "I'm so sorry you're going through this alone. I had no idea the lawyer would have such… unexpected news."

Emma stayed quiet. Her automatic response was to say 'it's fine' but right now they'd both know it was a lie.

Nothing about this situation was fine.

"When you get home, I'll be waiting at the airport to give you the fiercest hug you've ever gotten," Lizzy said.

Emma's eyes teared up. Again. She gave her head a shake of annoyance. She'd never been a big crier, and she almost never lost her temper. The memory of her outburst in the truck made her wince.

"You are still planning on coming back in six days, right?" Lizzy's voice was wary. "You're not going to let this whole sister search change your plans, are you?"

Emma's gaze caught on a deer in the distance and her lips curved up in a small, rueful smile. What her darling sister meant, of course, was would this search for the other O'Sullivan daughters change Lizzy's plans.

Not that Emma could blame her. Planning a wedding was stressful, and without her far-more-organized maid of honor, it was no surprise Lizzy was in a panic at the thought of her getting delayed.

She opened her mouth to reassure her sister that she'd still be home on time, but hesitated.

"I mean, you can make calls from Chicago, right?" Lizzy persisted. "You don't have to be there to do it."

Emma nodded, but Lizzy couldn't see her and she couldn't quite bring herself to make any promises aloud.

She wasn't sure what other secrets this sister search would reveal, or what new surprises would come her way.

The thought should have added to her tension, but the view was working some sort of magic on her heart. The way the land seemed to stretch on forever, the way the sun setting in the west kept subtly changing the colors of the sky and the landscape. The wildlife that moved so freely.

"Em?" Lizzy prompted. Anxiety was clear in her voice and Emma felt another stab of guilt. Her sister needed her.

The newfound family she'd never known now needed her too, though they might not know it.

Her gaze moved to the right where a faded red barn was silhouetted by the setting sunlight. Nash was in the doorway, leading a horse by the reins. The sight was so perfect. He looked so natural in this environment, like he fit. Like he belonged.

Her heart gave a sharp tug of yearning at the thought. What must it be like to belong to the land?

She could only imagine.

"Emma, please tell me you'll be back when you planned," Lizzy pleaded.

Emma sighed, jarred into the moment by her sister's voice. She couldn't just ignore the laundry list of responsibilities that filled her plate.

"You know I'll..." *Try.* That was what she wanted to say, but there was no way Lizzy would let that fly, so instead she settled for what she hoped would be the truth. "You know I will."

8

The sun was brutal the next morning. Of course, it didn't help that Nash had stayed up too late playing pool with the guys, or that even after a few beers and some distraction from his friends, he'd still tossed and turned with thoughts of Emma's tear-filled eyes.

"You look like moose scat," JJ said when he joined him in the stables.

Nash gave a grunt that made JJ laugh.

"Did you go into town after you left us last night, or what?" The ranch hand scratched at his scruffy beard, his dark brown hair pulled back in a low ponytail. The ladies seemed to find him appealing, but like with Kit...it certainly wasn't for the effort he put into his appearance.

"Not in the mood to talk, huh?" JJ said.

Nash just grunted again. He wasn't in the mood for jokes or small talk. There was work to be done, and he meant to do it....without chatter.

JJ laughed again at his silence. Like Kit, JJ was quick to humor. Not much fazed the guy. What was more, he was dependable and a hard worker.

His full name was Jesse Jamieson and he was a few years younger than Nash and Kit, and that was just about all Nash knew about the guy. With some prying over drinks a few years back, they'd learned that he'd been married briefly—a topic he seemed keen to drop immediately—and that he'd worked in the Dakotas for a few years before finding his way to Frank O'Sullivan's ranch.

He'd become a good friend, even if he didn't talk about himself much. And right now, he seemed to respect the fact that Nash wasn't in the mood to talk about himself either.

Instead, Nash went back to work, and JJ did the same, saddling his horse while murmuring something to it that Nash couldn't hear.

The man was born to be a cowboy, it seemed. It fit his personality to a tee—no-frills, taking life as it comes, and with a talent for working with his hands.

Over the years, Nash had never once heard JJ complain. Not about anything.

When JJ finished his routine, he turned to Nash, who was still scowling. He'd woken up in a foul mood, and it wasn't likely to go anywhere anytime soon.

Definitely not until he figured out how he could help Emma.

"Aw, come on, man. Snap out of it. You still bummed because Cody won your money?" he joked.

Nash gave a grudging huff of laughter. Cody was the third ranch hand and hardly ever won a game of pool. "That was a fluke. It won't happen again."

JJ pointed a finger at him accusingly, though his eyes were filled with laughter at Nash's expense. "No, Nash, that was you being distracted. Cody took advantage of the fact that you were barely with us even though you were in the same room."

Nash turned away, avoiding more conversation by putting away some supplies. He couldn't deny it. He'd hung out with JJ and Kit's brother, Cody, for hours last night at the cowboys' bunkhouse, where they stayed most of the year.

The bunkhouse had a small lodge of its own for the guys to relax after a hard day's work, and it was where they tended to gather in the evenings when they weren't up for making the drive into town.

He'd thought it would help last night, but no amount of jokes or trash talking could stop his thoughts from wandering back to Emma.

He'd sent her a text around dinnertime asking if she wanted to go out for something to eat, but she'd said she wanted to stay in and that she'd help herself to the kitchen if she got hungry.

So, fine. Good.

He sent a bale of hay flying when he shoved the stack too hard to move it out of his way.

He was glad she could take care of herself. It wasn't like he wanted her crying on his shoulder, right?

She wasn't his problem.

"How's the new owner settling in?" JJ asked.

Nash scowled over at him. "She's not the owner."

JJ arched a brow, but he didn't argue.

"She and her sisters will be selling the place the first chance they get," Nash said.

He assumed that would be the case, at least. And it was better for everyone if that was what happened.

It was definitely what his father wanted. It would be

73

the best scenario for his family. And every Donahue knew that family was all that mattered.

Family came first. Always.

"So, she's not sticking around?" JJ asked.

Nash shook his head, brushing dirt off his hands. "Nope. She's only here for a week."

Which was good. Great, even. The sooner she left, the sooner his life would go back to normal.

And normal was good. He was content with normal. He'd never wanted for anything, and what more could a man ask for?

"Too bad," JJ said mildly. Too mildly.

Nash narrowed his eyes in suspicion. "Why?"

"Rumor has it she's real cute." JJ wiggled his eyebrows.

Nash growled. He legit growled. The sound shocked him almost as much as it seemed to surprise JJ.

But then JJ's head fell back with a howl of laughter. "Oh man, you should have seen your face." He pointed a finger at Nash. "I've seen a grizzly protecting its cubs out in the wild up close and personal, and not even that was as terrifying as the look you just gave me."

Nash's jaw clenched shut with a click. He didn't trust himself to respond, so he turned around and headed to the main house. It was late enough. Emma should be up, and he felt like a mother hen because he'd been waiting all morning to check on her.

He wrenched open the door to the mudroom, kicked off his boots and stumbled to a stop in the kitchen. She was awake all right.

Awake and at home in his kitchen.

No, her kitchen.

He scrubbed at the back of his neck. Aw heck, this was getting confusing.

She was sipping on coffee and staring at a sheet of paper in front of her, her brows drawn together in concentration.

Her long blonde hair was piled up atop her head in a messy bun, with a few strands falling down around her cheeks. His fingers itched to brush it back and tuck it behind her ears so he could see every angle of her face.

He wanted to find out for himself if her skin was as soft as it looked.

The way her hair was up like that, it called attention to the long line of her neck, and from there his gaze fell to the oversized, faded college T-shirt that nearly swallowed her whole.

His throat tightened with the urge to laugh even as his heart squeezed with an ache.

Adorable. She was adorable.

Rumor has it she's real cute.

The urge to laugh died. JJ was wrong. Rumors were wrong. She was cute, yes, but she was so much more. She was gorgeous. A knockout in her own sweet, refreshing, wholesome, girl-next-door sort of way.

She noticed him then, her head snapping up and a smile instantly replacing her look of concentration.

"Morning," she said in that soft tone of hers.

It was a voice that made him think of babbling brooks and whispering wind. It was soothing, and for the first time all morning he felt some of his foul mood lifting.

"Did you sleep all right?" he asked.

She lifted a shoulder. "Fine, I suppose, considering the circumstances."

One corner of his mouth hitched up at that non-answer. "Which is another way of saying, you hardly slept a wink, am I right?"

Her cheeks turned a pretty shade of pink and she shrugged again. "The bed was comfortable, but I just couldn't turn this off." She tapped her temple.

"You had a lot to think about," he said.

She nodded, her smile fading a bit. "How about you?" she asked. "How was your night?"

"Good," he lied. But he couldn't exactly tell her he'd spent the better part of the night worrying about her, now, could he?

She held up her mug. "I hope you don't mind; I stole some of your coffee, but it was getting cold, so I put on a fresh pot for you. Oh, and I was making myself some breakfast, so I made extra in case you're hungry."

She pointed to a pan on the stove. He could smell the undeniable and mouthwatering smell of bacon and his stomach rumbled in response.

He was temporarily stunned. Making him coffee and some breakfast was hardly a big deal, but it still struck him in the solar plexus. He wasn't used to anyone taking care of him.

Oh sure, his mother always sent him off with leftovers after Sunday dinner, and his guys here on the ranch always did their share to pitch in, but that was about it. He was the one who took care of others, and he wasn't entirely sure how to react.

With a thank you, you dope.

"Er, thanks," he said after an awkward pause.

Her smile widened. "My pleasure."

And he could have sworn she meant it. His chest got all weird and warm, and he ducked his head to hide a smile as he headed over to the stove and helped himself.

He had a moment of trepidation when a silence fell. He

wasn't good with small talk at the best of times, but first thing in the morning? He headed back to the table and saw her bare feet which were crossed in front of her under the table. Pale blue toenail polish caught his eye. There was that urge to laugh again, that unexpected smile tugging at his lips.

He looked away quickly, trying not to notice the tanned, lean legs that were bare thanks to little pajama shorts.

How on earth was he supposed to make small talk with a strange woman who looked adorable as all heck in her pajamas?

This was going to get awkward.

"So, what's on your plate for work today?" Emma asked.

He let out a sigh of relief. Work he could talk about. He gave her a quick rundown of what a typical day looked like at the ranch. When he was done, she was leaning forward, gripping her mug with two hands. She was the very picture of a captivated audience.

She ended up asking him a bunch of questions that loosened his tongue and had him talking more during one breakfast than he typically did in a full day.

"Do you think…" She hesitated, biting her lip.

"What is it?"

She tilted her head to the side with a shy smile he'd never seen from her before. "Do you think I could see the property?" Before he could answer, she added, "Later today, I mean. I know you're busy this morning." She nodded at the paper she'd been staring at when he'd arrived. "I have some work ahead of me too."

"Of course." He leaned forward, resting his arm on the table. "Emma, you do know that this is *your* property now, right? You can explore wherever you like. This is your house, your land...your home."

Her gaze collided with his, and the mix of emotions there was nearly his undoing.

She looked lost. Frightened. But her chin came up and her smile was once more back in place as she said, "It's *our* property now, remember?" She tapped the paper before her. "Not mine alone."

"Yes, well..." He wanted to comfort her. So badly. He wished he had the right to tug her out of her seat and into his lap so he could hold her tight.

But that wasn't his place, and so he tried to find words to help. Never his forte, even at the best of times.

"You might share the property with your sisters, but you're the one who's here now, right?" He arched his brows. "And just because you're only part owner doesn't make this any less your land."

Her throat worked as she swallowed. "I guess you're right. In that case..." She looked at that paper again, and this time he could see her dread. "Exploring the ranch will be my reward for knocking one name off the list."

Ah. Understanding dawned in a heartbeat. "Your sisters," he said.

She nodded. "I need to start contacting them if I'm going to get a unanimous decision and be able to sell anytime soon." She frowned down at the paper and mumbled as if to herself, "If that's what we want to do."

Nash heard his father's voice in his head, of all things. *Convince her to sell.* He knew without a doubt what his father would do if he were here. It was what he'd urge Nash to do, too.

For the sake of the family, for their own ranching business...they needed Emma and her sisters to sell.

And it wouldn't be hard. He toyed with his mug as he watched her frown at whatever document she was studying.

She was confused and torn. Her emotions were all over the board. It likely wouldn't take much to steer her toward selling, to convince her that she had no place here, and that her life would be easier if she just went back to Chicago and her cozy little apartment that she loved so much.

He took a sip of his coffee. He had a hunch that all it would take were a few pointed comments, a couple of subtle suggestions, and her doubts about selling would be wiped away like marker on a whiteboard.

He knew that...but he still couldn't bring himself to say anything.

9

E mma eyed the sheet before her one last time after Nash left to go back to his chores.

It had taken everything in her not to throw out some desperate barter scheme. I'll muck out every stall if you'll just make this phone call for me.

She let out a sharp exhale, irritated with herself and her own cowardice.

How long had she been staring at this one sheet of paper? All morning. She'd been procrastinating for hours now. But after making breakfast and taking a shower, she was running out of ways to delay.

So she'd gone back to staring a hole into the piece of paper. It had been the top sheet in the folder Mr. Billman had given her. There was one sheet of paper for each of the sisters. All it held was contact details and some very basic info. Mother's maiden name, date of birth.

That was how she knew this woman was the first-born. Sierra O'Sullivan. Sister Number One, as Emma was starting to think of her.

This was ridiculous. Emma curled up on her bed and

pulled out her phone. Did she really think staring at the phone number would in some way make this easier?

No.

It was time to do or die. She took in a deep breath until it puffed up her cheeks, then let it out slowly as she dialed the phone number she now knew by heart.

Nothing. No answer. Not even a voicemail.

She frowned down at the phone. Well. That was an anticlimactic start.

She moved down the list to the next in order, after herself and Lizzy.

"Lucky sister number four," she mumbled as she dialed the number.

Dahlia picked up on the first ring, her voice brisk to the point of being curt. "Yes?"

"Dahlia?"

"Yes?" Irritation now at having to repeat herself, no doubt. Maybe she thought this was some sort of spam caller.

"Hi, I'm Emma." She took a deep breath. "Emma O'Sullivan."

There was a pause, and Emma waited for a response to the fact that they shared the same name. Any sort of response. All she got was silence, followed by a short, "And?"

"And…" She had to stop to clear her throat. Emma hadn't known what to expect with these calls, but this…was not it. "And your father, Frank O'Sullivan…he was my father as well—"

"Yes, I know."

That was it. The bored tone gave nothing away.

"Y-you know?"

A short sigh. "Of course I knew about you and the others."

"The others?" She sounded like a parrot echoing Dahlia's words back to her.

"There were six of us at last count, is that correct?" The woman sounded so aloof. Like she was talking to a random stranger about making a dentist appointment.

"Seven," Emma said.

"Ah." Finally, a hint of emotion and it was bitter amusement. "It appears I lost track."

"But you knew," Emma said again, trying to wrap her head around it. "About me and Lizzy, I mean."

"Of course I knew. My mother kept no secrets from me."

Emma's lips parted but she had no idea what to say to that. Or rather, she had too many questions that she wanted to ask and had no idea where to start.

Dahlia let out a sharp exhale. "Look, Frank was no father to me or my sisters except by blood, if that's what you're wondering. He married my mother shortly after he divorced yours, had us in quick order and then bailed."

Spoken so succinctly. Emma blinked in surprise. But then again, apparently this woman had had a lifetime to reconcile herself to Frank's many daughters.

She flipped through the file. "So, he had you and your sisters…"

"Rose and Daisy," Dahlia finished in an overly patient tone. Not rude, necessarily, but close. It was definitely patronizing.

"I see that you're… all named after flowers." Emma tried to lighten the mood, but all her observation scored was a derisive huff.

"Yes, my mother adores plants, but not her children, apparently."

Emma frowned. "Why—"

"Because she named us all after flowers, which tends to lead to a lot of irritating conversations. People find it very amusing. I, most certainly, do not."

Biting her lips together, Emma bailed on the line of conversation as quickly as she could. "So, you knew about Lizzy and me, and…" She found that first sheet and filled in the blanks before Dahlia could. "Sierra."

"Mmm, the first of Frank O'Sullivan's mistakes."

Emma blinked rapidly, her lips parting. Mistakes? They were people. Women. They were her *sisters*.

She shook her head, her stomach was coiling with tension at the woman's cold attitude. If nothing else, maybe Dahlia and her knowledge of Frank's offspring could help her track everyone down. "Do you know Sierra? Do you know how to get in touch with her?"

A short laugh from the other end. "Of course not. I have my hands full with my two *actual* sisters. The rest of Frank's children are none of my concern." A brief pause and then she added in a stilted voice, "No offense."

"None taken," Emma said quietly. If a little sarcasm slipped through, she found she didn't care. "I'm not sure I have a good number for her though, so if you have any way of contacting her—"

"I don't. Sierra was Frank's first daughter from when he was still a teenager, but she never made any attempt to talk to us and we respect that privacy," Dahlia clipped.

Emma straightened. The implication was that Emma was not respecting Dahlia's privacy.

"Well, maybe she doesn't know about any of us," she said.

"Possibly. But even if she did, why would she seek us out? We're complete strangers. The only thing we have in common is Frank's blood."

Emma wanted to argue that at least that's something, but she doubted this dismissive woman would agree. She really needed to wrap up this call, but she had yet to explain about the inheritance.

Before she could, Dahlia was continuing her lecture on Frank's offspring.

"All I know is that Frank and Sierra's mother met in high school. They were high school sweethearts, from what I understand. Until Frank knocked her up, and then his true colors shone."

"How so?" She should end this. Everything inside her recoiled at the bitterness in Dahlia's tone.

"Sierra's mother quickly found out he had no intention of marrying her. He gave her money, so that was something." Her voice turned bland and bleak. "The man was good for that, at least."

Emma opened her mouth to protest, but what could she say? It was the truth. All he'd ever given her and Lizzy was money.

"A birthday card, a Christmas card..." Dahlia gave a weary sigh. "At least the money was nice to look forward to."

A long silence passed and Emma had the craziest urge to cry. Not just for herself but for the sisters she hadn't known who'd all dealt with the same rejection.

"Who's the seventh?" Dahlia asked suddenly.

"What?"

"I knew about you and Elizabeth—"

"Lizzy," Emma automatically corrected. Her sister hated being called Elizabeth.

"I knew about you, Lizzy, Sierra, and my own sisters, obviously." She paused. "Who's the seventh?"

Emma glanced down. "April. The daughter of his last wife, Loretta."

"Hmph. I guess the old man just didn't know when to quit." She gave another rueful laugh. "He should've gotten a vasectomy decades ago."

Emma winced. Dahlia was kidding...she thought.

She hoped.

"Yeah, well, I'm sure you've heard that he's left us all his property—"

"We don't want it," Dahlia said briskly.

"Well, if that's the case, we're all on the same page so far. Which is good," she added. "Because Frank specified in his will that we have to have a unanimous decision in order to sell."

Dahlia uttered a curse under her breath, before saying, "Of course he did. Had to make this difficult for us all, didn't he?"

Emma didn't answer. She wasn't sure she was expected to. Dahlia seemed to be talking to herself.

"I'll get my sisters to sign in front of a witness once the others give the okay to sell." Dahlia's tone said she was ready to wrap this up.

"*If* they give the okay," Emma said.

Another sharp laugh that made Emma's stomach turn.

"Not if, *when*," Dahlia said. "I can't imagine any of Frank's daughters will be emotionally invested in that man or his legacy."

Maybe I am. Emma swallowed down the impulsive comment before it could slip out.

No, of course she didn't have an attachment—to the man or his land.

"You don't need to worry about my sisters. I will make sure they sign. But let me know as soon as you've contacted the others," Dahlia said.

And then Emma was listening to three quick beeps, followed by silence. Sister Number Four had just hung up on her.

She lowered her phone to stare at it. "So rude."

"I hope you're not talking about me." Nash's low voice from her doorway made her jump, and then she giggled at his smug little grin.

"Sorry," he said. "I didn't mean to startle you. Just wanted to see how you were getting on."

"Well, one call is done, and I think I hit three birds with one stone." She wrinkled her nose. "So to speak."

She pursed her lips, not sure if she was right about that.

Dahlia obviously liked being in control and handling things with quick efficiency. She indicated that her sisters would sign, but what if they didn't want to? She really should call them and check for herself. She felt it was her responsibility to make sure the decision was, in fact, unanimous.

The idea made her stomach twist into a tight knot. Would they all be as unpleasant as Dahlia?

Nash's low, warm chuckle distracted her, making her forget all about snide sisters and the fact that she had more calls to make.

"You almost ready for your tour?" He shoved his hands into his pockets. "I don't want to hurry you. There's no rush."

"Oh no, I am ready. I am so, so ready."

He laughed at her eagerness, but the moment her feet hit the floor she was stopped by one thought, a comment from Dahlia that had been nagging at her for the last few minutes. There was no way she could enjoy her tour until she cleared something up.

She held up a finger. "Can I just make one more quick call?"

"Of course." That slight little hitch of his lips just before he walked off made her knees go weak.

She put a hand out and braced herself against the bed. Goodness. It was probably for the best if Dahlia was right and she wrapped this up quickly.

Nash was too appealing for his own good. She had no doubt that he was only being nice to her out of some sense of duty. Or maybe even pity.

The thought made her cringe.

Please, don't let it be pity.

But even knowing that, it was getting harder and harder to remember that his smiles weren't meant for her. Not like that.

She gave her head a shake to clear it of thoughts of Nash as she picked up the phone to call her mom.

Her mom didn't answer. She was probably out with Lizzy running wedding errands.

She frowned down at her phone. She couldn't enjoy her tour of the ranch until she addressed that comment.

Of course I knew. My mother kept no secrets from me.

Which of course begged the question, had Emma's mom kept secrets from her? Or had she been just as in the dark as Emma and Lizzy?

She tried their home number but it was her stepfather Derek who answered.

"Sorry, hon, your mom is out with Lizzy. Who knows when those two will be back," he said with a good-natured laugh.

"Oh." She sighed. "Okay."

"Is there something I can help you with?"

Emma hesitated but then...why not? Derek was as much a part of their family as anyone. It came out quick and ineloquent. "Did Mom know that Frank had other daughters?"

His silence was her answer.

She fought a surge of hurt that left her winded.

"She knew about his first daughter. The one he had with his high school girlfriend." Derek's voice was low and gentle. "She only found out about the others when you did."

Emma pinched the bridge of her nose to hold off tears. "Why didn't she tell us we had a sister?"

Derek sighed. "We didn't think you'd ever need to know about her."

"But she's my flesh and blood."

"Who we never thought you'd meet," Derek said. "Look, sweetheart. From what your mother told me, Frank was a strange man. Very closed off and hard to communicate with." He hesitated and she could just imagine the frown that would be furrowing his brow and making his gray, bushy eyebrows come together like a muppet's.

The thought had a wobbly smile forming. She and Lizzy had been so lucky to have Derek in their lives. And she had to wonder what life was like for her sisters who hadn't been so lucky. She assumed by the bitterness in Dahlia's tone that they hadn't been blessed with a loving stepfather in their lives.

What were their stories?

She was torn between desperate curiosity and the urge to turn her back on this whole thing.

"Your mother really tried to make things work with

89

Frank, for your sake and Lizzy's. But when he offered to leave after Lizzy was born, she just didn't have the fight to tell him to stay." Derek sighed. "He disappeared out of your lives and became nothing more than a birthday card each year. Your mom didn't want you to face any of this heartache. She wanted you to have a normal, happy life and we've had that, right?"

"Yeah, Dad." Emma paused to swallow the lump in her throat. "I mean, yeah. Of course. Our life has been great." She rubbed at the bridge of her nose again. "I just feel so bowled over by this. It hurts that you didn't tell me."

"I'm sorry," Derek said softly. "We obviously should have."

A long silence followed as Emma breathed through another wave of hurt and anger. But what use would it be to throw out accusations now?

What was done was done, right? She took a deep breath and let it out slowly. The past was in the past—dead and buried right along with Frank. Now all she could do was face what was ahead of her.

"Seven. There's seven of us." Emma closed her eyes, exhausted at the thought of the work ahead, the calls she still had to make. "Dad, I don't know if I'm cut out for this."

"Yes, you are. I'm sorry it's landed in your lap, but you can do this, Emmy Girl. You've got all the skills required. You're a kind, caring person and you can relate to anybody."

She let out a little snort of disbelief. "I certainly couldn't relate to this Dahlia lady. Dad, she was awful. Rude and bossy. Her tone was caustic."

"There's always a reason behind bad behavior," Derek said. He was using his 'principal of a high school' voice, the one she and Lizzy always teased him about. "We're both in education, Emma, so we know this implicitly. Maybe Dahlia is hurting, but can't express it. Maybe she's having a busy day or work troubles. You don't know the full story, and the other sisters might all be delightful." He paused, a smile clear in his voice as he added, "You and Lizzy definitely are."

Emma grinned. "Thanks, Dad. I love you."

"Love you too, Emmy Girl."

She hung up with a sigh. That call hadn't exactly given her the clarity or the answers she'd hoped to find, but as she headed out of the bedroom toward the sprawling meadows outside, she let herself relax and enjoy.

Her time here was limited, after all. She'd do well to make the most of every second.

10

N ash was grinning like a fool when he pulled the side-by-side to a stop in front of the house.

Dirt was swirling around the open off-road vehicle as it bounced over some rocks, but that just made his passenger laugh harder.

She'd been doing a lot of that on this tour, and the sound was music to his ears. They'd been out exploring the range for over an hour, and he'd watched her relax more with each passing minute.

Emma turned to him with a wide smile, her eyes twinkling. "You did that on purpose."

She meant the last rocky bump. He put a hand to his heart. "I would never."

Her head fell back against the seat, her eyes crinkling at the corners with another laugh.

He would and he had, and she knew it. But he'd realized quickly that while she might not know how to ride a horse, which was a crying shame, she lit up like a Christmas tree the moment they'd started off-roading.

"Although," he added in a slow drawl as he held up

his arm to look at a nonexistent watch on his wrist. "I would say I beat your challenge."

She rolled her head to the side, her cheeks pink and her eyes bright as she bit her lip like she was holding back another laugh. "Um, I sort of forgot to set the timer."

He chuckled. "We'll just have to do it again then."

She nodded, her cheeks turned a deeper shade of pink that was downright enchanting. "I'd like that."

She started to unbuckle her seat belt, and he leaned over to help.

"Thanks," she said.

"No problem." He tugged on the strap. "These tend to get stuck."

"No, I meant…" She tilted her head to the side with a sharp exhale. "I mean, thanks for today. For *this*. For everything."

She ducked her head when he didn't immediately respond. In his defense, he had no idea what he was supposed to say, and he was a little shocked by what he'd wanted to say.

It was my pleasure. The shocking part was—he'd have meant it. What was more, he might have added, *I can't wait to do it again.*

"Well," she said as she clambered out of the UTV. "I'm sure you're busy, and I've taken up too much of your time as it is."

"Not a problem," he finally managed. He cleared his throat. "You ought to get a good feel for the property as you figure out what you're going to do next."

She nodded, and he could have kicked himself for bringing up that business again. Just the mention of the inheritance and the potential sale had her bright blue eyes clouding and that easy smile fading away.

"We'll do this again," he said, a little too quickly, to fill the silence and to bring that smile back.

It worked. Her lips curled up with enthusiasm. "Yeah?"

"Anytime you like."

She nodded. "I'd really love that."

He was getting out of the driver side, and gripped the roll bar as he faced her. "Much as the side-by-side is a fun way to get around the ranch, it's a shame you couldn't see it on horseback. That's really the only way to experience the range."

She sighed, and that sigh was so dreamy and sweet it had his lips twitching up in another grin.

"Oh, I would love that," she said.

"Maybe one day." The moment the words slipped out, he felt a kick of guilt. What was he doing talking to this woman about 'one days'? Especially at the ranch.

He was supposed to be supporting her efforts to sell and sell fast—to his family—not make promises about all the fun she could have here if she stuck around.

"Maybe one day." She repeated his words softly, like she was talking to herself.

Maybe she was. He'd caught her mumbling to herself more than once since she'd arrived.

"But for now, I'd better get back to business," she said, nodding toward the house. "I'll see you later?"

"I'll be back in time for dinner," he said.

His neck grew warm because...aw heck, that sounded too intimate. Like they were a couple or something, making plans to meet up again later.

"Great." She started to back away. "I saw there's a grill out on the back deck and some steaks in the freezer. How about I organize dinner?"

"That sounds great," he said, in what had to be the understatement of the year. What it sounded like was heaven.

He watched her walk away before turning toward the large barn structure that acted as a warehouse, shop, and also housed the small office Nash used for the property's paperwork.

One of the unsung glories of being the property manager was all the paperwork it entailed. He still had spreadsheets to update and wages to figure, not to mention all the onboarding paperwork that went along with the new seasonal hires.

But not even thoughts of paperwork could dampen his mood, and he found himself replaying every second of his time with Emma, cataloguing each smile and every laugh like he could store it all away for a rainy day.

"Well, well, look who finally made it." Kit sauntered past his office, then lounged against a tool bench to watch his younger brother, Cody, work on the stump grinder that'd been broken for weeks now.

Cody glanced over with a small smile of sympathy. Cody was a good kid—quiet and serious. Basically the opposite of Kit.

"Come on, man, give us the details," Kit said as he pushed away from where he'd been lounging.

"There's nothing to tell," Nash said. "The lady wanted to see the property and so I showed her around." He shrugged, keeping his gaze on the stack of mail he'd picked up and was shuffling through.

It was bills and junk mail, mainly, but he frowned down at it like each envelope required his utmost attention.

"Aw, come on, man," Kit said. "It's not every day we

get a gorgeous new owner on the property. What's she like? Did you ask her out?"

Nash glanced up. "Don't you have anything better to do than wait around here looking for gossip?"

Cody laughed at that as he continued to mind his own business.

"Nope," Kit said, undeterred. "I'm done for the day. I've got nothing to do but learn all there is to know about Aspire's newest pretty lady. Did you find out if she's single?"

Nash's muscles stiffened, and a flood of something toxic and green had him gripping the mail like he might shred it to pieces. He loved Kit like a brother but right now all he could think about were his jokes over the past couple years about needing to find a mama for his twins.

"Did I hear something about a pretty lady?" JJ strolled in, grease-stained and grinning.

Nash groaned. "Not you too."

JJ scratched at his scruffy beard with an unapologetic shrug. "I saw you two speeding up to the homestead in the UTV. What's the story there?"

Nash shrugged. "No story. Just giving the lady a tour. That's it. I didn't ask her out, and I don't even know if she's single."

All three men stared at him and JJ's eyes widened, dancing with laughter. "I just meant, did she say anything about her plans to sell, but clearly I'm missing something."

Dang it. Nash scrubbed the back of his neck, avoiding all three of their laughing stares.

"Oh, you missed something all right," Kit said. "Nash here was just going to tell us all about his lovely new houseguest."

"Want me to ask her if she's single?" JJ asked. "I don't mind."

"Oh no, no, you leave that to me," Kit said. His easy laughter made Nash tense even more. "I'll just ask her out and then we'll have our answer."

"You will do no such thing," Nash growled.

This made Kit and JJ crack up all over again.

"Leave him alone, you guys," Cody said with a tolerant grin as he swiped his dirty hands on a rag. "Nash here needs our help."

"Oh, he definitely does," Kit agreed. "When's the last time you asked a girl out, man?"

Nash shrugged. It had been...a while. Not only because his family and all their nagging about getting married had made dating feel like a chore, but because the ladies in Aspire and the surrounding towns made it unnecessary for him to do the asking.

The last three dates he'd gone on, the women had asked him out first. Maisie Traynor, the hairdresser from two towns over said if she'd waited for him, she'd have been old and gray before he got around to it.

She might have had a point.

He didn't have Kit's easy charm or JJ's confidence. Heck, he didn't even have that boyish appeal that made Cody so popular with the ladies.

Nash knew from gossip around town that he had his fair share of admirers, but that didn't mean he had a clue as to how to ask a woman out, let alone how to show her a good time once they were out.

Nash ignored the razzing going on around him, because apprehension was setting in. Was he really thinking about asking Emma out?

No. No, of course not. That couldn't lead to anything

good, and he well knew it. She was a city girl who wanted to go back home to her apartment in Chicago. That's what she'd said, and he wasn't about to keep her here for longer than she needed to be.

And then, just as he was starting to calm himself down, Cody kicked his pulse into red alert territory. "Hey Nash, your dad just arrived."

Sure enough, seconds later, his father strode into the warehouse like he already owned it. "Son," he greeted with his standard 'all business' nod. He turned to each of the men who called out a greeting. "Boys."

Ask anyone in Aspire and they'd tell you that Nash Donahue was the spitting image of his father. They shared the same features, for the most part, although Patrick Donahue's skin was weathered by a lifetime out in the sun, and his dark hair was threaded through with gray.

But they shared the same height and build, and on days like this Nash was reminded that they shared the same too-serious demeanor.

His father didn't even seem to notice the jovial, joking atmosphere he'd walked into, his brows drawn down in concentration as he strode toward Nash. "So?" he asked. "Any news on the sale?"

What sale? Some mischievous, rebellious part of him wondered what would happen if he just played dumb. If he got himself out of the middle and not give a flying fig what decision Emma and her sisters made about this place.

But, of course, he'd never been stupid, and he couldn't bury his head in the sand just because he liked the woman.

"No news," he said.

"Is the O'Sullivan woman here?" He meant on the

ranch, but his father looked around as if Nash might've been hiding her behind some equipment.

"No, she's…" Inside. "Busy."

"Busy, huh?" He sighed in irritation. "I was hoping to talk to her."

Nash straightened, knowing exactly what his father wanted to talk to her about—selling. He'd pester her until she gave in. Sure, he'd be polite about it, but Patrick Donahue had a quiet force that was hard to reckon with.

Every protective instinct Nash had was screaming to keep Emma safe. Not that his father would harm her—of course he wouldn't. But he'd press his case, and he'd push and pull until he got his way.

The last thing Emma needed right now was his father trying to pressure her on top of everything else she was facing.

"Well, she's not here," Nash said with a shrug, ignoring the curious looks from his friends. "And besides, she can't do anything with the property just yet. There's some legal holdup at the moment so it wouldn't do any good to talk to her until that's all figured out."

His father frowned. "What's the holdup? I thought the property went to some daughters from the big city. Thought they'd want to sell as soon as possible."

"Yeah, well, there were some unexpected holdups." Like the fact that there were now seven sisters whose support they'd need, not the three they'd anticipated.

"What kind of holdup?" his father asked, eyes narrowing.

Nash looked around at the four men he was closest to in the world.

He trusted them. Of course he did. But this wasn't his

story to tell, and he had to respect Emma's privacy. "Just some red tape the family has to sort through," he said.

His father gave a grunt of disappointment. The sooner this deal was done, the better, as far as his dad was concerned. His frown morphed to a slightly different shape as he smoothly changed the subject. "Found yourself a date to Casey's wedding yet?" Before he could answer, his father continued. "Your mother is driving me crazy. And you know how I feel about that. Don't tell me you haven't met at least one woman you could bring to the wedding."

"Uh…" Nash looked to his friends, as if they might have some new excuse he hadn't already thought of.

Kit flashed him a wicked grin. "Oh, he's found himself a date, all right."

Patrick's brows shot up. "Oh yeah?" He turned to Nash, but JJ stepped in.

"Her name's Emma."

Nash glared at his friends. What on earth were they playing at?

"Emma, huh? Don't think I know an Emma."

"She's new to the area," Cody said.

Nash turned to the younger Swanson brother with an accusatory glare. *You too?*

Cody shrugged with an impish grin.

Nash's father turned to him. "Do I know her family?"

"Uh…" Nash never had been much good at lying, but there was no way he wanted his father hassling Emma. He was trying to think of a little white lie that would protect her, but Kit beat him to it.

"Like Cody said, she's new to town." He crossed his arms and flashed Patrick an easy grin.

Nash knew he ought to shut this down. He couldn't

bring Emma, not when his family had their own agenda for her inheritance. And yet…

When he ought to be protesting and shutting down his friend's idiotic little games, he found himself daydreaming instead. Of all the bad times to become a daydreaming fool, his mind chose that moment to conjure an image of Emma in his arms, smiling up at him as they danced to the local bluegrass band at the reception.

He was jolted back to the present when his father clapped a hand on his shoulder.

Nash was stunned speechless at the sight of his father's beaming grin—a rare sight indeed. "Good for you, son." He shook his head with a low chuckle. "You know I don't get worked up about these things like your mother does, but it would make us all real happy to see you there with someone you care about."

Nash swallowed hard. He ought to protest. He should shut this down right now—

"Your mama's gonna be over the moon," his father was saying, walking away with an air of satisfaction that made Nash's belly twist with guilt.

"Dad, I—"

"We'll want to meet her first," Patrick said, not seeming to hear his protest. He turned back and pointed a finger in Nash's direction. "You make sure to bring her along to the family barbecue on Saturday, you hear?"

His father didn't wait for a response. And Nash was left to deal with three grinning idiots who were laughing themselves silly.

11

E mma narrowed her eyes at her new, makeshift therapist. "Don't look at me like that."

The big-bellied pig continued to stare at Emma as she chewed her food.

Emma sighed. "I tried my best, you know."

The pig grunted, obviously unimpressed.

"Rose didn't give me much to work with," she said. "I mean, she seems sweet and everything, but talk about indecisive. She couldn't give me a straight answer about anything."

The dirty, smelly pig had the gall to snort her response.

"Fine, fine. I get that. Big decisions and all. But I just want one little signature." Emma shrugged. "It was like she was afraid to make a decision without checking with her older sister first. And her older sister, Dahlia? Oh my word. She's a piece of work. Don't even get me started on her."

The pig didn't prod. Pigs, Emma had recently learned, were excellent listeners.

"Anyways, I tried my best, right? It's not my fault I couldn't convince her."

This was true, but guilt still nagged. She had one job while she was here and she was failing.

If anything, her second conversation with a long-lost sister had gone even worse than the first. Rose had seemed sweet but Emma got the impression she could be swayed in whichever direction her older sister chose.

Was it really right that they were all making this decision so quickly?

Emma rested her chin on her folded arms as she leaned over the wooden fence. "Don't any of them even want to see this place?"

Gnawing on her lower lip, her mind strayed to the purple bedroom. "April's seen this place, huh?" she said to the pig as it shuffled its big belly in her direction. "She even lived here for a while." Emma lifted her head and the pig gave a snort in response. "Do you remember her?"

The pig snorted.

"No, probably not. I guess it's been a while, huh?"

Two smaller gray piggies came running out of the barn, no doubt to see what all the fuss was about. The smaller one ran right up to the fence and made a snuffling noise that had Emma giggling despite her most recent setback.

Not that Rose was a setback, really. She'd most likely sell, because Dahlia would insist that she do.

And selling was for the best.

Emma frowned down at the cute, ugly, smelly little pigs. "It *is* for the best, right?"

They didn't answer. Not even a snuffle.

Emma rested her elbows on the fence and dropped her head into her hands with a sigh. She should call April soon. She kept putting her off, and she couldn't quite say why.

Or...maybe she could.

April was different from the others. She was the only one who'd had any real relationship with Frank O'Sullivan and Emma wasn't sure how to feel about that.

Was she curious about her youngest sister's life here on this ranch? Was she jealous? Did she want to know what Frank was really like...or was ignorance bliss?

"It's confusing," she admitted to the smallest pig.

She was pretty sure he... she... it... was the most sympathetic to her plight.

The larger pig came back in her direction. Was Emma imagining things or was that swine judging her?

"Okay, fine," she muttered. "I'm imagining things."

But she wasn't imagining this kick of guilt or the fact that there was one call she'd yet to make today. The one to her favorite sister, who'd no doubt be worried sick if she didn't check in.

"I think I have to stay." Maybe saying it aloud to the judgy pink pig would make it easier to tell her sister. "Not for long," she added quickly, aware of just how ludicrous she'd sound if anyone overheard. "Just another week or so. I mean, I've got the time, right? School doesn't need me back until mid-August, so there's really no rush." She let out a loud exhale. "Except Lizzy will be so upset with me. She'll argue that I can do all this from Chicago, but..." Emma gripped the fence, gazing to her left and taking in the breathtaking view. That blue sky, those green fields dotted with cattle.

Emma nodded. Staying longer was the right thing to do, she could feel it in her gut. It was clearly going to take more time than she'd thought to get ahold of each sister—she still didn't even have a clue how to contact Sierra, although she had plans to start cyberstalking her on social media just as soon as she found a spot with better wifi.

She looked around her at the wide open range and the utter lack of civilization. "Which is where, do you think?"

She arched her brows when Mr. Snuffles' sidekick lifted its nose with a snort.

Emma laughed. "Anywhere but here, amiright?"

They didn't laugh.

"Tough crowd," she muttered.

The sound of a throat being cleared behind her sent a cold shock running down her back. She bulged her eyes.

Oh no.

With her breath on hold, she dared to take a peek. Slowly. So very slowly.

Please, please don't be—

"Nash." She choked out his name, internally cringing at how ridiculous she must have looked while he stood there holding his cowboy hat and eyeing her with the most ludicrously sexy grin.

It was a smile that said he was trying really hard not to laugh at her, but somehow even that looked good on him.

She gave a small, awkward wave. "Hi."

"Hi yourself."

Oh, he was really trying hard not to laugh.

Her cheeks were on fire and her insides were melting into goo. "How, uh...how much of that did you hear?"

He managed to school his expression, and if it weren't for the laughter in his eyes, he might have even looked sincere. "I have no idea what you're talking about."

She burst out laughing, covering her blazing hot cheeks along with her eyes as she groaned. "So embarrassing."

"Nah, I think everyone at this ranch has taken advantage of Myrtle's excellent listening skills."

She peeked at him through her fingers. "Myrtle?"

He nodded toward the biggest pig. "Myrtle."

She dropped her hands completely. "You named your pig?"

"Not *my* pig," he mumbled. "And it's not just a pig, more like...a pet." He shifted from foot to foot, looking so much like one of her kindergarteners for a second that she had to press her lips together to stop a giggle.

"You have a pet pig?" She teased. Sure, she might have been the one talking to said pigs, but watching this manly man cowboy get all sheepish and defensive over his pigs was just too much fun.

He cleared his throat, dipping his head and arching his brows as he gestured toward the large barn in the distance. "Kit's kids fell in love with Myrtle when she was living on the Darby's property."

"Okay," she said slowly.

"Don't ask me how, but some kind soul informed Chloe of what happened to the pigs who were raised on the Darby's spread." He ran a finger across his throat.

"Ohhh," she breathed.

Nash shrugged, his expression pained. "What was I supposed to do?" He met her gaze evenly as she bit her lip to hold back a giggle. "There were tears, Emma." He widened his eyes. "So many tears."

She shook her head. "That's horrible."

Her voice came out choked as she tried valiantly to swallow down a belly laugh. She pointed to the other two. "And these guys?"

"Girls," he corrected. "They were a surprise gift from Myrtle here."

She gasped as she looked at Myrtle, who appeared bored by the conversation. "Myrtle, you sly little swine," she murmured.

Nash's laughter was so deep, so warm, so...so...*rumbly*, she was sure she felt it all the way to her toes.

Her cheeks ached from smiling as she met his amused gaze. She was filled with such a feeling of joy, it was hard to imagine she'd been so blue just a moment ago.

She glanced at the two little pigs who were frolicking in the mud. *You guys are good company, but Nash is better.* The thought had her swallowing whatever laughter was still bubbling inside of her.

What would Nash say if he knew she was comparing him to a couple of pigs?

"Did you name these two as well?" she asked.

"I didn't." He spoke so slowly she just knew there was a 'but' coming. He cast her a sidelong smirk that made butterflies spread their wings and fly in her belly. "But Chloe and Corbin did."

She clapped her hands together beneath her chin.

How sweet is this man?

First he adopts pigs to make the twins happy, and then he lets them pick the names?

"Tell me." She sounded breathless with excitement and he rubbed a hand over his mouth like he was trying not to grin at her goofy pleasure.

He pointed to the gray one with the sympathetic eyes. "That there is Snuffleupagus."

She sputtered out a laugh before clamping a hand over her mouth. "He does snuffle the most," she said when she was able to speak. "That's brilliant."

Nash's eyes seemed lit from within as he beamed her yet another smile. The sight made her knees weak.

"And that one?" she pointed to Snuffleupagus's sister.

Nash gave her a bland stare. "That's Big Bird."

She doubled over as she officially lost the battle with laughter. When she could stand again, she swiped at her eyes. "You have a pig named Big Bird?"

He shrugged.

Her gaze moved to the chickens who were pecking and clucking outside their coop nearby. "Do you suppose the chickens find that confusing?"

Nash's brows drew down and he took his sweet time settling his hat back on his head as he studied her as though giving the matter consideration. "You know, I hadn't thought about it," he said in that low, somber drawl of his. "I sure as heck hope we haven't been giving them a complex."

It was the oh-so-serious way he said it that had her cracking up again and then lightly smacking his arm. "You know, you're way more fun than I imagined you'd be."

His brows arched. "Oh yeah? And what did you imagine I'd be like?"

"Uh…" Her mouth went dry. Well, she'd set herself up nicely for that one. "I don't know. Cool, I guess?" She flinched in embarrassment as his brows hitched up even further. "Not that you're not cool. I just meant…you have the whole brooding cowboy vibe going on, you know?"

He arched a brow in response. If it wasn't for the way his lips twitched as he fought a smile, she'd think maybe she'd honestly offended him.

She bit her lip as she struggled to find a better explanation that wouldn't bury her even further in this hole of humiliation.

Oh heck. How did one tell a man he was too good looking to be so nice? It was hard enough to have an instant infatuation just by staring at him, but add in his kindness and his humor…

A girl like her didn't stand a chance.

He leaned in closer, his eyes still twinkling with mirth. "What I wouldn't give to be able to read your thoughts right now."

She let out an embarrassing snort. "Trust me. No one wants that."

He studied her for a long moment, but thankfully let that go. "There is one question I'd love to ask." His jaw worked like he was chewing over his words. "But it's kind of personal."

Her belly fluttered with nerves. "You can ask me anything."

Oh dear. Had that sounded flirtatious. She hadn't meant it to sound—

"Are you really planning on sticking around?"

She blinked up at him. "What?"

He nodded toward Myrtle. "I overheard enough, and it sounded like maybe you were going to stay here in Aspire longer than planned."

Her stomach sank, and she didn't want to consider why. Only a dang fool would think he'd been about to ask her something truly personal...like if she had a boyfriend. Or if she wanted to go out on a date.

She shut her eyes for a second and when she opened them her smile was firmly in place. "I am thinking of staying longer."

The flicker in his eyes was there and gone so fast she almost thought she'd imagined it.

Almost.

But no. She hadn't imagined it. Her newfound friend,

the guy she'd stupidly developed a crush on when she really ought to know better...

He was disappointed to hear she was staying.

12

The change in Emma was so sudden it made Nash's head spin. Her bright smile and playful laughter evaporated as she ducked her head and stared at the ground between them.

"Only for a week." She rushed out the words before he even had a chance to respond. "I just don't feel right about heading back to Chicago when I still have sisters to get in touch with, you know? And school doesn't go back for a while yet." Her hands nervously fluttered in front of her chest like they didn't know where to land. "I might actually stay for another ten days. Maybe? Or, not even that long. If it's too much trouble I can try to get to—"

"Emma." He reached for her arm and she stilled the moment he touched her. "I think that's a great idea."

She blinked. "You do?"

"I do." It wasn't a lie. It was clear Emma was torn about the inheritance and dealing with a world of emotions now that she had a new family to contend with.

He just didn't want her to have to contend with *his*

family as well. The moment she said she was staying longer, a flush of panic shot through him. How could he keep his father at bay? The longer she stuck around, the harder it would get. That man was like a dog with a bone when he had his sights set on something.

The protective instinct firing through Nash was strong and surprising.

Don't get too attached, man. She's still leaving. Her life in Chicago will call her back eventually and then where will you be?

He removed his hand from her arm, shoving it deep into his pocket and tipping back on his heels. "You staying here is no trouble. This ranch belongs to you, remember?"

She let out a half-hearted laugh and shrugged. "Well, me and six others."

"Staying here gives you time to deal with all that."

"I don't know how I'm going to tell Lizzy," she said with a rueful wince.

He smiled. "I bet she'll understand."

She chuckled softly. "You have a younger sister, Nash. Would she understand if you weren't doing everything in your power to make her wedding day perfect?"

He flinched. Her pointed question hit its mark, and then some. "Don't remind me."

"Why?" Her tone was teasing and she was starting to lose that odd insecure edge she'd had a moment ago. She reached out and pushed his shoulder playfully. "Are you in trouble with the bride?"

"Something like that." She waited for him to continue, and when he didn't, she moved on.

"Well, then, you must know what I mean. Lizzy needs me in Chicago."

He nodded slowly. He hadn't known Emma long but he wondered if she had any idea how many times he'd heard her talk about what everyone else around her needed and wanted. "What about you?"

Her eyes widened in incomprehension. "What about me?"

"What do you need?"

Her lips parted. She was clearly stunned. Almost like she'd never been asked that question before. The thought rankled him. This was a woman who was so selfless, so sweet, and it was about dang time she thought about number one for a change.

He leaned against the fence and crossed his arms. "Emma O'Sullivan, what is it that you want?"

She bit her lip and guilt flared in her eyes. "I want to stay." A smile tugged at his lips but she quickly added, "Just for a little while longer."

"You don't have to explain yourself to me," he said. "This is your property. You belong here."

She blinked, and her eyes got that dazed look again like he'd just stuck her with a cattle prod. Then she bit her lip again. "You think I belong here?"

His insides flushed. He hadn't meant to say it so openly like that, but his heart ached at the sincerity and vulnerability on full display before him. The woman didn't have a superficial bone in her body.

"I think people belong wherever they're happiest," he said quietly. "I think everyone deserves to get what they want sometimes. Especially those people that are always putting everybody else's needs before their own."

She dipped her head and the way she studied him made him feel like she could see straight through his checkered shirt and right into his heart. "And you're sure you're all right with me being here in your space?"

"I told you it's your—"

"Yeah, yeah." She waved a hand. "Legally I own this place. I get it. But it's your home. It's your world."

A smile spread across his face and pride swelled in his chest as he followed her gaze to the valley beyond. The sun was sinking low, casting the meadows and hills in shades of golden yellows and warm ambers. "It is my home," he agreed, his voice gruff. "But it's yours too, for as long as you want it to be."

She nodded, and he caught the flicker of indecision crossing her face before she blurted out. "Are you sure? Because you seemed unhappy about it when I first said I'd be staying."

His eyes widened in surprise. She was perceptive, all right. Most people accused him of being unreadable, at best. Not to mention too serious, too quiet.

His lips twitched. No one had ever accused him of being fun. He swallowed down a laugh. Or too cool, for that matter.

Emma arched her brows in a prompt and he realized he had yet to answer. He took a deep breath and let it out slowly. The fact was, if his father had stuck around a little longer or arrived a little earlier, they would have crossed paths.

He'd told himself earlier that he could keep them apart for the next six days, but if she was staying even longer?

He'd have his work cut out for him trying to shield Emma from his ambitious father.

"Okay, now you're starting to freak me out."

He dipped his head with a rueful laugh and took off

his hat to run a hand over his hair. "It's nothing, just..." He sighed. "My family owns that property over yonder."

"Over yonder," she repeated with a funny quiver in her voice. "I remember."

"My dad has his heart set on buying this property from y'all when you decide to sell." He caught himself quickly. "*If* you decide to sell."

She nodded, her brows drawing together. "That's likely a good thing, right? I mean, we want to sell, your family wants to buy...?" She trailed off with a question in her voice.

"It is, it's just..." He winced. "My father is a good man."

She grinned. "Okay."

"I don't want to give the impression that he's not."

"I didn't get that impression at all," she said. "You've very clearly told me that he is."

He smiled because...she was teasing him. And he liked it. Somehow it felt familiar, and it made her easier to talk to. Even now he felt the tension from his father's visit starting to crumble, and it helped him to be completely honest.

"He's a very single-minded man, especially when it comes to business. I just don't want him bothering you since I know you have a lot on your plate already. You don't need the added pressure of my father and his grand plans."

Her expression softened. "That's sweet of you to worry, Nash, but I'm a big girl. I can handle your father."

He met her smile with one of his own, but he wasn't so sure. His father wasn't some villain, and he had a heart as big as Montana, especially when it came to his family. Unfortunately though, all that love for his family meant he sometimes lost track of what was best for others. And when it came to his own family, he expected a lot from them in return.

He expected a lot from Nash.

And right now all those expectations felt like a ten-ton weight.

Emma reached a hand out and touched his arm with a soft smile. "Hey, you okay? Your face is very serious right now."

"I'm always serious," he said. "Ask anyone."

Her smile widened like he was teasing. He wasn't. He typically was too serious. Okay, maybe not around his buddies when they were shooting pool, or when he was spending time with his sister and cousins...

Or when he was around this woman.

Her hand dropped from his arm and he felt the lack of her warmth instantly. She leaned against the fence beside him. "Well then, so long as you're on board, I guess I need to tell Lizzy that I won't be back next week to help with the wedding."

He gave a little grunt of amusement and sympathy at the anxiety he heard in her voice.

He was so comfortable, the moment so intimate and warm...he did something he almost never did. He spoke without thinking. "And I just have to break it to Casey and my family that my ranch hands are idiots. Hopefully Casey won't murder me, and my mom won't die of heartbreak."

She laughed as she looked at him. "What? Why?"

He turned to tell her about how Kit, JJ and Cody had thought it would be funny to throw him under the bus, but the moment he caught sight of her expectant smile, her cute, upturned nose and her pointed chin, he forgot what he'd been about to say.

The way the dying light seemed to catch on her hair and make it glow like a crown…

He swallowed thickly.

He'd been about to tell her about the fictional girlfriend his pals had created, and how they'd used her name, but now…

Now a new thought was forming. A plan, really. His heart started to thud faster in his chest as he turned it over in his mind.

Was he really considering this?

Her smile was so bright it nearly blinded him. "What?" she laughed. "Why are you looking at me like that?"

It could be perfect. Not only would he have a date to the wedding, but everyone could get off his back about finding a bride. The pressure would be gone, just like that. And when Emma returned to Chicago, he could maybe say he was too heartbroken to be ready for dating again. He could drag that out for at least a few months. Not only that, but…

His chest lightened with an additional idea. A selfless, worthy one.

He could protect her. If everyone thought they were romantically involved, he could ensure that his father left her alone. He could stay close to her side and play running blocker when his dad tried to force a sale out of Emma.

His gaze focused on hers and he was hit with a wave of uncertainty, but her expectant smile drew the words right out of him. "I was thinking…that is…I think maybe you sticking around for a while might be a good thing for both of us."

She tilted her head to the side in a silent question.

Aw heck. He was already making a mess of this.

He cleared his throat. "My sister, my mother, all of my aunts and basically any woman over the age of fifty in this town, really wants me to have a date to Casey's wedding."

"Ahh." Her expression cleared with understanding.

"Yeah, they're a real romantic bunch…" He shook his head. "And the fact that I'm still single at the age of thirty-three really seems to stress them out. My mother and my aunts are obsessed with me meeting my future wife."

"Oh dear." She winced.

"Exactly."

"And weddings only add to the pressure," she said, with so much understanding he had to wonder if she was getting her own fair share of nagging with Lizzy getting married soon.

"That's exactly right," he said. "So, I was thinking…"

Her expression turned to curious anticipation.

"Would you maybe consider—that is, would you do me a favor and—no, that came out wrong. You're not dating anyone right now, are you? You don't have a boyfriend?"

She shook her head, obviously fighting the urge to laugh.

His insides started dancing. She was single. Yes!

That doesn't mean she's free to be yours. Stay focused, you idiot! Tell her your plan already.

He was making such a colossal mess of this. What would she think of him? Scrubbing a hand down his face, he softly groaned.

Emma giggled. "Just spit it out, Nash. I promise I don't bite."

He took a deep breath, then laid out his plan as succinctly as he could. "Since you're staying here a little

120

longer, I thought maybe you could be my date to the wedding and I figure if we're doing that, maybe you could pretend to be my girlfriend too." He rustled up a smile, trying to sell it without being cheesy, but then the words just slipped on out of his mouth. "I wouldn't mind pretending to be your cowboy."

Nash cringed like he'd just said something awful and it took Emma's brain a full second to register his words. And when she did, it felt like her mind was processing it out of order.

Wedding date.

Yes!

Girlfriend.

Whoa. Holy—

Pretend.

Wait...what?

She stared at Nash as her heart went on a roller coaster ride without her. It landed with a crash and a thud.

"Pretend...?" she managed.

"Yeah, you know...just a bit of fake dating." He flashed her that boyish smile, the one that made her heart double in size.

This was normally a nice feeling, but right at this second, as the poor organ recovered from a crash landing, it kinda hurt.

Nash kept talking. Some part of her was dimly aware

of his low, sexy voice filling the air with explanations, justifications, rationalizations…

"It's beneficial for both of us really. We could just tell everyone it was love at first sight and I'd get a reprieve while you're here. You don't have to commit to anything long-term, since I know you want to go back to Chicago as soon as this inheritance mess is all sorted out. So, when you leave I'll feign a broken heart and everyone will give me some space to recover." He beamed at her, going on to say something about his father, but she couldn't process his words.

All she could hear was her own voice chiding her. *Stupid, Emma. So stinkin' stupid.*

Had she really let herself believe that this crush might be reciprocated? She gave her head a shake to rid herself of that voice, but the self-recrimination was worse than her disappointment.

It was just that…she'd been here before. Many times. With every guy she'd ever actually developed feelings for. She was not the girl men like Nash dated.

Nope. She was the kind of girl they *pretended* to date.

Emma winced. Her pride was definitely stinging.

And it seemed Nash caught her wince because his tone changed, and the resignation in his voice brought her back to the moment. "Oh no. You think it's a terrible idea."

She blinked up at him. She'd yet to say anything but apparently her face was speaking for her. "I didn't say that."

He grimaced, taking off his hat once more and scrubbing the back of his head. It gave off such an apologetic *aw shucks* vibe, it was impossible not to feel a tug of sympathy.

"I didn't mean to put you on the spot like that," he

said. "I was just trying to help us both out. But I'm not very good at this sort of thing."

She arched her brows. "You're not good at asking girls to be your pretend girlfriend?" Her lips curled with amusement despite the lingering sting of rejection. "Do you do this often?"

He dipped his head with a rueful chuckle. "No. This would be a first."

"Good," she breathed. When he glanced up at her, she added, "I might be offended if I thought I was just another fake girlfriend in a long line of phonies."

His smile was adorable. All sweet and hopeful, and tinged with a hint of disbelief. Like he couldn't believe she was making a joke about this.

Truthfully, she couldn't either.

Her pride was stung, and yeah, her heart might still be a little rattled. But she couldn't bring herself to be mad at Nash. He was too sincere. Too genuine. And right now, she was even getting a glimpse of something vulnerable. A side of him she suspected few got to see.

"It's really that important that you have a wedding date, huh?"

He nodded. "I know it sounds ridiculous, but…" He sighed. "My family has a lot of expectations."

There was that tug again in her chest. "I'm sure there are plenty of girls in this town who'd love to go with you. Why me?"

He shrugged and glanced away, so clearly uncomfortable.

Well, too bad. If she was going to do this, she needed to understand why. She had to hear with her own ears why pretending to date her was the better option. Maybe she needed him to spell it out for her why they couldn't be more. No more daydreaming about what ifs.

She'd go into this with her eyes wide open.

Even as she thought it, she blinked in surprise.

Wait a second… Was she actually considering this?

He cleared his throat and finally dragged his gaze back to hers. "There are women I could ask. My family has a laundry list of potential dates, in fact." He shot her a wry grin but she couldn't quite return it.

A laundry list of single, no doubt beautiful women. How nice for him.

She threw her hands out wide. "And yet you want to settle for little ol' me?"

His grin fell flat and his gaze sharpened. "Emma, I didn't mean—"

"I'm kidding. Just kidding," she mumbled, heat creeping into her cheeks. She wasn't fishing for compliments, and she didn't need to hear his consolation speech.

He hesitated and Myrtle chose that moment to snort so loudly they both started to laugh, and the tension eased by several notches.

She shot the pig a sidelong glance. *Thank you, Myrtle.*

She liked to think the pig's head bob was an '*I got you, girl*' but in reality Myrtle was probably just scrounging for more scraps.

Nash ran a hand over his face and for a moment she saw his exhaustion. He was at the end of a long day of hard work—and he'd even thrown in hosting duties to boot.

"I'm doing a terrible job of explaining myself," he said as he stubbed the toe of his boot into the dirt. His gaze followed the movement and she had a moment to stare at that ridiculously handsome face of his.

His jaw was darkened by a five o'clock shadow and the area around his eyes was tight with tension.

She reached out and touched his arm, and his gaze snapped up.

She smiled. "You're not doing a terrible job. I'm just trying to understand."

He nodded, his Adam's apple bobbing as he swallowed. "I love living in Aspire," he said slowly. "I've always loved it here, and I've never dreamt of leaving."

Emma waited patiently for him to continue, her heart thudding painfully with each word he spoke.

What must it be like to live somewhere you love so much? Her gaze took in the spectacular view behind him.

What must it feel like to belong to a place like this?

You belong here.

His earlier words came back to her like a blow to the chest, just like the first time he'd said it. It was ridiculous but those words had felt like destiny, like...like the answer to her prayer.

"But as much as I love Aspire," he continued, his tone thoughtful. "There are some aspects to small-town life that drive me nuts."

"Like what?"

"Like everyone knowing my business," he said on an exhale. "Like the responsibility that comes with living up to a legacy name. Our family helped to build this town, and we're all involved in the community. My aunts and uncles, my parents, the cousins who didn't move away."

"That sounds nice," she murmured. "To know your purpose in a place." She shrugged. "To be so certain you belong."

"It is nice," he said quickly. He squinted one eye. "I sound like an entitled brat, don't I?"

She laughed. "Not at all. I'm guessing that there's a flip side to all that belonging."

"Exactly." He leapt on her understanding and his gaze grew intense. Almost eager, like he needed her to understand. "If I ask a local girl to the wedding, it's like making a vow before we even order appetizers on a first date."

She giggled softly at the metaphor, but nodded when she saw how serious he was. "Yeah, I can see that," she said.

"And as for my family," he continued. "They only want the best for me. But they don't seem to understand that I'm not looking for romance." He gave a little helpless shrug. "I'm no good at it. And I'm happy with my life as it is. I'm not looking for more. Not right now, at least." His brows drew together as his gaze turned pleading. "Does that make sense?"

She swallowed down a thick wave of disappointment as she nodded. "Yes, it does."

And if she'd wanted it spelled out for her, there it was. Written out phonetically so anyone could understand.

Nope. There was no way her heart could be confused if she went into this. Her eyes were open, and there was no doubt in anyone's mind that there was no future here. Not with Nash.

"So?" he asked.

Ugh. Her heart twisted. That glimpse of a boyish, sweet Nash was going to kill her one of these days. It was even harder to resist than his good looks and his sexy voice.

She'd do it. She knew she would. Heck, she'd known at some level what her answer would be before he'd finished asking the question. But...

You belong here.

His words were still ringing in her ears, echoing in her chest.

She wanted to feel that way. Just once. Not forever, but for right now. While she was here. She wanted to actually feel what it was like to belong in this world of magical sunsets and sweeping, awe-inspiring landscapes.

This was God's country, they said. And she wanted to know what it was like to truly live under this big sky.

She straightened, an idea coming to her so hard and fast it made her heart race. "I'll do it."

His brows arched. "Yeah?"

"On one condition." A smile spread across her face as she thought about what she wanted—what she truly wanted. "You have to teach me how to ride."

He blinked. "A horse?"

She giggled. "Yes, a horse."

His answering grin made her heart soar before she gave it a stern warning.

No more of that. This was a friend helping a friend. Nothing more.

And in return…

"I want to learn what it's like to actually live on a ranch."

He studied her like she'd just fallen from the sky. "That I can definitely do."

She stuck her hand out, ignoring a warning voice that told her she was diving headfirst into stupidity. She didn't care. Her eyes were open. She knew the risks and wouldn't let her heart get hurt. And in exchange, she'd get a taste of the life that was calling to her. Maybe it would be enough.

It would be. It had to be.

She'd go back to Chicago with a world of memories,

the closure she'd been seeking...and a totally uninjured and intact heart.

Nash took her hand in his, and all thoughts stopped at once. All she knew was the feel of his warm, large, calloused hand engulfing hers. She swallowed hard. She did know what she was doing...right?

"Then it's a deal," he said, his smile making her heart glow in her chest.

"It's a deal," she said.

14

The next day Emma sat out on the ranch's back porch and stared at her phone.

Once again, staring accomplished nothing.

"One call and then you can have a riding lesson," she reminded herself.

This time she glanced around to make sure no one was watching her talk to herself.

Was it crazier to talk aloud to herself or to pigs?

Maybe Nash knew the answer, because for Emma, the jury was still out. She tapped her fingers against the phone and let her gaze roam over the calming scenery.

The wind moved through the grass and trees, and birds flew overhead, their sweet twittering enough to make her smile. Other than that, the scene was peaceful and still. No one was in a hurry, there was no need to rush. She was so far removed from the bustle of Chicago that she could be on another planet.

Before she knew it, her blood pressure had calmed and when she lifted the phone to dial Daisy's number, she was no longer on the verge of a freakout.

Sure, maybe her younger sister Rose had been disappointingly wishy-washy and seemingly uninterested in Emma and the ranch. And Dahlia might have been brisk to the point of rude. But this was a new sister. Another chance.

Daisy answered on the first ring. "Hello? Is this Emma?"

Emma blinked in surprise. "Uh… hi, Daisy. Yes, this is Emma." She didn't hide the shock in her voice, and Daisy's light laughter filled the other end of the line.

"Rose told me you'd be calling," she explained.

"Oh. Right." Emma laughed too…at herself for not having guessed the obvious. "For a second there, I thought maybe you were psychic."

Daisy's voice was filled with amusement. "I like to think I have a special connection to the spiritual realm, but it doesn't give me telepathic caller ID."

Emma wasn't sure how to respond because she wasn't sure if her sister was serious. Daisy laughed again and Emma blinked, shifting the phone to look at it for a second to make sure she'd called the right number.

So far, Daisy was nothing like either of her sisters. Which she supposed wasn't a surprise. It wasn't like she and Lizzy were anything alike either. Aside from the blonde hair, they were as different as night and day.

Emma felt a stab of guilt and shoved thoughts of Lizzy aside.

She and Nash had walked back to the house together last night, and while he'd cleaned up, she'd started the grill. Once he joined her on the back porch, taking over at the grill while she put together a salad, she'd forgotten all about the fact that she owed Lizzy a call.

It wasn't until this morning that she realized she hadn't told Lizzy about her change of plans yet.

But Lizzy could wait a little while longer because Daisy was chatting away like a happy little parakeet. "Rose didn't tell me much, she never does. She just gave me a heads up that you'd be calling about Frank's ranch. So, what do you do, Emma? Are you a lawyer or something? Is that why you're sorting all of this out?"

Emma laughed. She couldn't help it. "Uh, no. I teach kindergarten."

"Oh, that must be so rewarding," Daisy said. Her entire tone was sweet and excited and...*kind.*

"I'm on summer break at the moment," Emma said. "So I thought I'd come see the ranch, and yeah... I guess, it kind of fell to me to sort this all out."

"Well, you are officially awesome for doing that."

Emma let out a relieved sigh. Finally, a newfound sister she felt a connection with.

"What about you?" she asked. "What do you do for a living?"

"I'm a musician," Daisy said in a sing-song voice. "I'll play just about any instrument put in front of me, but guitar is my favorite. Oh, and I sing too."

"That's amazing." Emma laughed. "I play the guitar. Although, I'm only good enough to strum a few chords so my students can sing along to their favorite nursery rhymes and kiddy tunes."

Daisy laughed. "I bet you'd be great if you practiced. Maybe I can give you lessons sometime."

Emma was all out beaming, sitting on the edge of her seat. "I'd love that."

And she meant it. Up until this very moment she hadn't

realized how much she'd wanted...well, to be wanted. These new sisters might be strangers, but they were family. And that meant more to Emma than she'd let herself admit.

"Rose is a pretty mean singer, too," Daisy said. "If you can get the girl out of her own way long enough to belt out a tune."

"Really?" Emma curled one leg under her, her gaze catching on the sight of Nash and one of the other cowboys riding in the distance. Her grin grew wider. "What about Dahlia?"

Daisy let out a derisive grunt, but then lowered her voice. "Don't tell a soul, but my twin sister can play a mean fiddle." She started laughing. "Oh man, she would kill me for telling you that."

Emma gasped. "No way."

"It's true. Our grandmother insisted all of us take lessons when we were young. Said we were naturals, not that she would ever admit our father's part in that. It can't have been my mom, though. She couldn't hold a tune if you paid her to." Daisy's melodic laughter rose like a song.

Emma stilled. She hadn't thought about what they all might have inherited from their father. "So you think we all got an ear for music from Frank?"

"I'd say so," Daisy said. She sounded so cool about it. So calm. Like the mention of Frank didn't put her on edge the way it did with all her other sisters. Even Lizzy seemed happier not being a part of the conversation when it came to their biological father, his death, or this property.

There was a lull in the conversation and Emma rushed to fill it. "Well, Lizzy has a really great voice. If we all get together sometime, we'll have to form a band."

Daisy's enthusiastic gasp filled Emma with joy. "Like the Von Trapp family singers. Only way more dysfunctional."

Emma laughed. "I loved *The Sound of Music* when I was a kid."

"Me too!" Daisy said.

They chatted a little while longer about movies and music and their careers, until the sight of Nash heading back toward the stables made Emma aware of how much time had passed.

Her first riding lesson would be starting very soon. A thrill whistled through her, killing the mild sting of what it was costing her to take them.

Fake-dating. Was she completely insane?

"You know what I mean?" Daisy asked.

Emma's eyes bulged. She had no idea. She shouldn't have let her mind wander. She currently had no idea what Daisy was referring to, but she nodded and said, "Uh-huh." Trying to hide her lame response, she cleared her throat and got down to business. "Daisy, I hate to cut this short, but I've got to run in a bit, and before I do, we should really talk about your thoughts on selling the property."

"Oh yes, of course," Daisy said. "I heard that Frank left us some land. Rose says you need a yes or no on the whole selling it thing."

Emma let out a sigh of relief. At least she didn't have to recount the entire will all over again.

"So, you're on board with selling then?" Emma asked.

"Maybe." Daisy's tone was light but distracted.

Emma heard her murmuring something to someone in the background. Her voice sounded muffled, like she had a hand over the receiver.

"Um, maybe?" Emma repeated.

"Yes. Maybe."

Emma could practically hear Daisy's smile. "You, uh...you do realize that the decision needs to be unanimous. We'd all need to sign."

"Of yeah, sure, sure," Daisy said. "That probably won't be an issue."

Emma bit her lip. She wasn't liking all of these 'maybes' and now a 'probably'?

It wasn't a good sign.

"When do you think you'll know for certain?"

"Well, it's important for me to get a good read on the place," Daisy said, her voice suddenly serious.

"O-kay," she said slowly. What did that mean?

"I need to see the ranch in person, be in our father's space," Daisy continued. Her voice wasn't just serious, it was solemn.

"Okay," Emma said again, even slower this time. She felt like she was missing something here. But even so... "I can understand that," she said. "It's one of the reasons I came. I needed to see the ranch with my own eyes."

"Exactly." Daisy's tone lightened, apparently pleased that Emma could relate. "I need to feel it. I need to know if the land speaks to my soul, you know what I mean?"

Emma blinked. She didn't know. She had no clue what that meant, but she didn't want to offend Daisy by saying so.

"Once I'm there, I'll know my answer," Daisy said. So calm. So at peace.

Emma oddly felt a pang of jealousy at the other woman's certainty. Emma was here and she was no closer to feeling resolve or closure than when she'd set foot on the plane back in Chicago.

"So, you'll make a trip out here then?"

"Yes, most definitely!" Daisy said. "I can't right away, but I'm so excited to see the ranch."

Emma started to smile. Maybe it was fate that she was extending her stay. With the extra week she'd tacked on she might even get to meet this sister in person. "So when do you think you can get here?"

"Oh, in about four months," Daisy said.

Emma blinked, pressing the phone even closer to her ear. "Four...four *months*?"

"I'm on tour." Daisy's tone was breezy. "I can't just bail on the band, I..." her voice trailed off and Emma listened to more muffled conversation. She had a feeling Daisy was going to hang up any second now. "But as soon as I'm done touring, I'll book myself a ticket. How does that sound?"

"But, you can't just take a couple days off or—"

"I've gotta run, Emma, I'm needed for a sound check," Daisy said.

"That's—I mean, we can't—"

"Bye sweetie, can't wait to meet you in person."

"Wait, Daisy—" Emma's protest was cut off by the call ending.

What was it with these sisters hanging up on her? Had they not been taught proper phone etiquette?

She lowered her device and stared at the screen.

Four months?

Well, it wasn't like she had to be here that whole time. Even so, her pulse accelerated at the thought of not having an answer for so long. Of not being able to move on, one way or the other.

She really wanted this wrapped up before she returned

to Chicago. She needed things to be done and dusted so she could put this behind her.

She'd never been good at open-ended *anything*. Secretly she suspected this was one of many reasons sexy, eligible men put her in the cute, girl-next-door friendzone the moment they met her.

No one looked at her and thought *fun, spontaneous fling*. And for good reason. She couldn't even handle the thought of not committing to a decision on a house for a few months, let alone a relationship that didn't have firmly established boundaries.

She fell back in her seat with a sigh. No wonder she was so terrible at dating. Men must be able to sense this about her. It was like her entire demeanor emitted a vibe that said *commitment*. It scared them off before they could even get to know her.

That's probably why Nash went straight for the fake-dating arrangement. He was safety-proofing himself against her and trying to avoid the very thing he was afraid of—being pressured into some kind of romance he wasn't interested in.

The sound of footsteps approaching had her looking up with a start. Nash. He was close enough that she could see the muscles in his forearm where he'd rolled up his sleeves.

She let out a shaky breath. No one should have sexy forearms. It just wasn't fair.

She tore her gaze away, but it was impossible not to be distracted.

From the faded denim jeans to the impossibly perfect way his buttoned-down shirt fitted his sculpted muscles, the man just reeked of masculinity and an old school allure that made her think of classic, movie-star cowboys like John Wayne.

He stopped in front of her. "You ready for your lesson?"

She gazed up at him, trying not to notice how good he smelled—like leather and sweat and everything manly in the whole wide world.

Fake-dating. Fake-dating. Fake-dating! This can never be real, and don't you dare forget it.

She gave him what she hoped was a serene smile and nodded. "I'm ready."

He reached a hand down to help her to her feet and her heart tripped over itself when she slipped her fingers into his grip.

Oh heck. Two weeks of pretending with this cowboy, followed by at least four months of not knowing if she had a home here in Aspire or not. It was going to do her head in.

She stopped short, so suddenly that Nash looked down at her in concern. "You all right?"

She nodded, but her mouth was dry.

Home. Funny how she'd never thought about it like that until now. They weren't just talking about selling a property and some empty house. They were signing off on a home. Her home. Nash's home. The O'Sullivan sisters' home.

She caught Nash's gaze narrowing on her with concern and forced a smile. "I'm fine," she said, letting go of his hand and starting for the stables. "Nothing a little fresh air won't cure."

His chuckle was low and lovely. "Spoken like a true cowgirl. You haven't even gone for your first ride yet, but I'd say you've already got the right spirit."

She laughed. "Me? A cowgirl?"

I wish.

The thought nearly brought her to a halt again, but she swallowed down her surprise and kept walking, managing just a soft rasp. "Hardly."

15

There was something wrong with Emma.

Nash had been able to sense it from the moment he'd spotted her on the porch, curled up on the seat like a kitten. She'd been frowning down at her phone, and then when she'd caught sight of him, she'd gotten all tense, like a cat about to spring.

But this was Emma, not some feline he could fix with a treat and a scratch behind the ears, so he was forced to pick his way gently through an emotional minefield.

"You sure nothing's bothering you?" he asked as they walked.

Her fingers balled into a quick fist, but then released and she tipped sideways, nudging him playfully with her shoulder.

"I'm fine," she said. She added a smile as if that would convince him.

He might not know much about women, but he could read this one.

She was not fine.

She smelled like heaven, but she was not fine. He

shook off the thought. He wasn't supposed to be noticing her scent, dang it. But he'd never smelled whatever it was she was wearing. Not a perfume, he didn't think. Maybe shampoo? Or soap?

All he knew was, it smelled like citrus and vanilla, and somehow made him feel like he'd just come home after a long trip away.

He looked down to see her tipping her face back, like she was soaking up the sun. Kinda like a cat. The thought made him snicker and she peered over at him. "What's so funny?"

He shook his head. "You just remind me of a cat soaking up the sunshine, that's all."

"Mmm." She smiled. "I've always wanted to own a cat."

"Why don't you?"

"Well, at first because they weren't allowed in the apartment I was renting, and then my sister and I moved in together about six years ago and she's… well, let's just say she's not really a pet person." She shrugged, like it was no big deal.

He found that sad. If Emma wanted a cat, she should have one.

Her closed-mouth smile couldn't hide her melancholy and it made his heart twist out of shape.

"I suppose that's one positive of Lizzy moving out after she marries, right?"

He couldn't tell, but it sounded like she actually wanted reassurance. "Right," he said.

Her smile grew a little, but still seemed heavy with sadness.

He picked up the pace the rest of the way to the stables. He was overcome with the urge to bring back the sunshine in her smile, to see those pretty blue eyes light with laughter.

He wasn't entirely sure how to do that himself, but he had a suspicion Duke would have the answers.

Once inside the stables, Nash steered them both toward the stall in the back where Duke was waiting. He'd already gotten his old stallion ready for the ride, but he wanted Emma to have a chance to get used to him before letting him out.

Nash held his hand out, looking over to Emma to show her she should do the same. She hesitated, then gingerly raised her palm for the horse to sniff. Its soft nose snuffled against her skin and she grinned.

"It tickles."

Nash's heart bloomed with affection. "Emma, meet Duke."

"Duke, huh?" She smiled at the horse, scratching the top of his nose the same way he was. "Who named this one? Kit's kids again?"

"No, ma'am," he said. "I've had Duke for ages, long before I took over as foreman here at the O'Sullivan Ranch. I named him after—"

"Don't tell me," she cut in. "John Wayne."

His eyes widened in surprise. "How'd you know?"

She started to laugh. "It's just perfect, that's all." She addressed the next comment to the Duke himself. "The perfect name for the perfect horse."

Nash chuckled. "Well, I don't know about perfect. But I think you two will hit it off." He turned to the stallion. "Duke, this is Emma. She's gonna take you out for your ride today, but you've got to promise to be on your best behavior, you hear?"

Duke's ears perked up and he let out a loud exhale through his big nostrils.

"That's my boy." Nash gave him another scratch on the nose before patting his neck.

Emma was grinning up at the horse, and Nash smirked, already thinking of how he'd have to tell the guys he'd made the right choice.

Cody had been afraid Emma would be intimidated by Duke's height. JJ and Kit were worried that Duke wouldn't take to being ridden by a newcomer. But one look at the way Emma was smiling at Duke, and the way Duke was pressing his nose into the palm of her hand, and Nash knew he'd made the right pick.

"We're going to be good friends, aren't we, Duke?" Emma said softly.

Duke answered with another huff and then leaned forward to nudge her softly, making her laugh.

"That's what I thought," she said.

Nash watched Emma with the oddest sensation in his chest. It was like his ribcage was trying to tighten and expand all at once. The result left him winded.

But truly, he'd never seen anything more beautiful than this. Emma's smile, the way her hair was pulled up, messy and touchable. She was dressed simply, in jeans and a tee, but everything about her was soft and feminine and...touchable.

He blinked and looked away. He had to stop thinking that word when he looked at her.

She might look touchable, but she wasn't his to touch.

"So where do we start?" Emma turned to him with wide, trusting eyes.

Another reminder that he had to keep his thoughts pure around this one. She'd be leaving soon, and she deserved a heck of a lot better than whatever he could offer.

Like a pretend relationship?

He shoved the thought aside. It would be for her own good, he reminded himself. Sure, he had something to gain, but he'd protect her while he was at it, and then she'd feel no obligation to stay once her time was up. She wanted to go back to Chicago. After all, it was her home. It didn't matter that she seemed to fit here with such ease. She was the type of wonderful person that could no doubt make anywhere work.

"Nash," she prompted.

"Right, well, first I'll show you how to sit on a horse, and a few basic commands."

She nodded as he went about the ritual of getting Duke ready to ride.

"Duke might be big," Nash said. "And he doesn't always have the most gracious manners. But he's a sweet-heart underneath it all. And besides, he knows this land better than anyone so he's the best tour guide you can find."

"I don't know," she said lightly. "I thought you did a pretty great job showing me around yesterday morning."

He dipped his head to hide a grin. Heck, that simple compliment should not make his chest puff up with pride, but try telling that to his ego. "Well, touring the place in a side-by-side is all fine and good," he said. "But there's nothing like viewing the range from atop a horse."

She nodded, her smile fading into a sweet, dreamy expression. "I can only imagine."

He laughed as he caught her by the waist and helped her find her footing in the saddle. She threw her leg over like she'd been born to ride, and he grinned up at her.

"You can do more than imagine, Emma. By the time you leave, you'll be riding the range like a pro."

She leaned forward and patted Duke's neck. "What do you think, Duke? Do we got this?"

Duke's whinny made them both laugh.

They started simple, and just like he'd suspected, Emma was a natural. A little timid at first, perhaps, but Nash kept a hold of the reins and Duke seemed to be in no hurry. In no time, Emma was taking the reins by herself and was riding in the saddle with ease.

"I'm doing it," she said with a grin as she and Duke made a loop around the lower corral on their own.

"And you look like a natural," he said.

Her cheeks stained pink as she smiled down at Duke and patted his neck. They were too far away for Nash to hear but he could have sworn whatever little words of love she'd been murmuring to him for the past hour, had put the stallion under her spell.

Nash could relate. The more time he spent with this woman, the more he felt like he was losing his wits. Last night, for example. The whole 'pretend to be my girlfriend' speech?

Yeah. He'd officially lost it.

But even as he'd told himself that while they made dinner together, and again this morning over eggs and toast, he couldn't bring himself to put an end to this plan before it even began.

After all, how else was he supposed to keep her close and make sure his father kept his distance?

And how else was he going to get through a family wedding without dealing with a million questions and more well-intentioned matchmakers than he could handle?

No. This was the plan, and he was sticking to it. But that led him to another dilemma he'd been grappling with all day. He wiped clammy palms on his jeans as Emma gently drew Duke to a stop beside him.

"You need a break?" he asked.

Her excitement was palpable. He'd never met anyone who was so open and genuine with her emotions, and right now joy radiated from her like sunshine.

"If I could, I would never stop," she said, leaning down to give Duke an impromptu hug.

Nash chuckled at Duke's satisfied whinny.

Oh yeah. His old stallion was a goner for this girl.

"Trust me," he said as he took the reins to hold Duke still. "Your legs will thank you tomorrow if you take it easy."

She sighed, but her smile didn't fade. "Ease in slowly, huh?"

"That's the best advice I can give a city girl when it comes to life on the range." He grinned when she feigned offense.

"City girl, huh?"

He arched an eyebrow. "Aren't you?"

She pouted but didn't respond. Instead, she slid down just like she'd gone up—smooth and graceful.

No sir, she definitely didn't move like some city girl. But then, he'd known from the first that she had an athlete's build, lean and toned. After a few days in the sun, her skin was even more golden than when she'd stepped off the plane, and her hair seemed blonder in contrast.

His heart stopped when she turned and strode toward him.

Beautiful. So dang beautiful.

He itched to reach for her—just to give her a hug. To

return some of that easy affection she was always doling out to everyone else. But he kept his hands at his sides, not at all certain that he'd be satisfied with a hug.

And this fake-dating situation was complicated enough without adding in stolen kisses.

"You getting bored with teaching a newbie how to ride?" Her gaze was flickering over his face, like she was trying to read his mind.

He had no doubt she'd caught a hint of his turmoil. Best to just get this over with rather than make the poor woman think he didn't want to be here helping her.

"Honestly?" One side of his mouth hitched up in a crooked grin as he admitted the truth. "There's no place I'd rather be right now."

Her face lit up at that, and he was sure he felt the warmth of that glow deep down in his chest. "Yeah?"

He nodded, turning to gaze out at the scenery. "I like seeing all this through your eyes. It gives me perspective. Helps me to appreciate all that God's blessed me with."

She hummed softly in response, an appreciative noise as she turned to follow his gaze. "You've been blessed, all right. This place is like heaven on earth."

He smiled. Not everyone would see it that way, but he did, and it warmed him all the way through that she obviously felt the same.

In the distance he could make out some cattle grazing, and across the way he could see the Darby's house, tucked off the main road. The back corner of his own family's property was in view too. It was much larger than the Darby's, and more sprawling and modern than the O'Sullivans.

The sight of his family's house in the distance brought him back to the moment—and to the task at hand.

"Look, Emma, you obviously should feel free to say no to this. I don't mean to put you on the spot and—"

"Oh no," Emma interrupted with a giggle. When he stopped talking she arched her brows. "You're not going to ask me to fake marry you now, are you?"

"What?" His chin jerked back. "No, of course not."

She laughed harder. "Because that little speech you just started was sounding way too familiar."

He took off his hat and twisted it in his hands with a chagrined grimace. "I told you I'm not good with all this."

Laughter still written on her features, she turned to face him head-on. "All what? What is this, exactly?"

He let out a huff of laughter at her teasing tone. She made it so easy to be himself, and he still wasn't sure how she did it. All he knew was, when he spoke to her, he didn't feel like he was being judged, and he definitely didn't feel like he was found lacking.

He felt like he was enough just as he was. And that was an incredible feeling.

She arched her brows to prompt him.

"A barbecue," he finally spit out. "My family's having a barbecue tomorrow and they're hoping you'll join us."

She blinked a couple of times. "They're hoping…" She cleared her throat. "You told them about me?"

He lifted a shoulder. "Sort of. They know you're going to be my wedding date."

"Ah," she said softly.

"So, what do you think?" he asked. He didn't even give her a chance to answer before he kept prattling on. "My mama makes a mean brisket, you should know that before you answer. And I can swear right here and now that she makes the best peach cobbler in the world."

Emma laughed. "The best peach cobbler *in the world*? That sounds like a once in a lifetime opportunity."

He feigned seriousness. "You definitely don't want to miss this chance."

"Then I have no choice." Her head fell back with another laugh and she rested a hand on his arm.

He arched a brow, trying not to notice how her palm seemed to burn a hole through the thin fabric of his shirt and sear his skin. "So, you'll come?"

She leaned in and bumped her hip against his in a move that was so playful, so affectionate, it made him wish like heck that she wouldn't be leaving quite so soon.

Or...at all.

She grinned up at him. "I wouldn't miss it."

16

N ash was in the kitchen grabbing a mug of coffee when Emma finally ambled in the next morning, bleary-eyed but happy.

"There she is," Nash said. His low drawl wrapped around her like a warm, cozy blanket as she tucked her legs under her at the kitchen table and accepted the steaming mug Nash offered with a mumble of thanks.

"Morning, sleepyhead." He grinned as she closed her eyes and moaned in appreciation at the taste of hot coffee.

She opened her eyes with a smile. She was sore everywhere and yet she'd woken up this morning feeling more relaxed and content than she could ever remember.

"I overslept," she informed him.

He slid into the seat beside her, though she knew very well he was probably in the midst of a million chores this morning.

Mornings on the ranch weren't lazy affairs.

"You must have needed the sleep," Nash said. His grin had faded to a sweet little smile. Almost...affectionate.

She looked down into her mug to stop that train of

thought. "I guess my body isn't quite used to all this exercise and fresh air."

"Or the stress," he added, his gaze knowing.

She didn't argue. It had been a stressful few days, emotionally at least.

"How're your legs feeling?" he asked.

She laughed. "I've learned there are muscles in my body that I didn't even know I had."

"I bet. We can take it easy today if you'd like."

She sat up straighter, a thrill of joy shooting through her that he was already planning on giving her another lesson. "Not on your life," she said. "I'll be ready to go again."

"You sure?"

She'd fallen asleep with a smile on her face the night before, thinking about the wind in her hair and the incredible sensation when she and Duke had started moving in unison, like there was an invisible bond between them she couldn't explain. "I'm positive."

"All right, then. But do me a favor and take it slow this morning. Your body needs time to recover, and I'm guessing the rest of you could use a rest from all the stress as well." He leaned forward and she held her breath as he tucked a stray lock behind her ear.

The gesture seemed to surprise her as much as it did him because he dropped his hand like her skin was a hot stove, and pulled it back quickly.

He looked anywhere but at her as he got to his feet. "Sorry, I... I should, uh...I should get back to my chores."

"Of course." She found herself fighting a smile at his discomfort. "I'll see you around lunchtime, for our ride?"

"Yes, ma'am." He had his hat in hand and was almost at the door when he turned back. "You still up for the barbecue later this afternoon? Because if you're not, I don't want—"

"I told you I wouldn't miss it," she said. "I was promised the best peach cobbler in the world and I mean to taste it."

The tension in his face eased. "All right then," he said gruffly. "Rest up and I'll meet you at the stables a little later."

She nodded. Her heart was oddly full when he walked out the door. It had been a long time since anyone had fretted over her like that. Lizzy worried, and she never doubted that her sister and her parents loved her unconditionally, but nine times out of ten, she was the one taking care of others. Which was great. She liked being needed.

Her gaze lingered on the door where Nash had disappeared.

But she supposed every once in a while it was nice to feel like she was the one being taken care of.

After breakfast and a quick clean of the kitchen, Emma did exactly as her new riding instructor ordered. She took her sweet time getting ready for the day. At one point she found herself facing the dreaded file again, her attention fixed on one name—April O'Sullivan.

She'd done a little digging on Sierra the night before and was no closer to a good number for the elusive eldest sister, but April's number was right there, ready and waiting to be dialed.

In the end, Nash's words came back to her, and she shut the folder with a decisive flip.

It was Saturday. She now had an extra week. Plus, she had a riding lesson and a barbecue to get ready for.

The call to April could wait one more day.

It wasn't until she got out of the shower and was

getting ready to meet Nash for her lesson that Emma heard back from Lizzy.

"Hey stranger," Lizzy said with a grin. Even on a video call, during her lunch break, Lizzy managed to look phenomenal—hair up in a stylish ponytail with large hoop earrings and makeup applied so perfectly that it high-lighted all her best features. She could have been a runway model, and had this ability to make whatever she wore look extremely cool.

"I tried you last night," Emma said. "Sorry we didn't connect."

"I was on a date with my soon-to-be-husband," Lizzy said. She started playing with her large diamond ring and it made Emma simultaneously thrilled for her sister's good fortune and just a little green with envy.

"I take it you had a good night," Emma said with a laugh.

"The best," Lizzy sighed. She filled Emma in on every detail, from the gourmet meal at the high-end restaurant to the concert after.

"Just like my night last night," Emma teased.

Lizzy laughed. "I'm guessing there aren't a lot of Michelin-rated restaurants in Aspire?"

Emma grinned. "Probably not. But I have been promised the best peach cobbler in the world."

"Oh, well then," Lizzy said. "You can't turn down that opportunity."

"That's what I said," Emma shot back.

"So where's this peach cobbler? Some bakery in town?"

"Uh, no. I've been invited to a barbecue." Emma took a breath to continue, but hesitated. Her entire life, she'd always told Lizzy everything. Even during their high school years when they'd bickered over clothes and who got to borrow the car, they'd shared all their secrets.

So the fact that Emma was hesitating now over whether or not to tell Lizzy about her new fake-dating situation was jarring. It made her wonder if she'd made the right decision, after all, if she didn't want to admit to it.

In the end, she didn't have to make a decision because Lizzy was already moving on to the next topic.

"You can tell me all about it when you get home." She flashed an impish grin. "All your stories from Aspire will help pass the time while we work on floral arrangements and make a final decision on which shoes will match our dresses the best. I also want you to check out the selection of fonts I've chosen for the order of service. There are three that I adore, but I want your help with the exact design before we print them out and start folding them all."

Emma laughed. While Lizzy's fiancé was loaded and had given Lizzy a fair chunk of money for the wedding, she'd spent most of it on the venue and her dress, which meant their parents had to cover everything else. Lizzy and Emma's parents weren't exactly rolling in the dough, so the sisters were trying their best to do most of the planning and execution themselves.

Lizzy sighed. "Oh, Em, I can't wait to pick you up on Wednesday. We have so much to catch up on. And so much to do!"

Emma winced. "Yeah. About that..."

Lizzy's face grew bigger as she pulled the phone in. "What's that supposed to mean?"

"Um, well..." Emma reminded herself of what Nash had said. It didn't always have to be about what Lizzy wanted, right? "I've decided to stay."

"You what?" Lizzy's voice got all high and tight.

Guilt flooded Emma's veins at the anxiety in her sister's voice and she rushed to reassure her. "Not forever, just another week."

"A whole week?" Lizzy sounded so distraught, Emma found herself pacing her bedroom, reconsidering all her plans.

"Dealing with this inheritance has been harder than I thought," she said. And that was putting it mildly. "I don't want to leave here until I've spoken to all of Frank's daughters and have at least some idea of what they're all thinking."

"We're all thinking we should sell," Lizzy said.

Emma arched her brows. "How would you know that? Have you talked to your other five sisters?"

Lizzy looked away from the screen, but not before Emma caught a flicker of guilt.

Emma sighed. She didn't mean to make her sister feel bad, but Lizzy had a tendency to ignore problems rather than face them head on. Derek once said Lizzy shared their mother's convenient blind spot, and Emma couldn't help but agree.

Their mother wasn't sure how to deal with the fact that their father had another daughter with his high school sweetheart, so what had she done?

Ignored the issue entirely. Out of sight, out of mind.

And she knew without a doubt that was what Lizzy was doing now with their newfound sisters. It was what she'd done their whole life when it came to their father.

They'd both loved Derek like a father, but while Emma often wondered about Frank and stashed his cards away like rare treasures, Lizzy had been content to pretend he'd never existed.

Her birthday and Christmas cards could always be

found in the trash the day they arrived—after she'd taken out the money, of course.

The silence grew too long and uncomfortable and Emma was the first to break it. "Look, I get that you don't want anything to do with them. But I have to see this through. It's important to me."

Lizzy turned her gaze back to the phone with a grudging smile. "That's because you're too nice for your own good."

Emma rolled her eyes. "I'm not *that* nice."

"Yes, you are. But please don't tell me you're going to stick around all summer, okay? I need you here with me. I can't do this wedding without you. And I still don't see why you can't make these calls from Chicago."

Emma wasn't sure either, so ignored the comment and focused on the wedding stuff. "You have mom to help you with wedding prep. And Sarah."

Lizzy pouted. "It's not the same."

Emma laughed at her sister's over-the-top expression that was partially teasing. "I'll be back in ten days. And hey, just be grateful I'm not sticking around for four months until Daisy gets here."

Lizzy's brows shot up. "Four months?"

Emma nodded and settled on her back to fill her in on her latest conversation.

"Well," Lizzy finally said when she was done. "At least this one was friendly."

"Mmm," Emma agreed. "That was a nice change."

"What about the other two? Anything new?"

Emma shook her head. "Still not sure how I'm supposed to get ahold of Sierra, and I haven't reached out to April yet."

Lizzy nodded. "Keep me posted."

"I will." She looked at the clock and sat upright. It was almost time for her riding lesson. "Lizzy, I've got to cut this short."

"I should go too. My lunch break is nearly over. Oh, Sarah and I are heading out tonight. She says we need to get all the girls' nights in before I become a boring, old married lady."

Emma laughed. "Somehow I don't think you'll ever be boring. Not when you're old, and certainly not because you're married."

"That's what I said!"

Her tone had Emma laughing again. "Love you, sis."

"Love you too. And have some fun today, you hear?" Lizzy started to giggle. "I mean, I can't imagine hanging out at the ranch is a lot of fun, but try your best."

Emma smiled, her heart already fluttering with the knowledge that even now Nash was waiting for her. "I'll try."

Nash could hear the crazy cacophony that was his extended family and friends the moment he stepped out of his truck.

He went around to Emma's side and opened the door, holding up a hand, even as he said, "And you're sure about this?"

Emma rolled her eyes, just like she'd done the last three times he'd asked on the drive over. She slid her hand into his, and let him help her down like it was the most natural thing in the world.

But that's how it always was with Emma, he'd noticed. From their meals together to the riding lessons to the quiet conversation they shared last night before saying goodnight…

It all felt natural. It all felt…right.

"I'm as sure as I'll ever be," Emma said when she was at his side. "I think maybe you're the one who's not certain."

He flinched. She wasn't wrong.

Her smile was sweet and understanding. "Look, it's

not easy to lie to your family. If you want to change your mind—"

"No," he interrupted. "I haven't changed my mind." He'd debated this six ways from Sunday, and he always came to the same conclusion. This was the best option for them both.

"Okay, as long as you're sure," Emma said.

"It's not a *big* lie," he said, sounding guilty even to himself. "We're just playing pretend. I mean, it's not the sort of thing where someone's gonna get hurt."

"That's true," she said. "And the fact that I'm leaving in ten days will make it that much easier to put an end to it all as soon as your sister's wedding is over."

"Precisely." He gave a sharp nod. "I'll just tell them that while we hit it off during your visit, we realized a long-distance relationship wasn't going to work."

"They never do," Emma said.

He couldn't tell if she was just being agreeable or speaking from experience, and he hated the stab of jealousy at the thought of her with any other man.

But of course she'd dated before. She was a grown woman. A beautiful woman. It was only a matter of time before some lucky fella figured out what a gem she was and swept her off her feet.

He clenched his jaw and started to walk for the house, then stopped and gazed down at her hand. Those small, delicate fingers had been tucked in his only moments ago when he helped her out of the truck, and well, since they were playing pretend anyway, maybe he just wanted that sensation again.

"Do you think…" He worked his jaw to the side.

Emma waited a beat, and when he didn't fill it, she ended up giggling. "Still don't bite, Nash. Just say it."

He let out a gruff laugh, then swallowed. "I was wondering if we should hold hands. I mean, can I hold your hand?" He cringed and rubbed the back of his neck. "Sorry to sound like a thirteen year old, but I... well, it just might make us look more like a couple and..."

Emma's grin made his words evaporate. It was so kind and sweet he could barely breathe. Without a word she slipped her hand in his and gave it a gentle squeeze. His large fingers wrapped around hers, a tingly sensation traveling up his arm. This was ridiculous. He was a grown man, but the simple gesture of holding her hand was making him light-headed. As they walked toward the front door of his family's sprawling ranch home, she felt like his woman, and that feeling was so good, he started doubting this fake thing all over again.

But he couldn't make it real. What they said before was true—long distance didn't work, and he couldn't keep Emma here when her heart was in Chicago. Just like he couldn't move to a big city when he was born to be a cowboy.

The party sounded like it was in full swing out back, and even from here he could smell the mouth-watering aromas.

"Come on, let's head around back," he said, steering them toward the side lawn rather than taking her on a tour of the house. He was impatient to get the worst of this over with, he supposed.

As soon as they rounded the house, he caught sight of Casey and Ryan who were talking to Casey's co-worker, Dexter Thermopolis, better known as Dr. Dex to most everyone in town. He was still pretty new on the scene, less than a year in Aspire, but when Dr. Merton retired, he wanted a young, enthusiastic doctor to take over his practice and Dex had started to win the trust of an old town set in its ways.

Nash's aunts and uncles were gathered around a folding table playing a card game while meat smoked on the grill. Some of his cousin's children were running around an inflatable pool, screaming as his mother chased them with a hose.

"A family barbecue, huh?" Amusement laced Emma's tone as she gripped his hand tightly. "This must be some family."

He chuckled, glancing down to see her watching the scene before them with wide eyes.

She didn't seem scared, but maybe a little nervous. He squeezed her hand. "They're going to love you."

Her eyes widened even further in surprise as she looked up at him. "You think so?"

"I know so." How could they not? Even now she was smiling, her eyes crinkling at the corners like she was happy as could be, even tagging along to a family event. She was dressed simply in a cotton sundress and strappy sandals, her hair loose around her shoulders, and he was positive she'd never looked more beautiful.

She bit her lip as if considering something. "If it's not their reaction to me that worries you, why are you so on edge?"

He blinked in surprise. Was that what she'd thought? That he was concerned they wouldn't approve of her? He turned to face her fully. "I'm not worried about them liking you, Emma. Like I said, they're going to love you. It's impossible not to."

That had her smile widening and his chest swelled in response.

"I'm more worried about what you'll think of them," he said.

She burst out in a laugh. "Seriously? They sound amazing." She gestured to the group. "Just look how much fun they're having. I can't wait to meet them."

"They're the best," he was quick to agree. "But if my father or any of the others corner you about the property—"

"I know, I know." She rolled her eyes. "I'll sound the alarm."

He laughed at her teasing.

She turned to face the backyard of people who had yet to notice their arrival. "So, is this really all your family?"

"There's actually a lot missing." He grinned when her jaw dropped. "A lot of my cousins have moved away over the last ten years or so. But not everyone here is family. Though they might as well be."

He pointed to a couple who were laughing and talking amongst themselves in the shade of an oak tree. "That there is Kit's parents, Anna and Jonathan. Kit will be here with the kids anytime now. JJ and Cody should be coming too."

"Oh good." She winked up at him. "Allies."

He chuckled. She'd only interacted with them a few times, but Emma and the guys on O'Sullivan Ranch had hit it off easily. Of course they had. She was sweet, outgoing, and eager to learn about ranch life. The ranch hands were all taken with her.

He caught sight of his father, laughing at something his younger cousin Boone was saying.

Boone was his Uncle Hansen's son, and the youngest of three. His two older sisters were both married and had moved out of town, but Boone had opted to go work for

Nash's dad at the ranch rather than following his own father into the hotel business.

Nash was about to give Emma another warning about his father's tendency to forget manners when he was focused on business, but they'd been spotted already.

A big grin split the older man's face as he headed toward them.

"You must be Emma," he said.

"Yes, sir." She stuck out her free hand and shook it while he introduced himself.

"Patrick Donahue."

Nash took a deep breath. "Dad, this is Emma O'Sullivan."

His father froze for just a fraction of a second while pumping her hand. But then his gaze narrowed slightly. "Frank's daughter?"

"One of them," she answered. If her tone was a little too mild, bordering on sarcastic, Nash was likely the only one who noticed.

"Well, what a pleasure." His father was looking from Emma to him and back again, clearly not sure what to make of this development.

Nash didn't give him a chance to ask.

"If you'll excuse us, we're gonna make the rounds," Nash said, wrapping an arm around Emma's shoulders.

She fitted against his side like they'd always been joined at the hip. "Lead the way," she said, smiling up at him.

He let out a loud exhale as they walked away and she laughed softly. "I didn't think he was so bad."

He winced. Guilt flickered through him. He hadn't meant to make his father out to be a bad guy. He wasn't. He just wore blinders, that was all. But the fact that his father had restrained himself just now rather than diving right into talk about buying the land was a good sign.

Maybe she hadn't needed him to protect her after all.

"So?" she asked. "Where to next?"

He spotted his grandparents sitting on lawn chairs by the fire pit. "Let's start with my grandma and grandpa. They know just about everyone in this town, and they have all the stories you'll ever want to hear about how this place was settled and its history going all the way back to the nineteenth century."

"Ooh, fascinating," Emma said. "I'd love to meet them."

But his mother spotted them first and dropped the hose, hurrying over with outstretched arms.

Correction. She was heading toward Emma with outstretched arms. She didn't spare a glance at Nash as she tackled poor Emma in a bear hug.

Emma returned the hug, flashing Nash a private smile over his mother's shoulder before she pulled back to answer the questions being flung in her direction.

"Ma, please," Nash said, groaning as his mother slipped an arm through Emma's and started to drag her off toward his sister. "Don't hog her all night."

His mother lifted a hand in a dismissive wave as Emma turned to give him one last laughing grin before being hauled off.

18

E mma was having a blast. She had no idea what Nash had been so worried about. From the way he'd been fretting on the drive over, she'd started to get a little nervous herself, wondering if maybe his family was full of hypercritical snobs or something.

Judging by the size of the house and the vast acreage of their property, it had been a distinct possibility. They were wealthy, that was for sure. Wealthy and large—she still couldn't get over how many people were at this gathering.

And she was pretty sure Nash's fears about his father and his family's interest in the O'Sullivan land was overblown too. Why, his father hadn't even mentioned it. And while his mother and sister had been surprised and excited to discover her connection to the neighboring property, they hadn't mentioned a potential sale either.

But then, they both were way more focused on the fact that she was dating Nash. And going to the wedding. Casey, in particular, was talking a mile a minute about the big day and Emma could only grin. The girl was a sweetheart. Younger than Emma by a few years, and filled with an infectious energy that made her a joy to talk to.

"...and that, of course, was a gift from Ryan's parents." Casey leaned in as if Ryan's parents might overhear. Doubtful, considering Casey had just told her that they'd be flying in for the wedding next week from their home in Michigan. "But honestly, Emma, what am I supposed to do with two insta-pots? I don't even cook!"

Emma opened her mouth to respond, but was cut short by Casey and Nash's mother, who caught her by the arm. "Casey, I need to borrow Emma, sweetheart. Everyone wants to meet Nash's new lady friend."

Emma bit her lip to smother a laugh. New lady friend, huh? From what she could gather, she was the first 'lady friend' Nash had ever brought to a family gathering.

Emma took a deep breath to squelch a little thrill. It didn't mean anything, obviously. This was only for show. She couldn't allow herself to forget that.

She had just enough time to catch sight of Nash deep in conversation with two older men—his uncles, maybe. He caught sight of her at the same time and raised a hand as if to call her over...but his mother wasn't having it.

"You two kids have all the time in the world to spend together," she said by way of apology. "But I'll never live it down if everyone here doesn't have a chance to meet you."

Emma laughed, allowing Delphine Donahue to drag her away to the kitchen, where a handful of older women were sipping lemonade around the table.

She had to blink for a moment to take in the modern splendor that was the kitchen. While the house retained a log cabin charm, it had all the upgrades and modern functionality of the grandest new home. The kitchen alone felt like half the size of the entire O'Sullivan ranch house.

"Here she is," Delphine announced, pushing Emma forward gently by the shoulders and showing her off like a new work of art.

She was treated to a whole host of curious stares, but as they were all paired with warm smiles, it didn't bother her.

Delphine made the introductions, ending with the elementary school principal Abigail Toulouse, a friendly middle-aged woman with a round face and dark hair.

"Something tells me you two will have quite a bit in common," Delphine said. "Emma here teaches kindergarten."

Delphine ran off to replenish snacks for the table while Abigail and Emma kept up a lively conversation about the local school and Emma's teaching career. By the time dinner was served and the crowd was pouring back outside to help themselves to the buffet-style meal, Emma felt like maybe she'd made a new friend.

"Are you coming?" Abigail asked as she gathered her things to follow the others outside.

"I'll be out in just one moment," she said. "Could you just point me toward the bathroom first?"

Following Abigail's instructions, Emma found her way through a hallway, pausing to check out the large den with its high-ceiling and big-screen TV, as well as a formal dining room and an office.

The home was the perfect blend of homey and spacious. Like you could cozy up with a good book in any of these dark-wood trimmed rooms but thanks to the large picture windows and skylights, you never lost the sense that you were out in the open, surrounded by nature.

It was perfect. Exactly the sort of feel she'd want to convey if she ever redid the O'Sullivan ranch house.

She stopped short in the bathroom, considering her reflection as she registered that errant thought.

She wasn't really thinking about redoing the house, was she? That would only make sense if she meant to stay and make it into a real home.

Her own gaze stared back at her until she gave her head a shake.

No, Chicago was her home. That's where her family was, her school, her life.

When she was done in the bathroom, she stepped back into the hallway. Her stomach growled, teased by the smells of dinner this past hour, but she'd rather find Nash first and eat with him.

She hadn't spoken a word to him since they'd first arrived and she'd been whisked away. Oddly enough, she missed him. Or...no. She just needed a moment with a friend, that was all. He was familiar, that was probably the only reason he seemed like home base at a party full of relative strangers.

"Emma!" The sound of her name had her stopping short.

She'd been so lost in thought she'd nearly run smack into Patrick Donahue, Nash's father.

They looked so similar, her face automatically creased in a smile. "Patrick. Sorry I didn't see you there."

He gestured toward the back porch. "You heading out to eat?"

"I was, yes."

"Then let me walk with you." He flashed her a grin. "This house can be a maze if you're not used to it."

"Thanks," she said with a laugh.

"And while I've got you alone for a moment..." The change in his voice was slight but for some reason, it put her on edge. "I'd love to chat with you about your plans and how you'd do well to sell the ranch to me."

"Oh! Uh…" Emma couldn't say she hadn't been warned. And yet, she'd gotten so comfortable chatting with Nash's family she was caught off guard. "Well, you see, there are a number of loose ends I need to tie up before we can take any next steps."

His smile fell slightly. "I see." His brows drew down. "But you *are* planning on selling."

She blinked. "Like I said, the family has to attend to some business before we decide what to do next."

That was clearly not what he wanted to hear. "When do you think you'll know?"

"Um…" She glanced around as if help might come rushing into the hallway. All at once she remembered her teasing comment about sounding an alarm.

Right now an alarm didn't seem like the worst idea. Nash's father wasn't being rude, by any means, but she was definitely put on the spot. His intense gaze made her skin itch just a little, made her feel like she'd been called into the principal's office or something.

"I'm afraid there's a lot to consider at the moment, but if we decide to sell, you'll be the first to know."

She'd thought that would put an end to it, but it seemed to make Nash's father agitated. "*If* you decide to sell? Don't you mean *when*?"

Her lips moved but nothing came out. Yes, she probably did mean when. But she couldn't bring herself to say it.

It felt too much like a promise she wasn't sure she could make.

A promise she wasn't certain she wanted to make.

The thought had her breaths growing short and

uneven. She couldn't really be thinking about *not* selling, could she?

No. Of course not. But she hadn't talked to April yet, and Daisy was on the fence and—

And the thought of her sisters relieved her tension. It wasn't up to her. Not entirely. She didn't have to make this decision alone.

She tilted her chin up. "I'm afraid I'm not the only one making that decision, Mr. O'Sullivan." She took a step away. "Now, if you'll excuse me…"

She started walking away before she even finished speaking, not wanting to hear his response.

She took a deep breath when she hit the backyard. All at once the stiff, awkward tension of that run-in with Patrick was replaced by the warm welcoming atmosphere of the barbecue.

No less than three people tried to wave her over to join them but she just smiled as she sought out one Donahue in particular.

He spotted her first.

"Emma," he said as he reached her side. He wrapped an arm around her waist. "How are you doing? You holding up all right?"

He wore a smile, but she caught the hint of concern in his eyes.

She smiled, resting against him as the last of her unease faded away. He'd warned her his father could be intense, and he was. But she'd handled it, and it was certainly nothing to stir up trouble about.

She had a hunch that if she ratted his father out, Nash would be furious, so she just smiled. "I'm doing great. But I'm starving."

He chuckled and dropped a kiss on the top of her head. "As soon as Dad's said grace, we'll get you fed."

As if on cue, a sharp whistle rent the air. Patrick drew the attention of the crowd, welcoming them all to the bbq and thanking his lovely wife for her exceptional hostessing skills. Wrapping his arm around her shoulders, Patrick kissed Delphine's cheek, making her smile grow even wider. Emma watched him closely, struggling to match the intense man she'd just walked away from to the seemingly carefree one grinning down at his wife.

"Grandpa Donahue, how about you say grace for us tonight." Patrick gestured for his father to stand.

Everyone bowed their heads as the patriarch of the family thanked God for the food and His abundant blessings.

"Amen," Emma murmured with everyone, her soft voice blending with the low rumble of Nash's.

A sweet warmth spread through her like molasses in her veins as he squeezed her waist and guided them toward the long line of tables filled with food.

She smiled up at him. "Your family is really great, you know that?"

"I know," he said simply. "I'm a lucky guy."

She nodded. "You really are."

"But I'm especially lucky that you said yes," he added.

She laughed. "You don't have to say that."

"I do." He gave her waist a squeeze before letting her go so she could fill her plate. "You're a really good friend, Emma."

Her smile faltered as she dropped her gaze to the plate in her hand. She was a good friend. How many times had guys said something like that to her?

More than she could count.

Cute but never beautiful. Funny but never charming. Sweet but never sexy. She just barely held back a sigh because...he'd meant it to be kind. A compliment. And that was exactly how she ought to take it.

"I might be a good friend." She forced another smile as she gave him a teasing wink and whispered, "But *you* make an excellent fake boyfriend."

19

There was something wrong. Nash had noticed it the moment Emma stepped out of the house and into the backyard.

He'd spotted her before she'd seen him, and he'd watched it flash across her face. What 'it' was precisely, he wasn't sure. And they hadn't had a moment alone for him to ask properly. The second their plates were full, they'd been surrounded by family and friends, everyone stopping by their picnic table to get their own take on his new girlfriend.

All the while, Nash couldn't stop watching Emma, looking for any sign of distress.

And she noticed. "Honestly, Nash," she said as their latest visitor walked away. "I know you're really invested in playing the dutiful boyfriend, but you don't have to worry about me."

He gave her a sheepish grin. "Was I hovering?"

She glanced pointedly at his arm which was wrapped around her tightly, like someone might steal her away.

He loosened his hold with a little grimace that made

her laugh. "Sorry," he said. "It's just...you got pulled away and I know people must have been pestering you—"

"It's fine." She waved off his concern. "I can handle some curious stares."

He glanced over at the porch where his father was standing with his brothers, Hansen and Mace. Patrick was talking to them but his gaze never strayed from Nash and Emma.

"Did my dad say anything to you?" he asked. "When you were inside?"

There was that flicker again. A hint of unease before her normal cheerful smile was back in place. "It's fine, Nash. Relax."

"Fine, huh?" He shook his head. He wasn't sure she even knew what an open book she was.

He leaned in, ready to ask more about what transpired inside, but they were cut off by two little ones racing in their direction, hands up like claws as they roared.

To his surprise, Emma didn't miss a beat. She held her hands up like claws and bared her teeth as she growled right back.

Kit's twins, Chloe and Corbin, stopped in their tracks, gaping at Emma with open mouths.

If Nash believed in love at first sight, he was sure he'd just witnessed it now between Emma and the twins.

Chloe recovered from her shock first.

"You're funny," she giggled.

"And you're cute," Emma shot back with a grin.

Corbin watched her with serious curiosity. "Are you a school teacher? My dad says you teach kids."

Emma nodded, matching his seriousness as though she were talking to another professional and not a little boy with ketchup stains on his shirt. "I teach Kindergarten."

Chloe gasped. "We're going to be in kindy-garten when school starts."

Emma's eyes widened. "Oh, how exciting."

Corbin shrugged, kicking the dirt at his feet.

Emma leaned forward so she was at his eye level. "You don't like school?"

"I like playing." His lower lip stuck out so far Nash had to bite his own lip to keep from laughing.

But Emma had no problem staying serious, her brows down as she considered that with a nod. "Well, playing *is* learning. That's what I tell the kids in my class. We don't do any work at school." She sat upright with a shrug. "We just play all day."

Nash noticed Principal Toulouse watching Emma from where she sat at the next table over. A smile played on her lips as she listened to Emma telling an enraptured Chloe and Corbin a story from her class last year, all about how they built a rocket ship out of cardboard and learned about the planets by flying through space.

"Did you go to the moon?" Corbin asked with furrowed brows.

"Oh yes, our moon landing was very successful. And you should have heard my kids." Emma beamed with pride. "They could tell you everything there is to know about space by the time we returned back to Earth. Plus, they learned a bunch of math, how to work as a team, how to construct things and explain how something works. It was very impressive."

"I know three planets!" Corbin lifted his chin with pride.

Emma leaned forward with obvious interest. "Okay, go."

Corbin straightened like a cadet being called to attention. "Mars, Jupiter and the one with the rings."

Emma arched a brow playfully. "Do you remember what the one with the rings is called?"

"Umm…"

"Sssss…" Emma whispered quietly.

"Saturn!" Corbin threw his arms in the air.

"Good job." Emma grinned. "Wow, you know what? I think you are going to rock the kindy world."

"If we get to build spaceships, I'll love it." Corbin's eyes were gleaming with excitement like he wanted to start kindergarten right this second.

Nash glanced over to see Principal Toulouse still watching Emma with a small smile and a light in her eyes like she'd just discovered a rare gem.

Maybe she had.

"Tell us something else you did," Chloe piped up. "Do you get to play with dolls and stuff?"

"Some of my kids practice reading to their dolls. They bring them in at storytime and read out loud to them. And at the end of last year, we did a cool project where my students got to design and make a teddy bear."

Chloe's eyes grew so wide it looked painful. "They made a bear?" she whispered in awe.

"Yeah, from scratch." Emma nodded.

Nash dipped his head with a chuckle. Now both Chloe and Corbin were gazing up at Emma like she hung the moon.

He snuck one last look at this woman who'd won over every member of his family in one foul swoop. He couldn't blame the kids for being in awe. He was pretty dang awed himself.

Out of the corner of his eye, Nash spotted his father peeling away from his brothers to head inside.

"Will you excuse me?" he murmured to Emma.

She flashed him a quick grin and a wink before turning her attention back to the litany of questions Chloe was rattling off.

He found his father alone in the kitchen, restocking some ice into a bucket for the cooler. Nash didn't waste a second. "Did you say something to Emma?"

His father turned around, a brow arched in wry amusement. "You didn't tell me she was an O'Sullivan."

Nash swallowed. "Yeah, about that…"

His father laughed. "It's all right, son, I get it."

"You do?"

"Of course." His father took a step forward and patted him on the shoulder, a knowing glint in his eyes. "At first I couldn't believe it, you only met her a few days ago. But I've been watching you two together all evening, and I can see why you think this will work. I've got to say, I'm impressed."

Nash's brows came down. "You are?"

The laughter faded and the wrinkles around his eyes grew deeper. "But, son…" The look of fatherly concern made Nash tense. "I appreciate that you always put family first, just be sure you don't break the poor girl's heart while you're at it, all right?"

Break her… "What are you talking about?"

His father backed up with another laugh, wagging a finger playfully. "I'd rather buy the property outright, but if worse comes to worse, marrying into the land is the next best option."

Nash blinked. Marrying? Who said anything about marrying?

And...marrying for the land?

Revulsion twisted his gut. "What?"

His father winked. "It's good thinking, son."

"Good..." He started to repeat his father like a dang parrot before sense kicked in. "Dad, I'm not—"

"There he is." Mace's voice filled the kitchen. "Patrick, you'd better get back out here. We need your help with the grill. You know how ravenous this family gets. Demands for seconds are already flooding in."

"Dad, wait—" Nash stopped abruptly because his father was already in conversation with Mace and heading out the door.

And Nash was left reeling.

How could it even occur to his dad that he was using Emma just to get to her land?

He ran a hand over his face. The fact that his father could even think about that let him know just how far gone he was with this obsession to better the family's prospects.

He sighed wearily but followed after his father and Mace.

After all, Emma was still out there. And whether she knew it or not, she needed his protection now more than ever.

E mma nibbled on her lower lip as she stared at the contents of the pantry.

"Need help finding something?" Kit's voice had her whirling around.

"Oh! You startled me," she said with a laugh as she clapped a hand to her racing heart.

"Sorry." His grin was unapologetic as he leaned back against the kitchen counter. "I was just going to ride into town if you want me to pick something up for you."

He nodded toward the pantry.

She shook her head. "Oh no, I'm fine, thanks. There's plenty here, I was just hoping to keep myself busy by baking, so I thought I'd see what I have enough supplies for."

Not much, was her answer.

"Well, whatever you can't find in there, you just let me know." His eyes brightened. "Or better yet, you can come into town with me if you'd like."

"I should really stay here and…" Her voice trailed off. And what?

In the two days that had passed since the barbecue, she'd managed to keep busy. Sunday was taken up with church and more "faking it" with Nash as her boyfriend, but she'd loved being in the quaint wooden building and listening to the pastor speak about God's blessings and how it was good to take the time to count them.

Nash took her for another riding lesson that afternoon and she sure felt blessed by that.

Yesterday was filled with more riding, learning how to feed the chickens and pigs, helping out with the cooking, and digging into her sisters' files.

Not that she'd accomplished much on the sister front. She'd tracked down a potential number for Sierra and left a message on a voicemail that had a robotic voice and didn't give a name, just the number she'd dialed. Was it Sierra's? And if it was, did she even check it?

Emma didn't know.

Then there was April. True to her promise, she'd called April the day after the barbecue. She'd called, texted, and sent an email over the last forty-eight hours and hadn't heard a peep in response.

Today she was restless and unsettled since her time was once again running out and she still had so much unfinished business.

And pacing around an empty house wasn't exactly helping.

She closed the pantry door with a decisive click. "I've changed my mind. If you don't mind me tagging along, I'd love a ride."

Kit's easy grin widened. "Great." He glanced out toward the range with a knowing look. "Should we tell the boss man, so he doesn't think I'm running off with his girl?"

Emma laughed because he was obviously teasing, but her cheeks grew warm as she ducked her head. Kit and the other ranch hands knew very well that this was just a temporary ruse, but they insisted on acting like it was real.

It was frustrating because she was having a difficult enough time as it was remembering that the hand holding and snuggling was just for others, although the laughter and the easy conversation when they were here alone was genuine. They stayed up way too late the night before playing cards and laughing their way through childhood stories. Nash was the easiest person to be around and leaving him next week was going to hurt. Fake boyfriend or not, she loved his company.

A fact that both confused and delighted her. She shouldn't want this so much.

She reached for her purse on the counter. All the more reason to get out, get some distance. Maybe being around others would help to clear her head.

On the way into town, Kit kept up an easy stream of conversation, filling her in on some of the local politics and making her laugh with his twins' latest antics.

"And boy, will they not stop talking about you." He chuckled. "I wish *you* were going to be their kindergarten teacher. Ol' Ms Grantham can be a real battleaxe sometimes. I still don't understand how she's taught five and six year olds for so long. But she's all Aspire has, so what can I do?"

"Aw, those older teachers bring a lot of experience to the table and really help the children pick up quick routines that will only enhance their learning. I'm sure Corbin and Chloe will be just fine."

Kit bobbed his head, but didn't raise a smile, his finger tapping on the steering wheel.

Emma had seen it a thousand times before. Parents naturally worried about their children, especially when big changes were on the horizon.

"So, I've got to go to the hardware store just outside of town," Kit said as they drew closer to Aspire's main street. "Nash's uncle owns the place."

"Mace, right?" she asked.

"Yes, ma'am. But there's not much to see or do around there, so if it's all right with you, I'll drop you off downtown and come back and collect you in an hour or so."

"That sounds perfect," she said.

She probably should have known by now that none of Nash's friends would let her get out of the truck and wander around on her lonesome. Nope. Kit got out too and escorted her into the local diner, Mama's Kitchen, where he seemed totally confident he'd find some friends to show her around.

Not surprisingly, he did.

"Kit!" An older woman behind the counter called out his name in a way that reminded Emma of *Cheers*. The silver-haired woman wiped her hands on her apron as she turned an expectant smile on Emma. "Who do we have here?"

Before Kit could reply, Casey leapt up from a large table in the back that was filled with people. "This is Emma, my brother's girlfriend."

The older woman raised her eyebrows, indicating that she knew exactly who Casey was talking about.

Emma blinked, but didn't have time to respond as Casey rushed over to give her a hug. She turned back to the group she'd just left and said in a loud stage whisper, "She's the one I was telling you guys about."

The reception was...overwhelming. Nearly a dozen

faces were beaming at her in welcome. Many of them were familiar, as she'd spied them at church, but hadn't had any formal introductions. It looked like that would be happening today. All were clearly eager to meet the woman who'd won Nash's heart.

She just barely stifled a sigh.

Kit patted her shoulder and gave her a sympathetic smile. "I'll be back soon. Good luck."

She nodded as she let Casey drag her over to the large group. There were a few familiar faces, including Nash's Aunt Lisa, a sweetheart she'd enjoyed chatting with at the barbecue, and the elementary school principal Abigail, who greeted her like they were old friends.

She met a lot of new people as well, too many and too quickly to catch all their names right away. But she found out soon why they'd pulled all these tables together in the back. They were having one last meeting before some big festival the following night.

"It's the Aspire Days Festival," Casey informed her, tugging her into the inner circle as if she belonged there.

"It's a celebration of the town's founding," the local librarian told her.

"An annual event since 1893," Aunt Lisa added proudly.

"Wow, that's quite a tradition," she said.

"It's a lot of fun." Casey beamed. She was decked out in her scrubs, clearly on a break from her job at Dr. Dex's office. "But it also serves a vital purpose for our local nonprofits and volunteer organizations."

The librarian, a cute little redhead who looked to be about the same age as Emma, stepped in to explain. "We hold a lot of fundraisers throughout the festival to raise money for the local food bank, the library, the fire station…"

With that, she gestured to a handsome young man who was built like a fire-truck. His large, muscular frame looked comically out of place with this table full of women. He gave Emma a sheepish grin as he said to Aunt Lisa, "I'm still not sold on this idea."

Clearly she'd come along in the middle of a conversation.

Aunt Lisa pursed her lips. "It's too late to back out now, Ethan."

He winced. "But a bachelor auction? It's so embarrassing."

Casey patted his shoulder. "Just think of all the money you'll raise for the fire station." To Emma she added quietly. "Except for Ethan and a couple other firefighters, it's a seasonal station that's mostly manned by volunteers."

Ethan sighed wearily. "I suppose you're right. But it's still humiliating."

There were a few chuckles but Aunt Lisa was already calling them back to order to discuss the next topic.

Casey whispered to her, "We won't make you sit through the whole boring meeting. I'm guessing you came into town for a reason."

"I just want to pick up some baking supplies," she said.

Casey nodded. "I have to get back to work, so I'll walk you over."

"I'll come too," Ellie said, flashing Emma a shy smile. "The library calls."

They made their excuses and headed out into the sunshine. Emma was struck all over again by the charming quaintness of it all. From the old-school movie theater to

186

the cozy-looking bookstore with a large sign reminding the townsfolk of the weekly book club.

Yep, this place had 'Hallmark movie' written all over it.

Emma couldn't help a grin. Just walking down Main Street made her heart feel warm with a sense of belonging.

You belong here. Nash's low, comforting voice whispered in the back of her mind. He hadn't meant it like that. He hadn't meant she belonged here forever, just for now because she technically owned the land.

She knew that logically, but it didn't stop her mind from calling up his words like it was a melody she couldn't stop humming. She gave her head a little shake and came back to the present just in time to hear Casey and Ellie laughing about poor Ethan's bachelor auction.

"It's all just for fun," Casey assured Emma. "He and the other single firefighters and volunteers do this every year." She flashed Emma a wicked grin. "Even Nash took part one year when he was a volunteer for the station."

"He did?" She laughed, trying to imagine the serious, quiet cowboy on some stage being auctioned off like a piece of meat.

"Oh yes," Ellie giggled. "He was so in demand, I thought a fight might break out between Misty Traynor and Olivia Munster. Do you remember?"

Casey nodded and both women were laughing.

Emma tried to ignore a stab of jealousy, though she supposed she ought to be grateful for the reminder that he wasn't hers to keep. The moment she was gone, he'd be fair game, and from the sounds of it, he could have his pick.

A sour taste filled her mouth and her voice was a little too forcefully cheerful. "Are either of you going to be bidding?"

Casey pursed her lips and pretended to consider. "Although I'd love to see Ryan's face if I bid on a bachelor days before our wedding, I'm gonna pass."

"Good idea," Ellie said with a laugh. "And I'm out too, I'm afraid. Although I don't think my husband would care all that much either way."

Emma caught a sympathetic wince from Casey but Ellie shook her head with a determined smile. "What about you, Emma?"

Emma hesitated, scrambling for what to say. "I don't think that's a good idea. I'm, you know… I'm with… he's my boyfriend and…" She huffed out a little laugh. Lying to these two was a tricky business. It didn't sit right, but she couldn't betray Nash's trust, so she cleared her throat and tried for a last minute save. "I'd be happy to donate money to the cause, though."

Casey snorted. "I want you to bid just so I can see Nash's face go green with envy."

Emma's stomach dipped with disappointment. He wouldn't be jealous. Not really. Maybe he'd pretend to keep up their ruse, but the thought of lying even more to these kind, welcoming women made her stomach turn.

She forced a smile and pointed to a shop in front of them. "Is that the grocery store?"

"That's it," Casey agreed. "And if you don't find what you're looking for, Hazel at the bakery can help you out."

Ellie paused in front of a narrow, two-story brick building. "This is my stop."

"We'll see you at the festival tomorrow?" Casey asked.

"Of course."

Casey turned to Emma. "I'm sure I'll see you there tomorrow, right?"

"I…I don't know," she said honestly. This was the first

she was hearing about it, and while she felt ridiculous even admitting it to herself, she felt a stab of sadness that Nash hadn't invited her.

"Well, I hope I see you there," Casey said, leaning forward to peck her cheek. "But if I don't, I know I'll be seeing you at my wedding."

Emma was still laughing at the high-pitched squeal Casey let out at the mention of her big day. Her unadulterated excitement was contagious, and Emma found herself still smiling as she perused the aisles of the small store, gathering ingredients for cherry pie. There was no way she'd be able to outdo that peach cobbler. It was definitely the best she'd ever tasted, but her cherry pie was pretty good too and the idea of making it for Nash had her insides bubbling with giddy joy.

As she loaded up her cart with butter, cream and flour, she tried not to think about what little time she had left in Aspire, but how best to use it.

She needed to stop thinking ahead and focus on the moment. Be present, count her blessings and enjoy this small town and the O'Sullivan ranch.

By the time Kit came to collect her, she was feeling more like herself again.

A trip to town was exactly what she'd needed.

T he smell of cherry pie hit Nash like a ton of bricks when he walked into the house later that afternoon.

His mouth watered instantly at the delicious aroma and he followed it into the kitchen like some cartoon dog being pulled by his nose. When he turned the corner into the kitchen, he stopped short.

His breath left his lungs in a whoosh at the sight before him.

Emma waltzed around his kitchen like she belonged there. She did belong there, obviously, being her kitchen and all. But he'd never seen her like this. Her hair was pulled up in some messy updo, her feet were bare, and she was singing softly along to the radio.

His lips twitched with amusement. He recognized the pop country tune, but he never would have guessed Emma was a country music girl.

He watched in a daze, his chest tight as she moved her hips in time to the beat while finishing some task at the standing mixer before turning to check something in the oven.

That was when she spotted him and she jumped with a gasp. "Nash!" She blinked a couple times. "Why is everyone sneaking up on me today?"

He chuckled. "I don't know that I was sneaking. I walked in here like I always do." He glanced toward the radio with a smirk. "It seems you were just distracted."

She wrinkled her nose, her cheeks flushing. "You heard me singing, huh?"

He crossed his arms and leaned against the doorframe. "You have a pretty voice."

The pink color deepened as she shrugged. "The kids in my class don't mind it. And as I've learned recently, it might just run in the family."

"Oh yeah?" He arched a brow, honestly curious, which surprised him. All these years trying to avoid family drama, including other people's families, but he couldn't stop thinking about Emma and what she was dealing with.

It seemed every morning when he woke and every night as he was drifting off to sleep, his thoughts kept returning to her. Every inch of him wanted to help. To sort out all her issues so he'd never see that crease of concern between her brows when she was staring at that dang file.

There were some days he had half a mind to call these sisters of hers himself just to give them a piece of his mind. There were seven of them. How was she the only one taking responsibility for this land and the inheritance?

It didn't seem right.

He hadn't wanted to pry, but she hadn't been forthcoming with information about her sisters these past couple days. He wasn't sure if that was because there was nothing new for her to talk about...or if whatever his father had said had made her wary of opening up to him.

The thought made him tense as he stepped further into the kitchen. He hoped she understood that whatever his father's interest in her property—and his too, if he were being honest—he'd never take advantage of her and her trust.

He eyed her now as she turned back to the counter to flick off the music, her gaze averted.

She did know she could trust him, right?

"What are you making?" he asked, thrilled by the thought she could create something that smelled so delicious. She hadn't mentioned her talent for baking.

"Cherry pie," she said. "It's kind of like my signature dish."

"That's my favorite pie."

"Really?" Her eyes widened. "I thought it was your mom's peach cobbler."

"That's cobbler, we're talking pie right now."

She laughed, and the sound wrapped around him like a hug. "It's done, if you'd like a slice." She gestured to the mixer. "I was just making some whipped cream to go on top."

"I'd love to try some."

Her smile was sunshine and rainbows and everything good in the world. It made his heart kick erratically and he was still trying to calm this ridiculous reaction as she turned away to slide the pie out of the oven.

He reached for some plates, and as she went to slice him off a piece, he noticed the flour that streaked her cheek.

He chuckled softly at the sight, a sudden surge of affection hitting him so fierce it made his ribcage feel like a vise as his chest ached with it.

"Here you go." She offered it up to him with an expectant smile, so sweet he knew without a doubt he'd gush and rave even if it tasted like asphalt.

Luckily he didn't have to lie or exaggerate. His eyes closed with a groan.

"Yeah?" she asked, excitement in her voice.

"This is amazing." He opened his eyes to meet her gaze. "This is even better than Mama's Kitchen."

She giggled. "Don't let Mama hear you say that."

He laughed. "I heard you went into town today. I take it you met Hattie May?"

"If that's the nice older woman behind the counter at Mama's Kitchen, then yes. Although I didn't get her name."

He pointed his fork at her. "Aren't you having any?"

She beamed. "I thought you'd never ask."

He chuckled as he watched her dish out a piece for herself and soon enough they were both sighing contentedly.

Now would be the time to ask her. He watched her as she sank into a chair at the table, her gaze distant, a smile tugging at her lips as she enjoyed the fruits of her labor.

A nervousness he rarely felt around Emma rose up all at once. All morning he'd been thinking about how he might ask her to attend the festival with him.

It shouldn't be a big deal, but try telling that to his pounding heart.

He'd already asked her to a wedding, for heaven's sake. And she'd been the perfect date at his family's barbecue, enduring their curiosity and prying with all the grace and charm he'd come to expect from this warm, vivacious woman.

Asking her to the festival was no different than the wedding or the barbecue. Except...

It was. He couldn't say why. Maybe because he honestly wanted her to go as his date. Not as his pretend date, and not for any other reason than...he wanted to spend time with her.

And that confused things. It made him question his own motives in asking her, and he couldn't help but wonder if she'd question it too.

It made him wonder if she felt this connection between them. The draw that made him want to tug her into his arms whenever she was near.

She looked up and caught him staring. If she was surprised, she didn't show it, she just flashed him a friendly grin. "So what're you up to now? Don't tell me you're already done for the day."

He laughed at her teasing. She'd mentioned several times over the last few days just how in awe she was of the hours he and his men worked and how much labor went into running this place.

"Not yet," he said. "I still have some chores to do before nightfall."

He set his empty plate down in the sink and was about to head out the door when she stopped him.

"Can I help?"

He turned to face her, eyes wide with surprise. "Pardon?"

She shifted from foot to foot, her empty plate in hand. "I don't really have anything to do this afternoon, and I know I'd probably just get in the way, but...if I can help at all, maybe you could finish up those chores a little sooner."

His lips twitched, yet another thrill racing through him.

It was driven by ample amounts of wonder and affection. She really was the best woman he'd ever met.

"Of course you can." He took in her cute little sundress and bare feet. "Why don't you put on some jeans and boots and I'll clean up in here." He pointed to the sink. "Meet you by the stables?"

There was that sudden beaming grin again, and he felt like he'd just won the Superbowl.

"I'll be there in ten minutes," she said in a rush, already hurrying out of the kitchen toward her bedroom.

Later that afternoon...he was standing in the stables, shaking his head in awe.

He glanced over at JJ and Kit, and immediately realized he wasn't the only one. All three of them were watching as Emma threw herself into mucking out the stalls with the same energy and enthusiasm she'd brought to every other menial chore she'd been assigned.

He'd tried to take it easy on her when they'd first set out, but it had become abundantly clear over the past few hours that, despite her self-deprecating jokes about being a city girl, she had no problem getting her hands dirty or working up a sweat. Sure, she'd managed a little Montana shoeshine when she stepped in cow dung, but after a gasp of shock, she'd laughed like it was the funniest thing. And then there was that moment when she touched the electric fence and nearly jumped a mile. Nash felt kind of bad about that one. He should have warned her, but she brushed off his apology with a wave of her hand and that easy smile he adored so much.

Kit leaned against the stall door behind him, a goofy grin on his face. "I might be in love," he murmured.

Nash shot him a sidelong glare. His friend was teasing. He knew that. For all his flirting and all his charm, Nash had known him long enough to see when he was truly taken with a woman, and Nash hadn't seen him that way since Natalie.

The twins' mother had been his first and last love, and sometimes Nash worried that her betrayal had hurt his oldest friend so badly he'd never let himself fall again.

In spite of that, he glowered at his friend now. While he wanted to see the man move on, he wasn't about to let the charmer anywhere near his girl.

His fake girl.

Whatever.

He turned back to Emma with a huff as he reminded himself that this was Kit. The guy wasn't serious about women. Although he had been joking a lot lately about finding a mother for his kids...

An image rose up in Nash's mind and it hit him like a sucker punch. He nearly bent over with the force of it. Emma with a babe in her arms. Not just a babe, *his* babe. Emma with a little girl with blonde locks just like hers. Emma with a houseful of kids running around her and making her laugh.

Aw heck. He had to banish that picture right here and now. Tempting as it might be, she'd be leaving soon enough, and thoughts like these weren't his to have.

She straightened then, turning to swipe a stray hair off of her face with the back of her hand. She laughed softly at the sight of him and the others watching her. "What? Am I doing it wrong?"

JJ was the first to respond. "No, ma'am." He removed his hat and held it over his heart. "We're all just wondering how we can convince you to stay here forever."

Emma's laughter was light and sweet as she shook off the idea.

She still had every intention of leaving and selling this place just as quickly as she could get all the signatures. That was what her laughter told Nash.

It was a good reminder, and it was exactly what he needed to hear.

No more letting his attraction for her mess with his head. They were friends, that was all. And so long as he remembered that, no one would get hurt.

She stuck her pitchfork in the dirt and leaned against it slightly, her cheeks flushed. "So? What's next?"

He walked toward her with a chuckle, taking the pitchfork so he could put it away. "Next, you and I head home for some supper."

"Oh." She looked so disappointed he wanted to give her a hug.

"You did great today."

Her lips curved as she peeked up at him. "Yeah?"

"You're a natural."

She laughed. "You said that about horse riding too. I'm starting to think you're just really nice."

This made Kit and JJ crack up.

"Em, if you think Nash here is one to throw around compliments while we're working, you clearly haven't met the man."

She giggled at that. Nash felt a muscle in his jaw twitch, not because he was offended. He wasn't quick to give compliments, that was a fact. But when did JJ start calling her by a nickname?

He took a deep breath. No more jealousy. It wasn't his place to be so greedy. And yet...it was his place to take her to the festival. Right?

This shouldn't be confusing. The town thought they

were dating, she'd enjoy the event—there was no reason for him to be overthinking this.

As they headed toward the house, leaving Kit and JJ to head to their respective homes, he removed his work gloves and slapped them against his palm. "Hey, Emma?"

She looked over with an adorable teasing smile. "Hey, Nash?" she echoed back.

He cleared his throat. He was making this weird for no good reason. Drawing in a deep breath, he spit it out. "Would you like to go to the Aspire Days Festival with me?"

She turned to him with wide eyes.

He swallowed hard. Much as he tried to remind himself that this was not a real date, his heart didn't seem to buy it. The organ was pounding away like he'd just run a marathon. "It's this yearly festival that they hold downtown and—"

"Yes."

He blinked. "Yeah?"

She grinned. "I heard all about it when I went into town for baking supplies. I'd love to go."

"Oh." He let out a long breath. "Good."

She linked her arm through his as they headed toward the house again. He tried not to notice the smell of her shampoo, or how good it felt to walk with her like this, side by side after a hard day's work.

"You sure you won't mind being the center of attention again?" he asked.

She tilted her head back to look up at him. "Of course not." She winked. "That's what a fake girlfriend is for, right?"

Right. That was what he meant to say. But his mouth

went dry and felt like chalk when he tried to speak. So he kept his lips sealed and nodded instead.

Fake girlfriend. As if he needed the reminder.

But he did. He needed that reminder constantly, because when he was standing this close to Emma... Close enough that he could wrap her in his arms and hold her tight?... It was way too easy to forget.

22

S he almost forgot.

    For a moment there she almost forgot that it wasn't real.

That was why she'd forced herself to say it aloud. *That's what a fake girlfriend is for, right?*

She wanted him to deny it.

Or no, she wanted him to *agree.*

Oh heck, she didn't know what she wanted from Nash Donahue. All she knew was that she was restless and unsatisfied when she reached her bedroom a short time later to clean up before dinner.

The afternoon on the range had been more fun than she ever could've imagined. It was hard work, sure, but she'd loved it. She'd relished the feel of having a purpose here on this land, and she'd loved the camaraderie of working alongside Nash and his men. The way they laughed and joked together, the way they teased her and made her feel like one of the team...she couldn't remember the last time she'd felt that happy.

Her arm muscles twinged as she stretched them overhead to remove her sweaty T-shirt. She had no doubt they'd be aching by the morning.

She laughed to herself as she got into the shower. Okay, so maybe she wasn't going to be quitting her day job just yet. But even so, this hard work had been rewarding.

She'd been in a great mood...right up until Nash had asked her to the festival.

Oh, she'd been happy then, all right. Too happy. The moment he asked, she felt her emotions ricochet in every direction like a pinball. Elated one second that he'd thought to ask her, then disappointed when she realized *why* he'd asked.

Because it would be expected. It would look weird if his new girlfriend didn't tag along as his date.

And Emma wanted to go with him, she just...wished it was a real date.

She closed her eyes with a sigh as the water streamed over her, easing the tension in her muscles and numbing her thoughts.

There was no use denying it anymore. In fact, it was almost a relief to finally acknowledge the feelings she'd been fighting so hard since her very first day in Aspire.

She'd gone and done the unthinkable. She'd let herself develop a real crush on her fake boyfriend. Not the fleeting, initial attraction, but the kind of feelings that would take time to process and get over.

What a moron.

Just because a handsome guy was nice to her she let herself believe there could be something more. Hadn't she learned her lesson?

Guys like Nash didn't want a girl like her. Nope. They used girls like her to keep other girls like her at bay.

A cynical snort escaped.

Yup. Definitely a good thing she'd be leaving just after the wedding. Any longer and she might actually return home nursing a broken heart.

She turned off the shower, and the sound of her phone dinging in the other room had her wrapping a towel around her and hurrying out. It was a text from her mom telling her to keep her calendar clear the weekend after she returned because she and Derek wanted her to stay with them at their home in the suburbs just outside Chicago so they could hear all about her trip.

She replied with a: *Sounds good. Looking forward to it...* including some smiley face emojis for good measure. She was kind of grateful they were texting and not actually talking over the phone. The other night, when she called to tell her parents she was staying longer, her mother tried to read every little thing she could out of her decision— nitpicking for reasons that didn't actually exist. Emma did have to concede that her mother's over-questioning may have been a result of the fact Emma refused to breathe a word about her fake-dating Nash Donahue. She made it all about the sisters and her mother could smell the half-truth all the way from Illinois.

She'd also missed another message which she hadn't even heard come through. The selfie from Lizzy and Sarah made her grin. They wore cheesy smiles, and Sarah was sticking out her tongue while Lizzy crossed her eyes. Such goofballs. The text beneath it read 'we miss you' and her heart gave a pang of homesickness.

She missed them too. Right now more than ever.

Both messages were the reminder she needed that while it might be hard to leave, there were good reasons to go back home.

It was home, first of all. She had a job there that she

loved and she had people there who needed her.

She responded to her sister's text, not trusting herself to FaceTime Lizzy. An actual conversation right now would undoubtedly end in tears, and she still had dinner with Nash to get through. She couldn't show up tearstained and pouting when it was going to take all her effort to keep a breezy smile in place.

Even so, she wished she could press Pause on her time here at the ranch and just spend a few hours at her home in Chicago with Lizzy and Sarah.

Some girl talk was exactly what she needed to get her head on straight.

She'd just set her phone down when it dinged again. Emma picked it up, expecting to see a response from her family.

Instead, she got a text from Nash's family. It was an unknown number but the message read: *Hey, it's Casey. Ellie and I are going shopping in the morning for something to wear to the festival tomorrow night. You should come!*

Emma's eyes widened in surprise. She didn't even have to think it over. *I'd love to.*

They exchanged some texts to work out the logistics of where and when, and by the time Emma put her phone away and went to join Nash for another too-cozy, too-easy dinner together, she felt a little relief.

She wouldn't be here for long, and she was determined to get through this without falling any harder for the ungettable cowboy. Until then, she'd enjoy some much needed girl talk—even if she couldn't actually talk to Casey about her brother—and a fun, small-town festival. Almost like a Sweet Home Montana or something.

The thought enabled Emma to shake off the restless blues and put a smile on her face again.

Casey and Ellie munched on hamburgers while Emma devoured a BLT as they took a much-needed lunch break from shopping.

Not that there'd been much shopping to be done. Lizzy would have cried at the lack of selection in this little town. There were a total of three boutiques, two of which were too pricey for Emma's school teacher salary. Apparently their target market was the crowd of tourists who descended on the weekends during the summer and the ski bunnies who came in from the surrounding mountains during the winter.

There was talk of heading to the hardware store after lunch because apparently here in the middle of nowhere, hardware stores stocked cute blouses in addition to wrenches and garden hoses.

Emma had found a gorgeous outfit at the third boutique so at this point she was just going along for the ride. Although, Ellie and Casey were both insistent that she at least look at cowboy boots at the hardware store. It seemed they didn't want her sticking out by wearing heels instead of the requisite footwear.

"So...what?" Emma asked, thoroughly amused. "You have to dress like a cowgirl or get booted from the festival?"

"It's not about the fashion," Casey said. "Or even about tradition." She nodded toward Ellie. "Take our lovely librarian here. She's not even from cowboy country."

Ellie nodded in agreement. "I'm from a small bayside town in Maine. But I learned my first year here that cowboy boots are a necessity."

Casey arched her brows, her serious expression reminding Emma of Nash, which was unfortunate. "One word." She leaned forward. "Dancing."

Emma sputtered a laugh around her BLT. "You make it sound scary."

"Between line dancing and the two-step, there are lots of opportunities to have your toes smashed tonight," Casey said.

Ellie nodded earnestly. "It's true. Do yourself a favor and get some sturdy boots." She flashed an impish grin. "Maybe even steel-toed."

Emma laughed because it was clear the other girl was teasing.

"She's not kidding," Casey said, but her wide eyes and hint of a smile said she was. "Some of the guys in this town are terrible dancers." She reached out and patted Emma's hand. "But don't worry. Nash knows what he's doing."

Emma dipped her head with a blush. It wasn't the first time Casey had mentioned her brother, but with each passing second that Emma grew closer to these women, the lie weighed heavier and heavier.

It made her wonder how Nash could do it. It had been easy enough for her to pretend at the barbecue when surrounded by relative strangers. But now, with these two watching her like she was their friend? Like they trusted her?

She looked down, setting the sandwich on the plate because her stomach turned with unease. She couldn't keep lying. Not outright, at least.

"I told you not to pressure her," Ellie hissed to Casey.

Emma smiled and lifted her head to find them watching her in concern.

"Is everything all right between you two?" Casey asked.

Ellie leaned forward, her eyes wide. "You don't have to tell us. We both know how complicated relationships can be, especially when they're new."

Emma nodded. "It is complicated, I guess. But everything is fine," she added with a smile that had Casey visibly relaxing. "We get along great and we're having so much fun spending time together."

True and true.

The women both waited, like they could hear the 'but' in her voice.

"It's just that the future is so uncertain, you know?" She winced slightly. *Please say you understand.* She didn't want to lie any more than she already had.

Casey nodded. "I heard you're still planning on heading back to Chicago. I hope you and Nash are good with long distance relationships. It'll take some effort, but I'm sure you guys can make it work."

Emma let out an awkward laugh.

"I also heard that your siblings aren't sure what they want to do with the ranch," Ellie added. "But that might be a good thing, you know? Give you more than one reason to keep coming back to visit."

Emma blinked in surprise and both women snickered as they shared a look.

"This is Aspire, Emma," Casey said with a pat on her hand. "Everyone knows everything."

They all laughed at that, but it didn't help ease Emma's guilt. They might know a lot, but they didn't know everything.

They didn't know the truth.

23

This was a night like any other night.

Nash kept telling himself that as he paced the front hall waiting for Emma to emerge from her bedroom. He'd barely seen her all day and that fact had him pacing like a tiger in its cage.

He didn't like not seeing her.

And that was the understatement of the century.

He glanced at his reflection in the mirror and winced, taking the cowboy hat back off even though he'd just put it on, and twirling it in his hands just to have something to do.

No, he definitely was not a fan of going a full day with only a glimpse of Emma. He'd been leaving the kitchen when she'd come in for breakfast, and that was it.

He knew from her and from texts from Casey that they'd had plans today, but he'd expected to see her every time he popped in for more coffee or lunch or...oh heck, that last time he'd just come home to see if he'd find her.

He hadn't. The house had been silent.

Which he should have been used to.

After years of being the only full-time resident of the house, it should have been weird to have someone there. It didn't make sense that the house felt so dang empty without her.

He'd felt like a man possessed the longer he'd gone without a glimpse of her. Even now, he knew she was here in this house, and his skin was crawling with impatience to catch her eye, share a smile with her. There was some part of him that wouldn't be appeased until she was in his sights, within his reach, her voice in his ears.

"You ready?" She sounded breathless behind him and he whirled around to face her.

He froze the moment she came into view.

Beautiful.

He wasn't sure he'd ever seen anything or anyone more stunning in his entire life. Emma's hair was down, the waves loose around her tanned shoulders, and she wore a pretty, flowy dress with tiny flowers and buttons down the front. But it was the boots and the hat that had him grinning like a fool.

"You're a cowgirl," he said.

Her cheeks turned bright red as she looked down at the pale blue fabric and the bright red boots. "Is it too much?" She glanced up at him with a wince. "Seriously, I need you to tell me if it's too much. I normally count on Lizzy to be brutally honest but she's not here and—"

He touched her and she went silent. His fingers curled around her upper arms, toned and slim. His biceps clenched to fight that urge to tug her forward, to hold her close.

"Emma, I promise you," he said softly. "It's perfect."

You're perfect.

He swallowed the words.

"Yeah?" She sounded so hesitant. So vulnerable. Which seemed rare for this sweet, confident lady. It made his heart ache with tenderness.

"Yeah," he muttered gruffly.

She let out a soft sigh and wet her lips, pulling out of his grip as she looked down at herself. "Casey and Ellie picked it out. They assured me it's suitable, but I don't know." Her nose crinkled up and her eyes lit with laughter. "There's one part of me that feels like a kid playing dress up."

He laughed. "And the other part of you?"

Her head jolted back like the question surprised her. And then those pink cheeks got even pinker as she bit her lip and blurted, "I guess the other part of me feels...pretty."

He was melting. Right then and there, his heart became a mass of liquid at his feet. She sounded so uncertain, but so sincere.

"You look beautiful, Emma."

She glanced down at the floor, and before he knew what he was doing, he reached a hand out to touch her cheek, to draw her gaze back to his so she could see the truth that was burning in his veins. "You are so beautiful." He drew in a deep breath and dropped his hand. "You should know that."

She stared at him for a long moment, startled and wide-eyed. "Thank you."

He looked away first this time, his throat feeling too tight and his pulse impossibly fast. "You ready to head into town?"

She nodded, hesitating to look behind them toward the back door. "Are we waiting on JJ or Cody or—"

"No." He interrupted a little too quickly. But he'd realized today just how little time he had left with this woman. Sure, it might be crazy to let himself indulge in this attraction, but she'd be gone soon enough and he could pay the piper then. For now...

Well, for now he meant to enjoy every last second of his time with Emma.

Even if it was a bad idea.

Even if everything in him warned him that this would only ever be a mistake.

She arched a brow in question and he added in a rough voice, "They'll be driving into town later," he said. "No need to wait."

She nodded. "Okay then."

He held out an arm, trying to ignore the way his heart rate accelerated the closer he got to her. "Shall we?"

She grinned, taking his arm. "We shall."

He chuckled at her obvious excitement when he led her to the truck and answered all her many questions about the festival and its history.

He knew all the answers...and well he ought to. His grandmother and grandfather had been organizing this event for the last two decades. It was time they retired, and judging by the way his Aunt Lisa and Casey had stepped in to take charge of logistics this year, he suspected they'd be leading the event in full someday soon.

Her questions and his stories about antics that occurred at festivals in the past kept them busy for the drive into town, and the moment they pulled into Aspire, Emma was gasping with delight.

"Look at these decorations," she said, in obvious awe of the lanterns stretching high across Main Street and the colorful flowers and banners decorating store fronts and spilling onto the sidewalk. Like always, a huge section of the road had been closed off for the evening with pop-up stalls and delicious smelling food carts lining the street and heading down to a temporary dance floor and stage area.

When Nash steered toward the designated parking lot, Emma pressed her face to the window, looking like a kid, which made Nash laugh. "It's so beautiful."

You're beautiful.

He just barely bit back the urge to tell her again. He wanted to tell her every second just how gorgeous she was. Not just because she was wearing the dress, or the hat or the boots...but because she glowed with this happiness that he felt blessed to be around. She had an energy and light that was impossible to put into words, but it sure made him thankful he was here with her. It made him want to be by her side tonight...and every night.

The thought hit him upside the head, and he stopped the truck with a jerky hitch.

Lord, what am I doing?

"Sorry," he murmured.

But Emma was still chatting away about the decorations, oblivious to his turmoil. "I saw them getting ready this morning, but seeing it all complete, and with the lanterns." Her voice rose at the end and she turned to him with wide expectant eyes as she waited for him to agree.

"The people of Aspire do know how to throw a party," he said.

She was bouncing with excitement when he opened her door and helped her down. The skirt of her dress was all uneven, longer in some parts then others. It wasn't crazy revealing, and he recognized it as some fashion trend, but it made him acutely aware of her toned, tanned legs and the narrow waist that felt warm beneath his hands as he hoisted her down rather than let her clamber like she normally did.

"Where do you want to start first?" he asked as soon as they arrived at the top of Main Street.

"Umm…" She looked around them with wide eyes. "Whatever smells so delicious right now." She looked up at him. "I want that."

"Yes, ma'am." He tipped his hat, making her grin, and then reached for her hand. The ease with which she slipped her fingers through his took his breath away. It was almost as shocking as the way he'd reached for her.

Like it was something they'd always done.

He led her to a food truck that was buzzing with activity and ordered them a sampling of everything.

"Is everything fried?" Laughter laced Emma's voice as she looked over her options. "What's that?"

He held out the paper plate. "Fried oreo."

"Fried…" She glanced up. "Are you serious?"

He kept his expression even. "I never joke about fried food."

She burst out laughing, like he'd hoped she would, and he found himself grinning back at her.

Heck. His face was starting to ache from all the grinning he'd been doing this past week. Since she'd arrived he'd done more talking, more laughing, more smiling than he could remember doing his whole life combined.

"Okay, if you insist," she said with a good-natured shrug as she reached for the Oreo. She moaned in ecstasy and he chuckled, although the sound of that moan had his gaze dropping to her lips and staying there.

A man obsessed. Yes, sir. That was him.

After she'd had her fill of fried foods, they went around to the games, trying each one until their arms were loaded with cheap stuffed toys they could have bought for a fraction of the cost it took to win them.

Not that he cared. Playing those games had made her happy, not to mention most of the money raised tonight was going to one local nonprofit or another.

They ran into Casey and Ryan while enjoying some barbecued meats, and were accosted by his cousin Boone on the way to catch some live music on the far end of the street.

"Nash!" Boone called out. The young, boisterous cousin approached with a grin, with JJ and the firefighter Ethan walking more slowly behind him. "I need your woman to bid on me."

"Boone," he said in a warning tone, but Emma was laughing beside him.

Boone pointed to her with a knowing grin. "Emma, my hopefully soon-to-be cousin-in-law, will you please bid on me in the bachelor auction?"

"Why would I do that?" she asked, her voice such a sweet sound when she was amused. Nash couldn't even bring himself to be annoyed with Boone for putting her on the spot.

Or asking her to...bid on him?

"Why on earth are you asking my girlfriend to bid on you?" he asked.

Emma only laughed harder.

"Because he wants to win a bet," JJ answered. His bushy beard was trimmed for once, and the dirt had been scrubbed from beneath his fingernails. "Seems Boone here thinks he can raise more money than me or Ethan."

Poor Ethan looked like he was wishing for the earth to swallow him whole.

Nash could relate. He'd been just as miserable when he'd had to take a turn as one of the bachelors for the ridiculous tradition. Ethan nodded at Emma. "Ms. O'Sullivan."

She grinned. "It's just Emma, Ethan. Ms. O'Sullivan isn't nearly specific enough for this town."

She'd sort of muttered the last part for Nash's ears only and they shared a little smirk that made him feel like the luckiest man alive, because he had inside jokes with Ms. Emma O'Sullivan.

But then she turned to Boone. "I'll bid on you to keep the price going up, how does that sound?"

His face lit up and Nash scowled. "Now, wait a second—"

"What about me?" JJ asked. "I taught you how to rope. Doesn't that get me any love?"

"I'll bet on you too." She turned that gorgeous grin on Ethan. "You too, Ethan."

"You can't bid on all of us," Boone whined. "That defeats the purpose."

"The purpose is to raise money for the station," Ethan reminded him.

Emma beamed at Ethan. "Exactly. It's for a good cause."

Jealousy coiled in his belly as Nash wondered where they'd met, but he didn't get a chance to ask.

"Nash, any chance you want to take my spot?" Ethan asked, hope and despair written all over the young fireman's features.

He opened his mouth to say 'not on your life' but Emma beat him to it, clutching his arm like he was being led away to his execution. "Don't even think about it. Nash here is *my* date, I'm not offering him up."

He grinned down at her. "What happened to 'it's for a good cause?'"

She giggled. "Good causes are all well and good but I'm not sharing you with some other woman."

His chest tightened. His heart ached.

He was gonna be in his dang grave before the night was through if they kept up this act much longer.

After promising to be at the auction at the top of the hour, they continued toward the music. The real dancing would start up later, but for now there was Jeff Havrem and his two buddies playing in their three-piece band. They were regulars at all the local bars, and always had a good turn out.

They'd just sidled up to watch them when Dr. Dex came over to say hi. "Nash. Emma," he greeted.

The doctor was young but already becoming a town favorite, even more so by the Donahues because he'd been such a good employer to Casey. They'd taken him in like he was a part of the family.

"Have you been to the other end yet?" Nash asked.

Dr. Dex grimaced. "I'm trying to avoid it till after the bachelor auction."

Emma laughed. "Don't tell me, you're a volunteer fireman too?"

He shook his head. "No, ma'am, but they didn't have many takers this year so they were asking anyone who's not married or taken." He looked between the two of them for emphasis.

Nash was taken.

He glanced over and caught Emma grinning up at him.

Yup, he was taken all right. He was more smitten than he had any right to be with a woman who was leaving in a week.

He caught sight of his parents on the other side of the crowd and returned their wave. Emma too.

The sight of his father was just the reminder he needed. It was for the best that she was leaving. It was best for his family, and ultimately for him. It was definitely best for her…

He glanced down at the top of her head as she leaned in toward him for a better view of the musicians through the crowd.

It was best for her to leave…if she still wanted to.

He found himself holding his breath, hoping for…what? That she'd have a change of heart?

Maybe.

Abigail Toulouse approached and gave Emma a big hug. "I'm so glad you're still here," she said. "I wasn't sure when you were leaving."

"Still here," Emma said, throwing her arms out wide.

The elementary school principal pressed her lips together and then reached into her purse. "Look, I know this isn't the time or place, but it just feels like fate that I'm running into you here."

Emma glanced up at Nash in question and he shrugged.

"Fate?" she echoed.

The principal handed over her business card. "We just found out one of our elementary school teachers can't come back in the fall so we have an opening to fill."

"Oh." Emma stared at the card. "For kindergarten?"

"Yes, in fact. Ms. Grantham's daughter is pregnant and

having a terrible time of it. She wants to move to Texas and help out the family for a while and has decided to resign rather than ask for leave."

Nash's insides were twisting oddly. He couldn't tell if it was excitement or terror, or something else entirely, as he attempted to read Emma's expression.

Emma blinked at the card, like she was trying to read it but couldn't make out the words.

"I know it's a lot to throw at you like this, and I know you already have a good job in Chicago. But if you ever think about staying here…" She looked between the two of them with a chagrined smile. "Sorry. Am I overstepping? It's not my business, but just know that you are more than welcome to interview for a job at Aspire Elementary." She smiled and leaned in to hug Emma. "I think you'd be such a great fit for our school, so I'll leave you with my card and let you think it over, okay?"

Emma smiled but still looked stunned. "Okay."

The principal walked away and Emma stared back down at the card, blinking at it like it'd been written in some form of Sanskrit.

"Emma? You all right?" he asked.

"Yeah." She nodded and turned back to the musicians. "That was just unexpected. I…" Her words trailed off and she shook her head.

He gave her a closed-mouth smile, not trusting himself to say anything.

What was he supposed to say?

Please stay, because the idea of you leaving is killing me?

That would be so unfair.

With his father watching them, and the entire town crowded in close, he told himself he didn't want her to stay. They created this fake relationship for really good reasons.

But as he watched her lips curve up in a smile as she listened, as she swayed to the beat beside him, he knew it for the lie it was.

He wanted her to stay.

24

E mma had always considered herself a fairly decent dancer. She and Lizzy went out to clubs on occasion and she'd always enjoyed getting her groove on. So, no, she never thought of herself as having two left feet.

But that was before she tried line dancing.

Emma fell forward, laughing too hard to even pretend to stumble through the steps.

"See?" Casey crowed from behind her. She was grinning at Emma as she flawlessly moved in time to the music, along with everyone else around her. "It's not as easy as it looks."

Ellie was giggling from the sidelines. "Aren't you glad you wore the boots?"

Emma nodded, tears streaming down her face. It was the third song she'd attempted to join in on, and it had become immediately obvious that it wasn't off-tempo dance partners she'd needed to worry about crushing her toes.

She was doing a heck of a job herself. She'd literally

stepped on her own toes trying to keep up with the group choreography, and she'd done it more than once.

"Keep going," one of the old men behind her shouted in encouragement.

But honestly, her pride was stinging watching the men and women more than double her age flow through the moves with ease as she fumbled over and over. She waved her arms, swiping at tears of laughter. "I give up."

Nash was watching her with a smile from the sidelines. She'd just started heading in his direction when Casey shouted again. "Nash, show your girl how it's done."

Emma laughed again, certain Casey was teasing, but to her surprise all the older women surrounding Nash, including his mother and aunts, were pushing an obviously reluctant Nash forward until he stumbled onto the makeshift dance floor that took up one whole block of Main Street.

"Fine, fine," he said, waving off the teasing shouts from his family and friends.

When he drew close, her belly flipped with nerves and excitement.

"Let's try it from the start."

She nodded, utterly speechless. He couldn't be serious, he could not possibly be—

"Start with the right foot," he called over to her.

Oh. My. Goodness. She blinked in disbelief before jerking into motion.

He was doing it. Nash Donahue, serious, smoldering, sexy-as-sin cowboy was line dancing like a pro.

And it was hot.

The sight of this athletic, capable man moving in time to the music with ease made her insides flutter. And she wasn't the only one affected. She spotted a couple of girls nearby, their mouths curving into appreciative smiles as they watched him move.

"Looking good, Nash!"

He shared a quick look with Emma, obviously noting their appraisal, and focused on shouting instructions to keep her on track. With his help, she actually managed to make it through the song without stumbling.

Well, without stumbling too much, at least.

When the band stopped playing, she turned to gape at him.

"What?" He scrubbed the back of his neck in that *aw shucks* way that always made her heart trip over itself.

"You." She forgot herself. She forgot that she needed to keep her distance. She forgot everything because she was having more fun tonight than she'd had in ages. Her hands fell on his chest as she moved toward him shaking her head. "You are amazing."

He grinned down at her, his eyes crinkling with laughter and that smile making her knees go weak.

When he was this close, and giving her that grin, it was impossible not to feel like it was real. That smile was meant just for her, and those girls watching from the side-lines were just that.

She was his and he was hers.

He had this way of making her feel like the only woman on the planet. The only one he saw. And that was a heady sensation for someone who'd grown so used to being unnoticed and unappreciated.

She went to take a step back, to move out of the way of the other dancers who were jostling for space, but she didn't get far. Her breath caught as his arms wrapped around her waist suddenly, holding her still.

"Where do you think you're going?" he asked, the

teasing note in his voice slightly different to the ones she'd heard before.

It was huskier, somehow more precious.

And she loved it.

"I don't know if I can take any more line dancing," she admitted. Her laughter sounded breathless to her own ears and she was keenly aware of her arm around his neck.

"Too tired?" he asked. Something in the glint of his eyes and the arch of his brow made her heart do a backflip.

"Too humiliated," she said with a good-natured groan.

He grinned. "Then why don't we try something a little easier."

The music started up again, another fast-paced country song that she didn't recognize but that made her want to tap her toes.

He started moving, his feet shifting in time to the beat as he snared her dangling hand in his.

"What are you—"

"The two-step," he said as he set them in motion. He leaned down so his lips were right next to her ear. "All you have to do is let me lead."

She blinked. He wanted another dance with her?

Before she could even process this turn of events, that was precisely what they were doing. The crowd around them hooted and cheered and sang along, but all she could do was stare up at Nash with a grin so wide it hurt her cheeks.

She was flying. That was what it felt like, at least. His grip was strong, his steps sure, and with no effort from her she was being led around the dance floor as if she knew what she was doing.

She didn't, but it didn't matter. Her head tipped back as the lights strung overhead swirled with the quick movements. But nothing was brighter than the light in Nash's eyes as he smiled down at her.

This...this was new. His easygoing, lighthearted grin, the way he winked before dipping her and making her laugh. This was an entirely new side of Nash...

And she loved it.

She loved everything about dancing with him, and she found herself wishing the song would never end.

But it did, of course. And she was breathless with laughter and this giddy joy as they slowed to a stop on the final chord.

"Where did you learn to dance like that?" she asked when they stood there frozen, the crowd cheering around them. For the musicians, not them, but even so, she felt like the star of her very own movie.

For the first time in her life, she was the lead in her life and not the supporting cast in everyone else's drama.

"My mama insisted that Casey and I both be able to dance," he said, his tone rueful as they glanced over at a beaming Delphine. "She figured this town held enough festivals and fairs and celebrations that being able to hold our own on the dance floor would be useful."

Emma laughed. "She was right. You must be in demand with the ladies." She instantly regretted the comment and the jealous thoughts that came along with them. The two sideline watchers were eyeing them like hawks. She quickly added, "I sure hope you've thanked your mother properly."

She went to move again, but he still held on tight, apparently in no hurry to leave the dancefloor. "You know," he said slowly, thoughtfully. "I don't think I ever appreciated the skill until tonight." A flicker of emotion in his eyes made her lips part. "Until you."

She blinked rapidly, her lips still parted with surprise as she tried to figure out what she was supposed to say to that.

It was...romantic. And sweet.

She cast a quick glance around.

No one was close enough to hear him and a sliver of trepidation raced through her.

What is happening right now?

It was too good to be true.

She knew this. But she couldn't bring herself to do anything but nod when he asked, "May I have the next dance?"

The music was already starting, and it was slow in tempo, the lyrics an undeniable love song.

She swallowed hard as she rested her hand on his shoulder. Did she have a choice?

No. Her heart and her body were both willfully ignoring that inkling of fear.

There'd be plenty of time after she left for regrets and indecision. But right now there was just this.

There was only Nash, and her, and the music that seemed to wrap around her and draw her into a dream.

He moved slowly this time. They barely shifted from the spot where they stood, merely moving back and forth in time to the music.

He held her so close she could feel the thud of his heart through his chest, echoing hers. She forgot where they were as his gaze met hers and held on.

She couldn't look away. She couldn't force a laugh to break this new emotion which formed between them like a thread, connecting them and tying them together in a way she couldn't understand.

It wasn't an awkward feeling, more like that weight of

anticipation. The fear and excitement and breathlessness that came just before diving headfirst off the high dive.

Her heart slammed against her ribcage as she felt it—that realization that she was standing on the brink. She could back away now or see where this led.

Nowhere, the voice of reason cried in the back of her mind. *This can't go anywhere. It's not even real.*

But that voice was a hushed whisper, drowned out by the far louder beating of her heart, utterly lost in the swell of music that carried her away from reality and left her in the most perfect fantasy.

She was living her wildest dreams when she looked up into Nash's fixed gaze. There was an intensity there that said he'd never let her go.

Her lips parted for air because she'd forgotten how to breathe.

And then he was leaning down, his breath fanning against her lips. He hesitated, giving her a chance to stop him. But hot liquid surged through her veins, and that voice of reason was dead and buried under the need to see this fantasy through.

Her eyelids fluttered shut, a silent yes to his unspoken question.

And then his lips brushed over hers.

And she was lost.

Warm, tender, firm—his lips pressed softly at first. Testing. Making sure she was okay with this.

Her lips parted beneath his on a soft exhale and he matched her movement, kissing her harder. Tenderness infused his every touch as their lips met and clung, moving together in a dance all their own.

The kiss was so perfect—a fantasy come to life. She felt like a cherished girlfriend. Like his real girlfriend.

And then the blissful moment came to an abrupt halt as the sound of a whistle cut through the pretty melody of the band. A cheer rose in the air and someone called Nash's name.

"That's right, cowboy! You kiss your lady!"

Emma pulled back with a start to see Nash gazing down at her. For a moment, he looked just as dazed as she felt, but then he blinked and grinned, glancing around at the cheering crowd. This uproar was for them. She ducked her head, letting it fall against his chest as heat swept up her neck and into her cheeks.

His chest rumbled with a low laugh as he let go of her hand to pat her back. "All right, all right," he called, in a good-natured tone, to his family and friends. "Show's over."

"It's about time you got yourself a girlfriend, Nash," someone shouted.

The words had reality returning with a sickening thud, settling into her gut like a lead weight.

"I know, I know," Nash called back. "I'm a lucky guy."

She lifted her head, spotting the women out of the corner of her eye. They were sharing disappointed smiles and that was probably what Nash was going for.

He was making it clear to the town that he was off the market.

She couldn't raise her gaze above the stubble on his jaw.

Fake. This was all for show.

He kissed her to make a statement.

And she…

She was the idiot she'd promised herself she wouldn't be. She'd gone and forgotten the fact that this wasn't real.

She'd gone and lost her heart for good.

25

Nash's heart was full to bursting.

This night couldn't have been any more perfect. His gaze fell on Emma as she laughed over something Casey whispered in her ear when the two said their goodbyes.

Emma couldn't have been any more perfect.

His sister and "girlfriend" were hugging, and a small crowd was waiting their turn to say goodnight. Emma was a hit. All night, everyone had wanted to talk to her, to dance with her. And he knew it wasn't because she was Nash Donahue's new lady.

It was because she was Emma. A beacon of warmth and love and joy, and everyone could see that.

"Glad to see you two hitting it off so well." His father's voice made him tense.

Nash turned to face him as his mother joined the group clustered around Emma. "Did you and Mom have a good night?"

His father didn't seem to hear him. Patrick's gaze was

on Emma, and Nash hated the predatory gleam he saw there. "What's the latest?"

Nash just barely held back a sigh. He wasn't about to pretend not to understand. "No decision yet."

"Hmph," his father grunted. Definitely not what he wanted to hear. "Maybe if I give them an actual offer and they see the number—"

"Not a good idea." Nash shook his head.

"But—"

"Dad, I'm handling this." Nash wasn't even sure where this tone came from. He was never so forceful with his father. Heck, he never even talked to his employees like this.

His father's brows arched slightly, and irritation flickered in his eyes. "Now listen here, son. I'm happy to see you hitting it off with the O'Sullivan girl, but don't you forget where your loyalties lie."

"I haven't—"

"This isn't for me," Patrick continued.

Nash bit back a bitter laugh. Wasn't it?

"Do you want to go on working someone else's land for the rest of your life?"

Nash pressed his lips into a grim line, his pride smarting and some childish part of him hurting that what he was doing wasn't enough for his father. He wanted to make his dad proud, he always had. And of course he'd like to own his own place someday, but he didn't share his father's driving need to expand and conquer. He didn't need some giant ranching enterprise, he just wanted what he had—he was his own boss, even if he didn't own the place. And that was what mattered.

He had a good job, great co-workers, and a place to call home.

His gaze flickered back over to Emma. Since she'd arrived, it'd felt more like home than it ever had. It'd become more than just Frank's big, empty house. The rooms had been lit with laughter and warmth. That was all Emma's doing, and Nash hated to think how hollow the place would be when she returned to Chicago.

"Everything I do is for you, your mother, and your sister," Patrick continued.

Nash barely had to listen. He'd heard this speech countless times before.

"And when I die, it will all go to you. I want to give you more than what I inherited. I want to leave behind a legacy—"

"I get it, Dad," he said.

Emma was pulling away from his mother's embrace, and she was starting to look around. For him. They were both exhausted, and he'd promised to take her home.

He felt like he was crawling out of his skin, he was so impatient to be alone with her. Alone with Emma in the dark quiet of his truck—it sounded like heaven right now, and he resented the heck out of his father for bringing this up again. Here. Now.

"All those daughters." His father shook his head, missing Nash's eye roll.

Nash didn't bother asking where he'd heard that. Word spread quickly in this town. It was just a fact of life.

"Are there really seven of them?" His father's voice was dubious, and Nash almost relished the idea of wiping that skeptical frown off his face. Almost.

"Yep. Seven O'Sullivan sisters."

"What did April say?" Patrick continued. "I could talk to her. I bet she remembers me."

Nash clenched his jaw. "Dad, don't get involved in this. Do you hear me?"

But his father clearly didn't. "We can't wait around forever, you know. I have it on good authority that some company out of Wyoming is scouring property in this area, and if we lose the—"

"Dad." His tone was curt as he interrupted, but Emma was angling this way as she gave one last wave. "I told you I'm handling the situation, now drop it."

"Hi." Emma smiled at them both, slightly breathless and her eyes still dancing with excitement. "Mr. Donahue, did you have a good evening?"

His father nodded and forced a smile that likely fooled no one. But he was polite enough saying his goodbyes, and Nash's muscles unclenched as they walked away from his father and the rest of the crowd.

He slid an arm around her shoulders and she burrowed into his side, leaning into him as she yawned. His heart slammed against his ribcage at the feel of her in his arms. At the ease with which she rested there, like they'd always been doing this.

"You ready to go home?" he asked.

He could feel her nod against his chest. "Mmm. I'm exhausted."

"But did you have fun?" He was teasing. He knew she'd had a blast. Between the dancing, the games and the delicious food, they'd spent most of their night laughing and smiling.

Except for that wretched auction, of course. Nash rolled his eyes, still disgruntled by the fact she'd accidentally won a date with JJ. She was initially horrified, but then she saw the look on his face and got a serious case of the giggles. All Nash could do was stare at her beautiful smile.

Emma tilted her head back and he saw that smile now, aimed at him and him alone. His chest squeezed.

"I had the best time," she breathed.

They reached the truck and he opened the door for her. "I'm glad."

His hands fit her waist as he lifted her into the cab, and once she was seated, she gave him a long look. "Did I interrupt something between you and your dad?"

He swallowed as guilt flickered through him, but he wasn't sure who he felt guilty toward—his father, because he wasn't pushing this woman to make a decision in the family's favor or her, because he wasn't being fully honest about his family's stake in her decision to sell.

Part of him wanted to come clean. To tell her everything.

Everything? A voice mocked him, and when she tilted her head, his mouth went dry.

Yeah. He wanted to tell her everything. He wanted to tell her that what happened tonight—it was real. All of it. Especially that kiss.

That kiss had rocked his world, and he wanted her to know just how much it had affected him. Just how much he wanted to do it again.

Concern started to fill her gaze. "Nash, is everything all right?"

The air rushed out of him. He couldn't stand to see her happiness fade, and so he quickly said, "Everything is great."

Her smile was back and he could breathe again.

"You're not still upset by the fact I won a date with JJ, are you?" Her nose wrinkled and he had to laugh. "I swear, I thought someone else was going to bid higher than me."

"I did too."

"At least you know I won't be able to go through with it. But you will have to find me someone to give the date to. Are there any girls around here crushing on the rugged Jessie Jamieson?"

Nash's chuckle was low and deep. He honestly wasn't sure. Avoiding who-liked-who town gossip was in his nature and he wasn't about to go changing that about himself.

He shut her door and went around to his own side.

They were both quiet for the first part of the drive. He saw her gazing out, her forehead resting against the passenger side window as she took in the open sky and the stars overhead.

He wished like heck he knew what she was thinking.

She'd gotten caught up in the fun tonight, he knew that. But had that kiss meant something to her, too, or was it just part of the laughter and the dancing?

He drummed his fingers against the wheel. Finally, when he couldn't take it much longer, he broke the silence. "You doing okay?"

She turned to face him, and even in the shadowy light he could see the strain in her smile. "Of course. I'm fine."

He snickered. "You do know you're a terrible liar, right?"

She laughed softly too. "Yeah, I know."

"Obviously something's bothering you, but if you'd prefer not to talk about it…" He trailed off with a shrug. He knew better than anyone that sometimes a person just needed space and time with their own thoughts.

He could respect that.

He glanced over, his insides twisting with concern. He could respect that, but it might kill him if she didn't let him help.

He wasn't sure at what point he'd started to think of her as his to protect, but there was no use denying it. Give him a sword because he was ready to slay her dragons.

Even if that dragon came in the form of his pushy father or her stubborn sisters.

"Maybe I could help," he offered. "If you tell me what's troubling you."

She gave her head a shake. "It's nothing. I'm just tired."

That wasn't the whole truth, and he knew it. But he wouldn't press.

"It's actually you I'm worried about," she said after a beat.

"Me?" He arched his brows.

She laughed softly, but it wasn't her typical light-hearted sound. "You did one heck of a job playing the part of the doting boyfriend tonight," she said. "Every woman there was jealous. I don't know how you'll be able to stay single for long after I'm gone."

After I'm gone. That was all he could hear for a second. *After I'm gone.*

Not *if I go* but a definitive *after.* He cleared his throat, trying to focus. He had this feeling that she was asking a question with that comment, but he wasn't sure what she wanted to hear.

He glanced over at her but her eyes were hidden by the darkness.

They'd always been straightforward with each other, but right now he felt like they were speaking in code. He was treading on dangerous ground and one misstep could ruin everything.

"Don't worry about me," he said, his voice a little too gruff. "I'll stick with my broken heart story for as long as I can."

She nodded. "Yeah. Okay."

Wrong answer. He'd given the wrong answer. He could hear it in the disappointment in her voice.

"So, what's going on with you and your dad?" she asked. "You guys seemed tense when I came over."

He shrugged. How much did he say? "Just business talk."

He felt her gaze and shifted uncomfortably. He tried for a lighter tone, despite the fact that his chest seemed tight and heavy. "Can we just talk about the fact that you bid on every guy in the bachelor auction?"

She giggled, and some of the tension eased. "Like I said before, I didn't actually intend to win a date."

He laughed. "Well, the good news is, you got the bidding so high, the fire station brought in more donations than any other year."

She sat up straighter in her seat, preening as she flipped her hair. "You're welcome," she teased.

He laughed. "The bad news is, JJ isn't going to stop harassing you to go out on that date with him."

She laughed. "Well, you need to find me some other girl, then. I honestly thought someone would bid higher than me. It was my last one before I stepped back." Holding her cheeks, she looked at him, her cute nose wrinkling. "He knows it's just for charity, right? He won't mind us passing it on to someone else."

"It's a matter of pride." Nash glanced over at her with a grin, relieved to see her smile back in place again. "No guy wants to be bid on just for charity. Make no mistake, he's going to insist on taking you out on the town."

"Well then, I guess it's a good thing I'm leaving town soon," she said. "Then I won't have to explain why I'm cheating on you with your ranch hand."

He laughed because she was joking, but they both sounded a little flat. If what they had between them was real, he'd be scouring the Aspire directory for any single woman he could find, because no way would he want Emma out for an evening with JJ. Some other lady could have that experience.

But it wasn't real, was it?

Emma was leaving.

By the time he pulled up in front of the house, the cab seemed to be filled to the breaking point with unspoken words.

They hadn't talked about the kiss, and he had no idea how to bring it up. But he needed her to know…

What? That he was attracted to her?

He frowned, cutting off the engine. No, that wasn't right. Attraction wasn't all he felt, not by far. That kiss hadn't just been about physical desire, it had been spurred on by something so much more.

Something he'd never felt before and was at a loss to name.

With the truck's headlights off, the night sky seemed to come alive around them. Stars gleamed bright against the ink-black canvas, and as he climbed out and took her in his arms to help her down, all he could think was how romantic a backdrop this was.

How, if things were different, he'd set her down on the ground...but he wouldn't let go.

As if she could hear his thoughts, she tipped her head

back to look up at him. His hands were still at her waist, and this close he could see the questions there in her gorgeous blue eyes.

His hands wouldn't move from her waist. He couldn't bring himself to let go. Not yet.

There were so many things he wanted to say, but he didn't have the words for any of them.

And even if he could think of the perfect sentiment to tell her how much tonight had meant to him—how real it felt—would she want to hear it? She'd never once talked about staying here for good, even if her sisters decided to keep the ranch.

She'd never made false promises or given him any reason to believe that this was anything more than a temporary situation.

She had a life in Chicago, one she wasn't about to give up.

"Nash?" she whispered.

He swallowed back the words that were forming in the back of his mind. *Don't go. Stay with me.*

Forever.

He took a step back like he'd been sucker punched and dropped his hands from her waist.

Her eyes brimmed with emotions, but not one of which he could decipher.

She was waiting for him to speak, to say something. Anything.

He turned to head to the house. "Goodnight, Emma."

26

E mma was a fool.

And a coward.

Also, she couldn't figure out how to do her hair to save her life. "Stupid...tangled...ouch!"

The sound of her phone ringing to announce a video call cut through her efforts to tame hair, which had decided today was the day to be thoroughly unmanageable.

Lizzy's face popped up on the screen. "Hey, Em—uh oh, what's wrong?"

Emma let out a rough exhale. Apparently, she looked as bad as she felt. "My stupid hair won't cooperate."

She sounded like a petulant child, and she knew it.

"Okay," Lizzy said slowly, in a condescendingly gentle tone like she was talking to a petulant child. "Here's what you're going to do. You're going to set down the brush before you tear your hair out."

Emma threw down the brush with a sigh.

"Next, you're going to sit down, take a deep breath,

and tell me what's got you so upset." Before Emma could reply, Lizzy added, "Because I know it's not your hair. You've never been one to freak out over your hair."

Emma fell onto the bed, taking a deep breath like her sister ordered.

"Okay," Lizzy said after a beat. "Let's start with the fact that you're wearing your good dress."

Emma rolled her eyes. "I have more than one dress, you know."

"Yes, but this is the only one you ever wear to fancy events, so spill. Where are you off to and why are you freaking out?"

Emma didn't know where to begin and after a few stutters and huffs, she launched into the truth. The whole truth. From how nice Nash was on her very first day to the fact that she'd agreed to pretend to be his girlfriend to help ease his family's pressure, to the epic kiss that had taken over her brain and made her physically incapable of thinking about anything else.

"I'm such an idiot," Emma ended, covering her face with her hand.

"Oh sweetie, you're not an idiot." But Lizzy's tone said she wasn't entirely convinced of this. She sounded like she was trying to reassure them both that her older sister hadn't lost her ever-loving mind. "It's so like you to go along with something so ridiculous even though you have nothing to gain."

Emma sniffed. Tears were threatening but she refused to cry. She was a big girl and she'd known what she was getting into.

Had she hoped that maybe Nash would have a change of heart? Had she been a total coward after the festival and tried, but failed, to nudge him into confessing that the kiss had been real?

Yes and yes.

But she wasn't going to cry about it. She refused.

It's so like you…

Her sister's words had her brows furrowing in annoyance. "What's that supposed to mean? I've never pretended to be someone's girlfriend before."

And she'd certainly never fallen for a fake boyfriend. She would definitely have remembered this particular brand of pathetic self-pity.

Lizzy gave a little snort of disbelief. "You may not have pretended to be a guy's girlfriend, but you have to admit, you have a type when it comes to men."

Emma sniffed again. "I do not."

Lizzy nodded, her expression pained and knowing. "You do, sweetie. You tend to fall for guys who don't actually see you, they just see what they can get from you."

"I do not—"

"Remember Todd?" she asked.

Emma frowned. Todd was a former teacher at her school. She'd been head over heels for him, and she'd thought he'd liked her too. But when he transferred to another school, she realized he'd liked her as a friend—a friend who helped him do all his lesson plans in addition to her own.

"Or that guy who strung you along just so you'd feed his pets while he went on vacation?"

"Mark," Emma muttered. Humiliation was an unpleasant addition to all the other toxic emotions juggling for supremacy. "You make it sound like I'm some…some doormat."

Lizzy sighed. "Not a doormat. You're just nice. And

generous. And too giving for your own good. I just wish you'd find a guy who didn't try to take advantage of that."

Emma wanted to deny that Nash was taking advantage of her, but a memory of that kiss stopped her and had her battling another wave of tears.

Had it meant anything to him or was it just his way of making a really clear statement to the people of Aspire? *Nash Donahue has found a woman, so all you pining ladies and matchmakers can back off now, please.*

She wished she could get enough time and space to sort it out—what she was feeling and what she wanted from him—but the last two days had done nothing to settle her emotions. She was more confused than ever.

Casey's rehearsal dinner started in less than an hour and she'd already agreed to go. It was part of the deal, and she wouldn't back out just because she felt confused. She'd known what she was getting into when she agreed to Nash's plan. At least she thought she had.

She let out another pathetic sigh. "Oh Lizzy, I wish you were here."

"If I was…" Her eyes sparked with fire. "I'd give this new user a piece of my mind."

"He's not using me," Emma said. This time the protest came quickly. Despite the confusion around the kiss, Nash had been nothing but straightforward with her about where this was going—nowhere. If she'd let herself become confused about their friendship, that was on her. She took a deep breath. "Nash isn't like that."

Lizzy didn't respond but her silence felt like an accusation.

"He's not," Emma said. "He hasn't led me on. I knew what I was getting into when I agreed to this."

Lizzy just stared at her through the phone, and

Emma's cheeks burned at the memory of his kiss. Hearing herself say it aloud gave her clarity but not comfort. She'd felt so certain there had been real emotions behind that kiss, but hearing herself talk now in the cold light of day...

He hadn't meant for her to get the wrong idea. He'd probably be horrified if he knew that she had.

But it'd felt so real. She sank back into the pillows as the memory played on a loop for the millionth time. The soft look in his eyes, the way the world had blurred around them so, in that moment, they were the only people on Earth.

It was the sort of kiss she'd always dreamed of receiving. The kind of kiss that made her believe she was cherished and special and...

Stupid. She sat up straight with a huff. She was doing it again, romanticizing something that she should just forget.

"I just have to get through tonight's rehearsal dinner and then the wedding. After that I'll be flying home, and I can go back to my normal life." The fact that going back to her normal life made her want to cry was too depressing to talk about. So, she swallowed the thick wave of emotion instead.

She was living in a fantasy, but once she got back to Chicago, she'd be able to put this time in Aspire into perspective. "I'll be fine once I'm home."

A silence followed, and Emma wasn't sure who she'd been trying to convince, herself or Lizzy.

"Oh Emma, I'm so sorry you're going through this," Lizzy said. "I wish you'd just come back on Tuesday like you were supposed to and then none of this would have happened."

Emma didn't respond. She wasn't sure it would have

been any easier to leave Nash a few days ago. Even before the kiss, she'd been feeling too attached by far.

A glance at the time had her sitting up straight again. "Lizzy, I've got to go. But thanks for listening."

"I'm always here for you, sis. You know that."

Emma nodded. "I know."

"You are still coming home after the weekend, right?" Lizzy's mouth grew tight with anxiety. "I need you here."

Emma felt the tiniest pang of annoyance that even this conversation somehow came back to what Lizzy needed and wanted. She shook it off. It was frustration talking, because she couldn't even figure out what she needed when all her energy was being devoted to figuring out what her new sisters wanted.

"Just before you go, any news on 'the sisters' situation?" Lizzy asked.

Emma shook her head. "I've left April so many messages I'm starting to feel like a stalker, but she's ignoring me. And I don't know if Sierra is ignoring me or if I'm leaving messages on an old voicemail. The message is automated, so who knows if I have the right number."

And then there was Daisy with her plan of visiting four months from now, Rose who wouldn't give a single decisive answer without conferring with Dahlia, and— "Ugh. What am I even doing here?" The question came out louder than intended. "I shouldn't have come in the first place."

A noise had her looking over to see Nash hesitating in her doorway. He looked decidedly uncomfortable as he backed away. "Sorry. Didn't mean to intrude, I was just coming to see if you were ready."

"Almost." She forced a cheerful smile, as if he hadn't

just heard her ranting and raving. She held up the phone to offer proof that she wasn't talking to herself again.

Or to the pigs.

"Lizzy, I've got to go," she said, as Nash walked back down the hallway.

"Good luck tonight," Lizzy said. "And Emma?"

Emma paused, raising her eyebrows at the screen.

"Messy bun." This was said with all the solemnity of newlyweds speaking their vows.

"What?"

Lizzy gestured to the top of her head. "When in doubt, messy bun. You've got this."

Emma choked on a laugh. "Thanks, sis."

A little while later, her messy bun, exceptionally messy, and her favorite cocktail dress on, she sat next to a silent Nash as they rode into town.

The rehearsal dinner was at The Valley Bistro, the only place with candles and white tablecloths in a fifty mile radius, according to Nash. The restaurant was noisy when they entered, and she spotted several people she recognized standing at the bar that lined one wall.

"There they are." Patrick Donahue's voice boomed from where he stood at the far end of the bar talking to one of his nephews.

Nash turned to her, his smile strained. "Casey reserved the private room in the back. Why don't you go on ahead and tell her we're here? I'm sure she wants to get this dinner underway."

Emma nodded, but her smile felt stilted. Was he sending her away? She had the unsettling feeling she was being dismissed.

Nash had seemed kind of tense and awkward since the

festival. She assumed it was because of the kiss, but maybe it was something to do with his father.

Her gaze shifted to the senior Donahue. He was watching her with a glint in his eyes that she couldn't decipher. But it made her uncomfortable.

"Yeah, okay. I'll see you in there." She backed away toward the room where Casey's voice could be heard, along with her mother's.

Nash headed across to his father. While she walked the other way, Emma couldn't help but remember how the two men had gotten so quiet and awkward when she'd approached them the other night.

All she'd heard Nash say was 'handling it,' and then they'd both gone silent. She'd had the distinctly unnerving sensation that they'd been talking about her, but had been too distracted by the kiss and the high of such a wonderful evening to give it too much thought. Now it was crashing over her again, adding another brick of confusion to the growing tower in her mind.

Casey's face lit with a smile at the sight of her, and Emma shook off the paranoid thought. Even if they had been talking about her, there was no reason to think it was anything bad, right?

Her stomach twisted in spite of her assurances.

"I'm so glad you're here," Casey practically squealed as she wrapped Emma in a hug.

"I'm glad too. You look stunning."

Casey was always pretty, but tonight she seemed to glow in a pale pink silk sheath with her hair twisted up atop her head.

Casey beamed. "Thanks. But I feel like I'm going to burst right now. I'm so impatient to be married."

Emma smiled, ignoring a stab of envy.

Casey looked past her. "Where's Nash?"

"He's talking to your dad out by the bar."

Casey rolled her eyes with a groan. "It's always business with those two. They seriously cannot be in the same room without going on and on about ranch stuff. So boring." She made a funny face, but Emma couldn't bring herself to laugh.

Instead, she forced a smile. "Want me to go break it up?"

Casey's brows arched. "Would you? Toasts are about to start, we're gonna do a couple before the meal is served, and I don't want you to miss them."

"Of course." Emma turned back the way she'd come. Her smile still felt strained as she returned the greetings of Nash's aunts and uncles on her way to the bar.

It wasn't that she didn't like Nash's family, it was that she *did*. Way too much for her own good.

After spending all that time with them at the barbecue, church, and then the festival, it was hard to imagine how Nash could keep up the pretense around these people who loved him so much.

Personally, Emma wasn't sure she'd be able to do it much longer even if she was staying in town. Her mind flashed back to the kiss.

No, she knew she couldn't keep this up any longer, and not because of the guilt. Her heart couldn't take much more of this. It already felt like it was breaking in two.

She spotted Nash and his father, their heads tipped together as they talked. They were so deep in conversation, they seemed oblivious to the world around them.

Emma's stomach turned with unease at the glower on Nash's face. He looked so different from the Nash she'd been getting to know. A Nash who was quiet and serious, yes, but who wasn't quick to anger or even frustration.

He was even-keeled, which made this dark expression that much more concerning.

She inched a little closer, wondering how she was supposed to interrupt whatever they were talking about.

"I told you I'd handle it," Nash was saying.

Patrick raised his hands as if to pacify him. "I know you're trying your best to do right by our family. But we need to own the O'Sullivan Ranch."

"You know family means everything to me, Dad, but you have to let me do this my way."

They still hadn't seen her hovering at the edge of a crowd, and her feet had frozen at the mention of her family name.

"Nash, I trust you." Again, Patrick seemed to be trying to calm his son. "I know you'll get us the ranch." The older man gave a short laugh. "Even if you do have to marry the girl."

The floor shifted. The earth seemed to tilt.

She held her breath as she waited for Nash to say something. Anything. She wanted him to look confused and ask what on earth the older man was talking about. But he didn't do that. He seemed to know exactly what Patrick was saying.

They were talking about Nash marrying the girl, using her to get the land.

Oh my gosh. I'm that girl!

Hearts must be able to freeze over. What else could explain the cold pain expanding in her chest?

She wasn't sure if she made a noise—some kind of pitiful whimper or a heart-wrenching sound of disbelief—

but something had Nash looking over, his gaze colliding with hers.

She saw his eyes widen in horror.

Busted.

The flash of guilt on his face only made her feel worse.

She didn't wait to hear what he had to say. She couldn't stomach whatever excuse he'd no doubt come up with. Instead, she turned and bolted out the front door before he had the chance.

27

Time seemed to stop when Nash caught Emma's gaze.

Those blue eyes. So wounded.

His heart was in his throat and his gut twisted into knots as time came to a crashing halt.

The look on her face nearly killed him.

How much had she heard?

What conclusions was she jumping to?

And then she was gone, and time kicked into motion again. He tried to follow her out but got caught in a crush of rehearsal dinner guests who were making their way to the back room for toasts.

"Sorry about that, son," Patrick said from behind him. "I didn't know she was standing right there."

Anger flooded his veins, fast and fierce. Anger with himself, mostly, but he had plenty to spare. "Even if you didn't know she was there, how could you say such a thing?"

His cousin Boone stopped beside them, wariness written in his features. "You guys okay?"

Nash clamped his mouth shut. He got Boone's point. They were surrounded by people. And at his sister's rehearsal dinner. Now was not the time for a fight.

He leaned toward his father, lowering his voice to a fierce whisper. "I'm going to go find Emma and make sure she's all right, but you..." He gave his head a shake. "You raised me to be a better man than that. Do you honestly think I would date a woman just to seal a business deal?"

His father's eyes widened. He looked stricken but Nash didn't wait for his response. He was angry with his father, yes, but he could barely stand himself right now.

He shouldn't have let it get so far with his dad. He should have told him to steer clear of Emma no matter how much it might have angered him. He'd handled this all wrong, and now Emma was hurt.

Which was exactly what he'd been trying to avoid in the first place.

He ran into Casey as he tried to fight against the tide. "I'm sorry I'm going to miss the toasts—"

"Are you kidding me?" Her eyes were wide with disbelief. "I saw the way Emma rushed out of here. What happened?"

Nash couldn't look his sister in the eye, instead scrubbing a hand over his face and clenching his jaw.

"Nash Donahue." Casey's brows came down. "I don't know what you said or did to make her so upset, but you'd better go fix it." She jabbed a finger toward the door. "Now."

He was already shifting to squeeze past her. He didn't need to be told twice. His heart was thudding rapidly in his chest at the memory of the look in her eyes. So hurt.

And all because of him.

Once on Main Street, he glanced up and down, frantically searching. He spotted plenty of familiar faces coming out of the stores and bars further down the block, but no sign of Emma.

He headed to the truck, not that she had the keys to drive herself but maybe she'd wait there for him.

But no. She wasn't waiting there.

He ran down the street in one direction only to stop and turn, racing down the way he'd just come. Where would she go? He glanced into stores along the way, catching curious looks but no sign of his Emma.

Finally, when he reached the little park that fell between the library and the candy store, he spotted her. She was sitting in the gazebo, her elbows on her knees, her heels dangling from her fingers, and her head down like she was fascinated by the sight of her toes.

His heart crashed to the ground. She looked so sad. So...defeated. He swallowed down a surge of guilt and fear. "Emma."

Her head came up, and his chest ached at the detached expression. Her gaze was unfocused and her eyes...

Oh heck, her eyes. They were red-rimmed and puffy.

She'd been crying.

The realization nearly took him down at the knees. "Emma, I'm so sorry my father said what he did."

She stared at him for a long moment. "Is it true? Was all this..." She gestured to herself, to the heels. "Was all this just to get close to me so I'd—I'd fall for you? Marry you? Just so you could get a hunk of land with your name on it? Why even bother pretending in the first place? Some fake relationship? I don't even understand what you were thinking!"

Her voice wavered, and his heart cracked in two.

"It wasn't like that. That wasn't my plan."

Her lips trembled. "How do I know that's true?"

That stung. Worse than he ever thought it could. "I've always been honest with you, Emma."

She gave a little scoff of disbelief that was so out of character, it might as well have been a slap across the face. "You're lying to your family and friends just to avoid telling them the truth about what you really want in your life." She arched a brow. "Why should I believe that you've been honest with me?"

He winced. Her words cut. But then, he supposed the truth was brutal like that. He hated that she had a valid point. He hated it even more that she didn't trust him. That she couldn't see how he felt, when it seemed like she was the only one to truly see him for who he was.

He loved the way she looked at him. Well, he *had* loved the way she looked at him—until now. He recognized the distrust and disappointment in her eyes. It would no doubt haunt him for the rest of his life.

He moved closer, entering the gazebo. When she stiffened, he moved to the bench opposite her, afraid of scaring her off again. "You're right. I don't exactly have much credibility right now, do I?"

She didn't smile. The hurt in her eyes was like a dagger to his heart.

"I only wanted to protect you," he said, his voice so gruff he was surprised she heard him.

"Protect me? From what?"

He shrugged. *Everything.* "I saw how much stress you were under with the inheritance and finding out about all these sisters." He shook his head. "I didn't want my father pressuring you."

Her brows drew down. "So you asked me to pretend to be your girlfriend?"

He swallowed hard. When she put it like that, it sounded ridiculous. "I really did need a date to the wedding," he said. Nodding toward the restaurant, he added, "And the rehearsal dinner."

She stared at him for a long moment.

He huffed and admitted just how selfish he'd been. "It's been nice not having to make excuses with all those relentless matchmakers in town as well. Having a girl-friend definitely makes my life easier."

She shook her head. "And by staying close, your dad would believe that you were working an angle to get your hands on the land."

It wasn't a question, and he flinched at the bitterness in her tone. But he couldn't deny it. Even if he hadn't set out to make his dad think he was weaseling his way into her life and her inheritance, his father had leapt to that conclusion, and he'd done nothing to stop it.

They sat there in a long silence, and when she dropped her gaze to the ground again, he nearly fell to his knees to see her expression. Did she believe him?

She had to believe him.

He reached for her hands, but she shifted away before he could touch her.

Such a subtle shift, yet it felt like a punch in the guts. "I didn't mean to hurt you, Emma."

Her gaze flickered up and moved over his face, like she was trying to read something there. He stared back, hoping his expression was open enough. All he wanted her to see was raw honesty.

"I think I believe you," she finally whispered.

He tried to smile, but couldn't.

She didn't say it, but he heard it all the same. He hadn't meant to hurt her, but he *had*.

She nodded toward the rehearsal dinner. "You should get back. Casey will be disappointed if you're not there."

His heart twisted in his chest. Always thinking about others. That was just one of the reasons he loved her.

His heart stopped. His lungs froze.

He loved her?

Oh heck, what was the point of trying to deny it. He was falling head over heels for his fake girlfriend.

"Well?" She nodded toward the restaurant again, impatience in her tone. "You don't have to stay out here with me. I'm fine."

She was such a terrible liar. She wasn't fine, and the fact that her pain was his fault made it that much more unbearable.

"Come with me." He stood and held out a hand to help her to her feet.

"What? Why?"

"Because I want you there… beside me." His heart was racing wildly. Would she trust him this much? Would she believe that they were friends, at the very least?

He couldn't expect her to accept that this was real for him. It *had* been real since...since he didn't know when. Maybe from the very beginning.

But that didn't change much.

What am I even doing here? Her words from earlier in the evening came back to him with a jolt. She'd been talking to her sister on the phone and she'd said it loud and clear. *I shouldn't have come in the first place.*

His feelings for her changed nothing in the long run. She was still planning on leaving—couldn't wait to get back to her life in Chicago by the sounds of it. And he'd be left here. Miserable and sad, and aching for this beautiful woman.

But she wasn't gone yet.

She stared at his outstretched hand like it might bite. He just barely held back a sigh. "Emma, please. My father can be pushy, but he's not a bad man. My family and friends adore you. And I'm pretty sure you like them too."

Her lips pouted like she wanted to deny it but couldn't.

"I'm so sorry I let my father believe the worst. It wasn't fair to you. But I've been loving our time together, and I don't want you leaving here thinking that all of this was phony."

For him, none of it was fake. But he held his tongue. She didn't want declarations of love. But he could make sure they parted as friends.

She gazed up at him—a deer in headlights, still not sure what to believe.

He forced a smile, trying to make his voice a little lighter. "I think we get on pretty great you and me. Let's make the most of our last few days, huh?"

If nothing else, he needed her in his life as a friend.

Because somehow this woman had made her way into his heart...and she was fast becoming the closest friend he'd ever had.

S he was only doing this for Casey.

That was what Emma told herself the next day as she applied concealer to cover the dark shadows left behind by a sleepless night.

That was also the only reason she'd returned to the rehearsal dinner and sat through the sappy, sentimental toasts. That was definitely the only reason she'd cried when Nash stood up to say a few words about the happy couple.

Yup. She was only in this for Casey now, because despite what Patrick Donahue might think or what Nash had led her to believe, she honestly did value Casey's friendship. And his mother's.

And every single one of Nash's family and friends, for that matter.

Her phone buzzed with a text, but she ignored it. She'd stopped hoping that she'd hear from April or Sierra before her flight on Tuesday. It was a stupid idea to try and stick around until every *T* was crossed and *I* dotted.

Mr. Billman would be able to handle the signatures,

and she could make pointless phone calls and leave unanswered voicemails from anywhere.

For the first time since she'd arrived in Aspire, Emma was homesick for Chicago. She missed Lizzy and Sarah. She missed her parents.

For a moment, she'd entertained that notion that she belonged here—in Aspire, at this ranch—but now she had to wonder how much of that sense of belonging had been tied up in her infatuation with Nash.

She wasn't some cowgirl, and she never would be.

She got ready for the wedding in record time and with nothing better to do, headed out to say hello to Myrtle, Big Bird, and Snuffleupagus. She'd miss them, and Duke.

Emma sighed as she leaned over the fence, careful to keep her dress away from the dirty wood. She hoped no one noticed she was in the same outfit as last night, but she'd thrown the dress into her bag on a whim. She certainly hadn't been thinking of wedding dates when she initially packed in Chicago.

But Lizzy always made her take one nice dress. *"You never know what life will throw at you and there's nothing worse than not having the right thing to wear."*

It was funny how right and wrong her sister could be.

Life had definitely thrown Emma a curveball, but right this second, she didn't really care what she was wearing. Pretty fabric wasn't strong enough to keep a wounded heart from hurting.

"I'll be back to visit," she said to Big Bird, her voice trembling as she wondered if that was, in fact, true. "I'm sure I'll have to come back to sort out the signatures. Maybe I'll visit when Daisy's here too, you never know. It might be nice to meet the one sister who actually seems nice."

Snuffleupagus snuffled.

She nodded. "Exactly. So you see, it's not like I'm leaving forever, now am I? I'll be back." Her voice pitched on the last word and she sucked in a breath to stop herself from blubbering.

The pigs didn't seem to care that she was an emotional wreck.

She dabbed her eyes quickly before her mascara could smear. This was ridiculous. She was homesick for Chicago and yet somehow homesick for this ranch—and she hadn't even left yet.

"Honestly," she said to the pigs. "Is it even possible to be homesick for a place that isn't home?"

They didn't answer.

"Careful now," Kit's voice behind her made her start. "Don't start taking advice from Myrtle." He stopped beside her, looking better than ever in a suit and tie. His too-long blond hair was slicked back neatly, and his jaw was freshly shaven.

Even JJ was neatened up, wearing a button-down shirt with a bolo tie, his hair pulled back into a low ponytail, as usual. "No, ma'am," he agreed with Kit. "Kit's right. Myrtle here has been known to give some horrible advice."

She found herself torn between a sob and a laugh. She really had to get her emotions under control before Nash showed up to give her a ride to the church. "What kind of bad advice?"

"Well, she convinced Cody here to ask out Paige Luellen and that ended with Cody getting a black eye," Kit said.

Cody was walking over to join them with a rueful shake of his head at his brother's antics. "Not from

261

Paige." He put a hand to his heart. "I'm a proper gentleman."

Kit leaned forward with that easy grin of his, his eyes dancing with laughter. "It seemed no one told little Cody here that Paige already had a boyfriend."

Emma laughed at Cody's rueful shrug, and the fact that this big man who towered over her was referred to as 'little' anything.

The guys kept up their teasing and their laughter, and Emma laughed along with them, her heart full with emotion.

She knew what they were doing. They were trying to cheer her up, and while they did get her to laugh a bit, the fact that they were trying made her want to weep.

She'd miss them when she left.

They hadn't been at the rehearsal dinner last night, but they must have caught wind of the fact that she was upset —or maybe she was just doing a terrible job of covering up the fact that her heart felt bruised and battered.

Either way, their obvious attempts to cheer her were so sweet it made her heart ache in a whole different way.

"Uh oh," JJ said, taking two exaggerated, long strides away from her like she had cooties. "Boss man comin'," he hollered to the others.

Kit and Cody made a show out of scrambling away from her, too. For a second she was confused, but then Kit leaned forward. "Nash might seem like a good guy, and all, but we've noticed he's lost his head over a certain blonde ranch owner."

She snickered, embarrassment warring with wariness as she felt Nash's eyes on her as he strode toward them.

"My brother's right," Cody said. "I mean, Kit's an idiot, but he's right on this count."

JJ nodded, eyes wide as if scared. "Yes, ma'am. Nash is awfully protective of you."

Her smile faltered. *I only wanted to protect you.* Wasn't that what he'd said? And she actually felt like he meant it.

Did that make her a fool?

Maybe. Or maybe she was just seeing what she wanted to see.

You tend to fall for guys who don't actually see you, they just see what they can get from you.

Much as Nash's words were in her head, it was Lizzy's voice that echoed as Nash drew close, his gaze wary after the silent, tense way they'd parted the night before. Barely a muttered goodnight had passed between them. And now they had to pretend all over again at a wedding.

She drew in a deep breath that did nothing to loosen the knot in her chest.

"You look beautiful, Emma." Nash ignored his friends, who were giving them plenty of space now, though Kit gave her a wink from behind Nash's back as they headed toward JJ's truck.

Nash's gaze was filled with appreciation as he took in the gauzy, flower-patterned dress and the hair that she'd managed to curl into soft waves. At least today her hair was cooperating. That was a step up from yesterday.

"Thanks," she said, feigning cheerfulness as she took Nash in from his perfect hair to the tips of his boots that were shined to perfection.

It was truly unfair how handsome he looked in formal wear.

"Shall we?" He gestured toward the truck and helped her in like always.

And just like always her skin burned beneath her

clothes where he touched her waist. Unlike every other time, she held her breath as he settled her into the seat.

She wasn't sure she could handle his scent right now, not when the mere sight of him had her heart fluttering like a hummingbird.

He stood next to her for a little too long, and when she glanced over she saw him watching her with one hand on the passenger side door. His expression was taut. Grim, even.

"Nash, what is it?"

"I hate how things are between us now," he said on a rush of air. "I know that's my fault. But I need you to know—"

"It's fine." She cut him off rudely, and she knew it. But she didn't want to hear another apology, or worse, another explanation for why he'd let his father think he was wooing her.

"It's not fine, Emma. You're not fine." Frustration laced his voice. "You know I can tell when you're lying to me."

"I'm not lying," she said. Anger and hurt had her clenching her fists in her lap even as she told herself she was over it. She understood why he'd done what he'd done. She could even believe him when he'd said he hadn't meant to hurt her. But the truth of the matter was, he'd withheld information from her. He hadn't trusted her to handle his father, and he hadn't trusted her with the full truth.

He'd let her go into this situation blind, and that still hurt, even if she understood his motives.

"You're not fine," he said. His lips were set in a stubborn line as he crossed his arms.

She sighed, staring straight ahead. "Does it matter?"

"Of course it matters. I don't want you upset."

She shrugged. "I'll be out of your hair soon enough and you won't have to worry about it."

"I don't want that either."

Her head snapped to the side quickly at the frustration in his voice. The anger in his eyes left her temporarily speechless. It wasn't at her—she knew that. It was at himself. Or maybe his father.

Whatever it was, it made her insides coil with fear.

"Be careful, Nash." She barely recognized her voice. He looked more emotional than she'd ever seen him, and she was terrified of what he might say.

She was scared stiff at what she might believe.

Every ounce of self-preservation told her to run. To run now before her heart was mangled any further.

Because no matter what he was about to say, this couldn't end well. She'd never truly know how much of his interest was for her, and how much was because of this cursed land she'd inherited.

All of this, everything they had—it was all based on lies and half-truths.

She tore her gaze away from him and took in the house, the land that seemed to stretch into eternity, the cattle and the birds that dotted the scenery, and the man before her who she'd known from the beginning was too good to be true.

This wasn't her life.

She didn't get the handsome, noble cowboy and the home out of some Hallmark fantasy.

This was never her reality, and it was about time she remembered that.

29

Be careful, Nash.

She'd sounded so wary—of him. She was warning him off. And the look in her eyes...

He let out a sigh as he reached for her hand just outside the church doors.

She'd looked like a skittish colt, ready to bolt with one wrong move. And it was his own fault. He knew that. He'd lost her trust and he had no idea how to regain it, or if he should even try.

She slid her fingers into his, but she kept her gaze fixed straight ahead, like there was something more interesting on the church door than the date it had been founded.

The moment they walked inside, they were surrounded by a blast of cold air-conditioning and more arms than he could keep track of. He lost hold of Emma in the midst of all the hugging, but maybe that was for best.

When he caught sight of her she was smiling a genuine smile as she returned his Aunt Lisa's embrace. Those two had hit it off, and his Aunt Angela was quick to join them, nudging Lisa out of the way to talk to Emma.

He caught her eye through it all, and for a second, it felt like the night before hadn't happened. They were talking without saying a word, just the way a married couple would.

Ridiculousness, obviously, but being with Emma was like that. It had been from the start. There'd always be this connection between them...unless he'd broken it for good by not telling her the whole truth about his father's ambitions for her property.

"So glad you're here, man." Ryan clapped a hand on his shoulder, looking every inch the excited groom.

"I see there's no cold feet here," Nash teased.

Ryan rolled his eyes. "Are you kidding? I feel like I've been waiting for this day for an eternity. I can't wait to spend the rest of my life with your sister."

Nash nodded, his chest swelling with happiness on Casey's behalf. She deserved this—someone who would love her unconditionally. Someone who would be her partner and her best friend.

The thought had his gaze seeking out Emma before he could stop himself.

"You got the rings?" Ryan asked his best man.

Nash turned to watch the guy pull them from his pocket.

"Of course I do," he said with a laugh.

Nash didn't know Ryan's childhood friend that well. He lived in Boseman and had come over with his young wife for the wedding weekend. Nash hadn't really gotten a chance to speak with him at the rehearsal dinner.

He grinned at Nash. "Should we go take our places?"

"I'll be there in just a second." Nash nodded at the two men while Ryan straightened his suit jacket.

"Let's do this." His laugh had a nervous edge to it, but it was fueled by sheer excitement. That was obvious to everyone.

Nash chuckled at his almost-brother-in-law's boyish enthusiasm. He made a beeline through his aunts, stopping only to greet the cousins who'd traveled from out of town and hadn't been able to make it to the rehearsal dinner last night.

When he reached Emma's side, she was already shooing him off.

"Go, go. Casey will never forgive me if I hold up one of the groomsmen." She laughed, and to anyone who was watching, she looked happy.

But he could see the strain in her eyes. It seemed this kind, thoughtful, amazing woman had put aside her own emotions for this big event, and was doing her best not to spoil the day. Not for the bride, her family...and not for him.

"Will you be all right?" he asked, looking around for one of his aunts or cousins to sit with her.

"Of course." She gave a little sigh. "I'm not a child, Nash. I don't need you to protect me all the time."

His gaze shot back to her and he caught a sad tinge to her smile. That, plus the edginess of her words, told him...she wasn't just talking about right now.

"I know that," he said slowly, his voice a deep rumble. He led her into the foyer, for a little privacy, and turned to face her head on. She had to know he wasn't talking about right now either. He reached a hand out to touch her cheek because he couldn't stop himself. She was so dang touchable, and he never had been much good with words. "I guess…" He cleared his throat. "I guess I take one look at you and see someone who only ever worries about everyone else. You're a natural born caretaker, Em, and while that is a beautiful, precious thing, it makes me wonder who takes care of *you*."

Her lips parted, and her eyes widened, a glint of wetness making them shine.

His own voice grew lower and gruffer as he added, "I wonder who asks you what you want. What you need. And…" He glanced away and took a deep breath before looking back. "I know you're strong and you don't need my help. But I hate the idea of anyone taking advantage of your kindness."

She stared at him, the deep emotions in her eyes hard to read.

"Does that make sense?" he asked.

She swallowed and gave a jerky nod. He wasn't sure what else to say after that, so all he could do was gaze down at her.

Her blue eyes flickered over his face, then down to the plush carpet at their feet.

And then little Chloe appeared in her flower girl dress, with a basket of roses perched precariously in her arms.

Emma laughed at the adorable girl, straightening the wreath of flowers on her head. "You look like a princess, sweetheart."

Chloe beamed while Nash felt his heart cracking wide open.

How could he have screwed this up so badly?

This beautiful, kind-hearted woman was the perfect fit. He wanted her as part of his family, his life.

"Nash!" his mother's harsh whisper made him spin.

She bulged her eyes and pointed to the front of the church. "Casey will be here any second."

"I'd better, uh…" He gestured toward Ryan and the other groomsmen.

"Yeah. I saw Ellie before. Her husband couldn't make it so we agreed to sit together," Emma said.

He nodded. "I'll see you after?"

"At the reception. Of course." Her smile still seemed strained, but there was amusement there as well. "Wouldn't miss it."

He gave a huff of laughter as he turned away, that tension in his chest loosening now that he'd said…something. It wasn't all he wanted to say, but it was a start.

Would she want to hear the rest of it?

Would she give him a chance to fumble his way through the words he'd never said to another woman before?

The sound of the bridal song playing on the organ brought him to attention and he shuffled into place, his mind and eyes fixed on his sister as she walked down the aisle.

Casey was radiant with happiness. He assumed the dress was nice and the veil and makeup. He was sure the ladies of Aspire would have plenty to say about it all— giggles and gushing were a definite part of their imminent future.

All Nash did know was that he'd never seen his little sister glowing quite so brightly.

And because of that, she'd never looked more beautiful.

As she and Ryan exchanged vows, all he could think about was the true meaning behind the words. The commitment. The promises.

All of which he'd shied away from for years because he'd never been able to imagine wanting to make those vows. He couldn't fathom them being anything but an albatross around his neck. He couldn't imagine ever wanting his life to change in such a drastic way.

He'd always been so content with what he had. But now…

His gaze stole over to Emma as the minister spoke.

Now he couldn't imagine going back to life the way it had been. He didn't want to imagine a future without Emma's laughter and her teasing. He didn't want to picture a day when he didn't see her smiling face.

A partner. A best friend. She could become that so easily. She'd already started to, and in such a short time. His head was spinning.

Time. He didn't have much left. The clock was ticking too fast, and soon she'd be on a plane back to Chicago.

He winced at the memory of her words just before the rehearsal dinner. If he'd had any hopes that she'd change her mind about staying, overhearing her say she wished she'd never come at all had certainly squashed them.

She'd go back to Chicago, to the life she'd known before arriving in Aspire. Before him. His heart thudded so loudly it was a wonder it didn't interrupt the service. He knew without a doubt that he couldn't do the same.

He couldn't imagine going back to life before Emma. But he could perfectly imagine a future with her in it. And it was a future with her by his side, with a family of their own and a life filled with love and joy and laughter.

He could barely breathe, the onslaught of images were so vivid and filled him with such longing.

His gaze flitted over his mother and his aunts in the

first row. He could only imagine what they'd say if he told them this new revelation.

All these years he'd said he didn't want to get married.

But maybe he did.

He wanted to marry *Emma*.

The one woman who definitely didn't want him in return.

30

The ceremony was perfection. Everyone said so, and Emma couldn't agree more. Despite her own heartache, she'd been so grateful to see such a beautiful display of love and happiness.

And if her heart had ached just a little more at the sight of Nash at the front of the wedding...

If she found herself daydreaming about him being the groom and her the bride...

Well, that was an issue she and her brain were going to have to tackle at a later date. Like, after the reception.

She looked at the clock on the wall. They'd moved to the reception hall, a separate building adjoining the church, about forty minutes ago. Elaborate starters were laid out on tables in the smaller room, so guests could nibble while they waited for the bridal party and family to join them. Emma had taken a peek into the main hall and it looked stunning. Whoever was on the decoration committee for this wedding had done a phenomenal job, turning a plain church hall into a rustic fairytale. She snapped some pics for Lizzy who was always looking for ideas, although she doubted her sister would be interested in this quaint wedding, oozing with country style and warmth.

Emma guessed it was more her thing, and the thought that she'd probably never get it made her throat constrict.

She sipped from her champagne flute while she waited for the festivities to begin. Surely it wouldn't be too much longer. As she chewed her lower lip and spun the glass between her fingers, she couldn't stop her foot from tapping.

The pictures were taking forever.

She flinched when she saw Nash's Aunt Angela wrangling a group of Donahue cousins for yet another family photo.

Please don't see me. Please don't see me.

"Emma?" Ellie's voice caught her off guard as she sidled up beside her.

Emma stopped her inner pleading and turned to her new friend with a smile. "How's your husband feeling?"

Ellie slipped the phone into her handbag. "He's fine. He just doesn't like weddings, that's all."

"Oh." Emma wasn't sure what to say to that. She could make a flippant joke about how he'd played hooky but there was a sadness in Ellie's eyes that made her think her marriage wasn't a joking matter. "I'm sorry."

Ellie shrugged. "I'm used to it."

To her husband bailing on weddings? Emma didn't think that was what she meant, so she kept quiet. Ellie's gaze moved from her to Aunt Angela who was shouting loudly for all cousins and their spouses to gather together outside for pictures on the lawn.

"Aren't you going to join in?" she asked.

Emma bit back a sigh. Oh Ellie. So sweet. So naive. She

actually believed that Emma belonged here. That she was practically a member of the family.

Guilt left an unpleasant taste in her mouth. Of course, she only believed that because Emma was a big fat liar. When she'd agreed to this ruse, she hadn't imagined she'd make friends in this town so quickly. She hadn't expected to be so accepted and treated like a member of the family.

No. The sooner they put an end to this, the better for everyone. Particularly her guilty conscience.

But in the meantime...

"Emma, get over here, girl," Aunt Angela called.

Emma smiled but shook her head resolutely.

"Why not?" Ellie whispered. "Are you camera shy?"

"Um..." Emma couldn't bring herself to lie any more than she already had. "No. But I don't feel comfortable being in family photos."

"Why not?"

"Because I'm not family?" Her throat felt too tight.

Ellie laughed. "Could've fooled me." Her grin was knowing as her dimples flashed. The redhead's eyes sparkled with amusement. "Everyone who saw you and Nash at the festival the other night is convinced this is just the first Donahue wedding of the season."

Emma made a noise that she hoped sounded like a laugh.

She was a little afraid it sounded more like a sob.

Ellie was watching her closely, like she was expecting some sort of answer. Emma feigned a keen interest in the young cousins being jostled out the door, their shirts being straightened and their hair combed back into place with their mother's licked fingers.

She wasn't about to explain to Ellie that everyone had it all wrong. Because then she'd find herself blubbering about how *she'd* gotten it all wrong. Next thing she knew, she'd be crying over the wedding cake telling Nash that she'd gone and done the unthinkable. She'd fallen in love with him even when he'd made it clear that was precisely what he didn't want.

Not from anyone, but especially not from her.

Oh yeah. It was definitely time to go back home so she could start to heal this broken heart.

Ellie's gentle hand on her shoulder made her tense.

"Emma? Sweetie? Is everything okay?"

Emma's cheeks hurt from the strain of all this smiling. "Fine," she said. "Just fine."

Ellie's brows came down. Clearly she wasn't fooled. But when she opened her mouth to speak, Emma cut her off. "Will you excuse me?" She gestured toward the corridor. "I'm just going to go to the restroom before the reception starts."

"Of course." Ellie took Emma's champagne flute and watched Emma flee.

She could sense her gaze, and it forced her to slow down and not sprint the way her body wanted to.

Running away was exactly what she was doing. She was so grateful she'd been invited, so glad she'd met the Donahues and all their friends. But being at a wedding was a cruel and unusual torture for her already mangled heart.

Every time she looked around her, she saw *what ifs* and *what might have beens*.

Except…

She'd seen honest affection in Nash's eyes, she knew she had.

She picked up her pace, her heels tapping against the hardwood floor as she navigated the corridor, bypassing the restrooms when she spotted double doors leading to temporary freedom.

She believed Nash had been looking out for her best interests. But that somehow made it worse. Knowing that he'd been so very kind and was actually trying to protect her only made her fall even harder.

He wanted to make sure someone was looking out for *her*.

How sweet is that?

He's the kindest man I've ever met.

And that just made it all the more unfair. Now she couldn't even curse him as a selfish, lying jerk when she cried her heart out to Lizzy. Oh no. Even Lizzy would agree that she'd finally gone and fallen for a good guy. A selfless guy. A guy who'd only wanted to make sure she wasn't taken advantage of by—

"Patrick." She stopped short at the sight of Nash's father in the back alcove.

He slipped the phone into his jacket pocket, his handsome face creasing with a warm smile that reminded her so much of Nash her belly twisted into knots.

"Emma," he said, as if he was happy to see her here. He probably was. Maybe he thought she and Nash had made up and were back on track. "You look beautiful," he continued.

Which for him meant back on track to getting his hands on her land.

A surge of protectiveness had her hands clenching into fists at her sides. After days of stewing over what to do with the property, of trying to figure out what her sisters wanted and what her father had been thinking when he'd left it to all seven of them...

All that faded away in the face of this one fact. It was her land. It was their land. It was O'Sullivan property.

And she didn't want that to change.

The realization was so stark and sudden, it left her wide eyed and gaping at the older man.

"Emma, are you all right?" He took a step toward her, his brow creased in concern.

Yeah, right. Bitterness filled her mouth and made her stomach turn.

He wasn't concerned about her. He was just concerned with getting what he wanted—no matter who got hurt in the process.

"Emma, honey, do you want me to get Nash?"

"No." Finally, she was able to speak. "No, I don't want to see Nash right now."

That was the truth. She couldn't see him when she was this irrational and so very shaky. But while she might feel like she was walking on quicksand when it came to her feelings for Nash, facing his father gave her more clarity than ever about why she was here in the first place.

"Emma? Are you sure you're all right?" Patrick asked again.

"I'm fi—" She stopped, blinked and realized she was about to give him her automatic response, which was the wrong thing to do. With a tight smile, she shook her head and looked Mr. Donahue in the eye. "No. I'm not all right," she said. "Quite frankly, Mr. Donahue, I'm angry."

His head jolted back with surprise.

Emma took a deep breath, some of that tightness in her chest easing with the admission. She could have sworn she heard Lizzy's voice cheering her on, and the thought of her sister had her chin coming up further. "That's right,

I'm angry at your assumptions. You already think my father's property is yours, don't you?"

He held his hands up, and his voice was soothing to the point of being condescending. "Now, Emma, I'm not sure this is the time and place for discussing this, but you've got to understand. We've been taking care of that property—"

"No," she interrupted. "*Nash* has been taking care of it. Frank employed him to do that job. And while I appreciate that he's been looking after the land, the cattle, the house, since Frank left, the O'Sullivan ranch does not belong to you."

Patrick opened his mouth as if to protest, but she wasn't done.

"And you can't marry your way into it."

His mouth snapped shut. Some of that self-righteous anger sputtered slightly at the flicker of guilt in his eyes.

"I'm sorry about that," he muttered gruffly. "I never would have pushed him to do something like that if I didn't think he honestly cared for you. But I saw the way my son looked at you and I...I..."

He shrugged as if at a loss for how to finish.

To his credit, she saw shame in his eyes.

Emma never had much of a temper and she could feel her anger melting despite her best attempts to cling to it. Anger was so much easier than hurt. She wet her lips and took a deep breath.

"Well, you were wrong," she said simply. She wasn't about to explain to this man how it had all been for show.

He didn't deserve her explanations, and it wasn't her place. This was Nash's father. If anyone ought to explain, it was her fake boyfriend.

She took a deep breath and said a silent prayer asking

for the strength that she so badly needed to make it through this conversation and this day. "Nash is never going to ask me to marry him," she said. She managed to get the words out, despite the fact that they felt like daggers scraping her chest and throat on the way out.

But it was time to face facts. To speak the truth, even if it hurt.

Patrick was frowning at her again, and this time she was almost certain his concern was genuine.

It was that concern that had her voice wobbling when she continued. "But even if I was lucky enough to have him ask for my hand, the property still wouldn't be yours. It's O'Sullivan land, and it will never belong to a Donahue."

31

Nash stood frozen in the corridor, tucked out of sight, but able to see and hear everything. His chest swelled with pride at Emma's calm but forceful pronouncement.

But that pride was nothing compared to the other emotion that hit him like a tidal wave.

Even if I was lucky enough to have him ask for my hand…

Did she mean it?

His heart slammed in his chest as his gaze took in the sight before him with new eyes. His Emma. So sweet. So kind.

She'd been right, she didn't need his protection.

He watched Emma's lower lip quiver with emotion, but her shoulders were back and she was facing down his father in a way he rarely had. The way he should have done when he'd first realized just how obsessed his father had become with possessing the O'Sullivan land.

"Now, Emma," his father said, his voice taking on a patronizing tone that made Nash wince.

"No. Don't you 'now Emma' me," she said, steel in her voice and in her spine.

Nash fought the urge to intervene on her behalf. She didn't need him to, and he had a hunch this was something she had to do for herself.

"My offer would be more than fair," his father continued, not seeming to understand that the more he fought, the more she'd dig her heels in.

Emma might be generous to a fault, but it was obvious she was no pushover, and it was about time his father realized that.

"I'm sure it would be," she said. "And if my family decides to sell, we'll take *all* offers into consideration. But, I have to be honest, I'm not certain we will sell." She nodded as if confirming this to herself.

Nash studied her face, trying to read the emotions there.

"If we do, who we sell to will be up to my sisters and me," she continued. "No one else. And I assure you, Patrick, the more you try to push and cajole, the more you try to manipulate my feelings for your son, for your own gain, the more I am absolutely certain we won't entertain any offer from you, no matter how good the price."

"Well, I...I..."

Nash winced at his father's useless sputtering. Not many people had put Patrick Donahue in his place, and he clearly had no idea how to handle it.

Nash ought to intervene, but he didn't want to step on Emma's toes. This was her moment, and he wasn't about to ruin it for her or take her power away by showing up like some unwanted and unnecessary knight in shining armor.

He'd already made enough of a mess by trying to fight

her battles behind her back, and he wasn't about to repeat his mistakes.

Between his father's blustering and the way Emma's clenched hands shook, Nash nearly lost his resolve and rushed in. But then, just when he thought his father would lose his temper and say something rash...Patrick surprised him.

"I...guess I can respect that," he said grudgingly.

Emma's shoulder slumped slightly in obvious relief.

"I, uh…" Patrick looked down at his boots, his voice gruff. "I'm sorry, Emma. I know I come on strong…"

Emma arched one brow and Patrick let out a little huff of amusement.

Nash just barely held back a snort of laughter as well. He now knew exactly why Emma was so good with little children. She didn't have to raise her voice to express her dissatisfaction with Patrick's excuses. One look was more than enough.

"All right, all right," his father said. "I was out of line, and I apologize." He met her gaze evenly and without any of his earlier condescension. "I've only ever wanted what's best for my family, but I know that sometimes means I have blinders on. I get so focused on the end result, I lose sight of who I might be hurting in the process."

She nodded. "I can understand family loyalty. And I'm sure you can understand that my first priority is connecting with all of Frank O'Sullivan's daughters and ensuring that whatever decision we make going forward, is in the best interest of all of us."

Patrick's expression was serious, and Nash was almost certain he caught a gleam of approval in his father's eyes. "I do understand that, Emma."

There was a silence, and this was Nash's cue. He took a

deep breath, ready to announce his presence, but his father's next question, quiet and gentle, caught him off guard.

"If you don't mind me asking, why are you so certain Nash will never ask for your hand? Do you not see a future for you two?"

Nash's throat went dry and his lungs seized up in panic. Even if he'd wanted to intervene, he couldn't say a word. It felt like his entire future hung in the balance.

All that self-righteous anger seemed to seep out of Emma, and she wilted right in front of his eyes. Oh, she was still standing straight and proud, but he felt like he could see her deflate, and the sight nearly killed him.

Had he done that? Had he hurt her more than she was letting on?

She looked down at her feet. "I'd rather not talk about Nash with you, if you don't mind."

She wasn't looking at Patrick, but Nash saw his father's pained expression and it matched how he was feeling perfectly. Helpless in the face of her sadness.

"I know he cares about you," his father started, sounding just as uncomfortable as he looked.

Patrick was just as averse to talk of love and romance as Nash was, if not more.

Nash should be the one telling her how much he cared, but he couldn't stop staring at Emma. Would she even want to hear it?

"Maybe," she said so softly he almost missed it. "But my life is in Chicago. I don't belong here."

His chest felt like it was being torn in two. She did belong here, couldn't she see that?

Or was it his actions that made her want to run back home?

Or maybe it was the fact she never thought of this place as home. She was a city girl after all, even if she made life here look so easy.

His father spotted him and froze, his mouth twisting in a grimace of regret—maybe even pity.

"Nash," he said. "There you are. We were just talking about you."

Emma's head came up quickly, her eyes were wide with surprise...and maybe fear.

Aw heck. His chest throbbed in pain. He'd done this. He'd taken this kind woman's trust and let her down.

"Dad, Aunt Angela's looking for you," he murmured.

He couldn't bring himself to address his father in the eye. He couldn't tear his gaze from Emma's face. Right now, all he wanted was to ease that pain in her eyes. He had to make this right.

"Sure, sure," his father said as he stepped away, casting one last regretful look in Emma's direction.

A tense silence fell in his father's wake.

"How much did you hear?" she asked.

"Enough to know that I'm real proud of you," he said as he moved toward her.

He thought she might turn away but to his surprise, she turned into him and buried her face against his chest with a quiet sob.

"Oh sweetheart," he murmured, stroking her back.

"I never get angry," she said. "I shouldn't have said all that."

"Yes, you should have." Nash took a deep breath. "He needed to hear it, and it's exactly what I should have said to him rather than…"

She pulled back, biting a lip that still trembled in an

attempt to regain her composure. She swiped at her eyes. "Do you regret it then?"

He stared at her, trying to make sense of the question.

"D-do you regret asking me to play the part of your girlfriend?"

Nash was at a total loss for words. His inability to speak to women had fled around Emma, but right here and now, he had no clue what to say. But not because Emma was so hard to talk to. He just had no idea what the answer was.

Did he regret getting close to Emma? Kissing her and dancing with her?

Heck no. He wouldn't trade that for anything in the world.

But he hated that his lies had led to this mistrust he saw in her eyes. He hated that their newfound friendship was based on half-truths on his end.

She shook her head when he didn't immediately answer. "It's okay. I didn't mean to put you on the spot."

He opened his mouth and closed it abruptly.

His mother's voice in the corridor cut him off before he could try again. "Nash, honey, Casey needs you. She says you're in charge of the music?"

His mother's flustered expression transformed into a smile. "There you are, Emma. We were afraid you'd taken off when you didn't join in for the pictures."

Emma's smile probably seemed genuine to his mother.

Nash knew better.

She mumbled some excuse about not wanting to get in the way. It appeased Delphine, and she turned back to Nash with a warning look. "Don't make your sister wait. I don't want her turning into a bridezilla on us. We've gotten this far."

288

He and Emma both chuckled because it was expected, and Delphine disappeared back into the main hall.

"You'd better go," Emma said. Her gaze held a look of resignation that killed him. There was a finality there that made him want to drag her out of this church hall so he could kiss her and tell her everything that was in his heart.

"Emma, no. There's still so much I want to say." A surge of love so fierce took hold and made it impossible to hear anything but the pounding of his heart.

"Later." She gave him a smile that made his heart break with its bravery and strength. She gave him a little push toward the door. "There will be time later. But right now, you have big brother duties to attend to."

"Emma—"

"This is *her* day, Nash." Again with the serious teacher expression. He couldn't fight that look. She pointed toward the door. "Now, go. I'll be fine."

He took a hesitant step back. "We'll talk later?"

Her lips pressed together in a thin line but after a second she gave a jerky nod.

"Nash!"

They both heard someone calling his name and he winced, heading away from her. He looked back at Emma —the woman he loved. The woman he hoped he could convince to stay. "Later," he promised. "We're going to talk later."

32

W*e're going to talk later.*

His words hung in the air even after he walked away.

Emma slumped against the wall with a sigh.

There's nothing left to say. That was what she should have said. He hadn't made her any promises, and if anything, he'd told her right from the start how this would end. She couldn't pretend to be surprised now to find out that he only liked her as a friend.

And that was what he'd been about to say. She could see it in the sympathy that warmed his eyes. It was honest affection he felt for her, but then...it always was, wasn't it?

You're such a good woman, Emma, but I just don't feel that way about you.

You'll make some lucky man a wonderful wife some day, Emma, but...

But...

There was always a *but*.

Because she fell for the wrong guys, a fact even Lizzy couldn't deny.

The tears that had been threatening for the past hour finally trickled down her cheeks until she swiped them away with an irritated sigh.

This whole ruse had gone on for too long. She felt bone tired and weary in a way that had nothing to do with her sleepless night and everything to do with the Donahue family.

Okay, fine, Nash.

Although that altercation with Patrick hadn't exactly left her feeling heartened either. All it had done was make her doubt everything she thought she knew.

Namely, her decision to sell the property. Her words to Patrick had felt right coming out. It was the O'Sullivan property. It belonged to them. To *her*. For a second there she'd actually found strength in her family name, in the inheritance and the daughters that her father had left behind.

She had six sisters, a ranch that was too good to be true, and in a town that felt more like home to her than Chicago ever had. So why was she so intent on getting her sisters to sign off on selling?

What if she decided to keep it instead?

The thought made her head spin and she shut her eyes. That confrontation with Patrick, followed by the look she'd seen in Nash's gaze…

She couldn't make any decisions. Not here. Not now.

Pushing away from the wall, she headed outside. What she needed was fresh air. Maybe then she could get her head on straight long enough to remember what she was doing here and why she couldn't stay.

She threw open the doors and nearly collided with Cody. The younger Swanson brother was toting Chloe on one hip while Corbin rode atop his shoulders with a grin, pretending to control Cody with reins like he was a horse.

"Oh!" She laughed at the sight of the smiling but harried uncle. "Sorry, I didn't realize there was a horse show going on out here."

Cody laughed as Corbin informed her, "I'm training my new pony for the rodeo."

"Oh, I see." She eyed Chloe who clung to his front. "And are you a pony too?"

"Of course not," she said with a giggle. "I'm grooming the horses."

Cody's eyes shut as he shook with silent laughter.

"You are a very indulgent uncle," Emma said as she watched the little ones clamber all over him.

"Yeah, well, what can I say? Everyone's got to have the fun uncle, right?"

Emma grinned at that. She supposed there was some truth to it, but with her mother and Derek being only children, she'd never experienced a big family.

She smiled as she sank down onto the steps and rested her chin in the palm of her hands. She'd certainly never had an uncle like Cody.

He neighed loudly as if to make her point, and she and the twins burst out laughing.

Kit stuck his head out. "Where are my little curtain crawlers?"

"Daddy!" Chloe leapt off Cody as Corbin slid to the ground.

"Is it time for cake?" Corbin asked.

"Not yet, but if you eat all your dinner, I promise to snag you the biggest piece I can find. Deal?"

"Deal!" Corbin shouted.

Kit winked at Emma as his kids ran through the doorway, leaving her and Cody outside.

He fell onto the steps beside her. "Sorry if me and the kids ruined your hiding spot."

She shot him a rueful smile. "Is it that obvious?"

He eyed her kindly, not pointing out the fact that her mascara was no doubt smudged under her damp eyes.

"I'm not judging," he said. "Heck, it's no coincidence that I brought the twins out here to play during the picture time."

"*You're* camera shy?" Emma teased. She nudged his arm. "A handsome guy like you?"

He shrugged, his grin sheepish. "What's your excuse? You don't like cameras either?"

It was the nicest possible way he could ask what was wrong without directly asking what was wrong and Emma's appreciation for the ranch hand grew tenfold.

"Something like that," she said.

He sat quietly beside her. Kind of like Nash, he seemed comfortable with silence, and for a moment she wondered if that came from spending long hours alone on the range or if the cowboy lifestyle just appealed to that type of man.

Finally, his comfortable silence got to her and she found herself admitting, "I just don't want to be that girl."

"That girl?" he asked, his gaze still fixed straight ahead.

"Two years ago my best friend from college got married," Emma said. "I was her maid of honor."

"Okay," Cody said slowly.

"One of the groom's cousins was the best man and he brought a date." Emma cleared her throat, humiliation and pain making her throat feel too tight. "Anyway, when picture time came around the photographer and the

parents dragged the best man's date into all the pictures."
She glanced over at Cody with a wry smile. "Two weeks
later they broke up."

Cody's brows arched. "Ahh."

"So," Emma finished with a shrug. "Now she's 'that
girl' whenever my best friend and her family post pictures
of the big day or look through the album to relive the
happy moment."

Cody nodded slowly, clasping his hands around his
knee. "I see."

Emma turned to him. Something in his quiet, gentle
demeanor made her think he really did see. Maybe more
than she wanted. He looked out across the small yard.
"Does that mean you're going back to Chicago?"

She swallowed hard. "That was always the plan. You
know that."

He nodded, glancing at her. "I guess I thought maybe
things had changed."

She bit her lip to keep from crying but her throat was
too tight to speak. She couldn't admit how much she
wished he was right.

But things hadn't changed. Not in the ways that
counted.

She'd be boarding a plane Tuesday morning and there
was no stopping that.

"You going back inside?" he asked.

She shook her head. She couldn't even talk, how was
she supposed to smile and dance and make small talk the
rest of the night?

Cody nudged her elbow with his. "You want a ride
home?"

Home. The word hit her chest like a hammer and she
felt her heart reverberate from the impact. *Home.*

He was talking about the ranch, and that was exactly what it had come to feel like. Her home. The house, the land, this town, her new friends...

And Nash.

Nash most of all. He'd come to feel like home.

She pressed her lips together, but it was no use. She was already starting to blubber like a fool again.

"Yes, please," she managed through her tears. "If you don't mind."

"Of course not," he murmured. "Let me grab my keys and I'll be right back."

She nodded, swiping at tears as she waited. She should tell Nash where she was going, but she couldn't go inside looking like this.

And she couldn't bear to see the sympathy in Nash's eyes again if he caught sight of her crying over him.

"Ready when you are," Cody said when he stepped back outside.

She liked all the guys who worked on the O'Sullivan Ranch, but right now she was grateful it was Cody who drove her back to the house, because she wouldn't have been able to bear it if she'd been riding with someone who thought they had to cheer her up or pester her with questions.

Cody dropped her off with a few murmured comments about how she ought to get some rest and how he'd make her excuses to Nash and the rest of the family.

She nodded, waving him off and waiting until she was inside before bending forward at the waist as a heaving sob choked out of her. She covered her mouth but it was no use.

Thank goodness no one was home.

Her sobs seemed absurdly loud in the otherwise silent,

empty house. She headed toward her bedroom, but caught sight of the folder which had been plaguing her stay and turned right back around.

She'd spent what felt like weeks working so hard to find her sisters so that they could sell, and now she was having second thoughts. She fell onto the couch where she'd spent evenings relaxing with Nash, talking and laughing and feeling more comfortable than she could ever remember.

She leaned back and looked up at the high ceiling. Yes, this place had come to feel like home. But how much of that was thanks to Nash?

She hugged a cushion to her chest.

Would it be the same when they were no longer spending so much time together? Would she still feel like this was her home if Nash wasn't here to share her meals with her and say goodnight at the end of every day?

She squeezed the soft cushion with a little moan.

Somehow she didn't think so. She loved this place, all right. And she adored her newfound friends.

But it was Nash who'd filled her heart in a way that no one else could.

33

"Smile!" Aunt Lisa beamed at him from behind the camera.

Nash tried to oblige, but he wasn't in the smiling mood. From the amount he'd been forced to smile this past hour during photographs and greeting all the guests, he was pretty sure he'd never smile again.

Aunt Lisa checked the photo she'd just taken with a satisfied nod.

Nash didn't have the heart to remind her that the photographer had already taken hundreds of pictures of him and the rest of the family. His favorite aunt liked to think of herself as the family's memory keeper, and who could argue with that?

"Now I just need one with your girlfriend." She frowned down at the camera, like she might be able to find Emma with the zoom feature.

Good luck. He'd been looking for her for the last half hour in between pictures and the chores Casey thrust at him.

She'd disappeared.

Frustration had him fighting to keep his temper. He loved his sister and wanted nothing more than her happiness, but this reception felt interminably long and it had only just begun.

Where could Emma have gone?

"When you see Emma, you make sure I get a picture, you hear?" Aunt Lisa said.

"Yes, ma'am." He watched his aunt walk away before threading through the foldout tables and chairs that he'd helped to set up. White linen and table dressings hid their cheapness. The hall really had been transformed.

Their father had offered to pay for a big wedding and pull out all the stops but Casey and Ryan had opted to follow in her parents' footsteps with a relatively simple affair at the church hall.

Simple, Casey had claimed, meant she'd be able to relax and have fun rather than worrying about the details on her big day.

He watched her dancing with Ryan and her bridesmaids to the music that was being piped over speakers from her phone. She and Ryan had put together the playlist and they were grinning like maniacs out on the dance floor.

He chuckled when Delphine, and Ryan's mother, stepped out onto the dance floor hand in hand to join in the fun. They swayed over to Kit and Cody's parents, who were dancing with Chloe and Corbin in the middle of the makeshift dance floor.

His eyes scanned the crowd automatically for some sign of Emma, but it was hopeless. He checked his phone once more to see if she'd texted him back, but nothing there either.

"Great wedding." Cody's voice was quiet but Nash heard him when he sidled up beside him.

He nodded his response and pointed at the dancing couple. "It's great to see them so happy."

Cody cleared his throat. "I thought you might want to know, I took Emma back to the house."

Nash whipped around to face his friend. "You did?"

"She, uh...wasn't feeling well." Cody scratched his temple, squinting in obvious discomfort.

Nash's heart took a plummet. "Was she..." Ah heck. He and Cody were not cut out for this conversation. "Was she crying?"

Cody's wince said it all.

Nash muttered an oath under his breath. He hadn't been able to shake the sight of the pain in her eyes...or the sound of her voice when she'd told his father her life was in Chicago.

But then again, she had said she'd be lucky to marry a guy like Nash. Was she just being kind or had she meant that?

He'd been clinging to those words like a lifeline since he'd heard them, and he'd been itching to ask her if it was true.

"We were supposed to talk," he said to a no-doubt confused Cody.

Cody shrugged in response. "It seemed like maybe she needed some time alone."

Nash glowered at his friend. "Did she say that? Did she say she didn't want to see me?"

She left, moron. Of course she doesn't want to see you.

Cody didn't have a chance to reply. Kit came over and clapped a hand on his brother's shoulder as he looked Nash over. "What did I miss? Why does the brother of the

301

bride look like he's gonna start a fight with one of the guests?"

Nash turned his glare to Kit. He was definitely not in the mood for his best friend's jokes right now.

Kit held his hands up in mock surrender. "Hey Cody, can you go help Mom and Dad with the kids for a minute? Looks like they could use a break from the sugar-high twins."

"Sure thing." Cody slumped with relief as he walked away and Nash felt a pang of guilt.

"I wasn't mad at your brother," he mumbled.

"Yeah, we all know what's really bothering you," Kit said. "What I want to know is, what are you going to do about it?"

Nash didn't reply. He turned and stared at the dancing and laughter before him. Emma should be here. Even the twins had come up to him asking where she'd gone.

She belonged here. With him.

But did she want to stay?

Kit exhaled loudly. "You know you could just tell her the truth, right?"

Nash stiffened. "Which is?"

"You're falling in love with her."

The words hit him hard. He'd admitted the depths of his feelings to himself, but hearing his best friend say it aloud made it feel even more real. It made it impossible to deny and even harder to avoid.

He could feel Kit's eyes on him, waiting for some sort of reaction. No, he couldn't deny it. But that didn't change anything right now. It wasn't about what he wanted. It was about Emma, and what she deserved.

"Well?" Kit prompted. "Don't you think you owe her the truth?"

Nash flinched. He was no longer seeing the dancing family and friends before him because his mind's eye was filled with the image of Emma's wounded expression. She'd said she believed him, but wariness still lingered in her gaze. She didn't completely trust him anymore, and he wasn't sure how he'd ever fix that.

He crossed his arms over his chest, as if that might alleviate this pain. "I broke her trust. I'm not sure she'd believe me now."

Kit scoffed. "Nash, *I* believe you're in love with her, and I'm a skeptic when it comes to romance. You saw what happened to me."

Nash frowned over at his friend. He hated the bitterness that tinged Kit's voice whenever he talked about his ex. It was so at odds with his naturally laidback, easy going demeanor. "None of us saw that one coming. Natalie fooled us all."

"She did." Kit nodded, his brows coming down in a surprisingly serious expression. "Thing is, I don't think Emma's faking it. You two at the festival. The way you were laughing together, looking at each other, that kiss…" He met Nash's stare head on. "There was nothing fake about that."

Nash shook his head in frustration. "I know. I mean, for me, there wasn't."

Kit arched a brow. "Then what's holding you back?"

Nash huffed. Where to begin?

He settled for, "Relationships are complicated."

And that was putting it mildly. He'd never even been in a real relationship, because they always seemed like too much work. He didn't know how to talk to women, he couldn't read their minds and figure out what they wanted.

Add to all that the fact that Emma had a family and a career in Chicago, the fact that she didn't trust him any longer thanks to his father's agenda and his own actions, and things went from complicated to doomed.

Maybe if he had more time, but she was supposed to be on a flight back home early Tuesday morning. Two days wasn't nearly enough time to prove to her that his interest had nothing to do with the land or his father.

"Complicated, huh?" Kit's voice was filled with disbelief. "I've heard the right ones are easy. Look at my parents. Look at your parents, your grandparents, your aunts and uncles. Happy marriages are everywhere, man."

Nash swallowed hard. He knew Kit was right. Happy marriages did exist. And when it came to Emma, he'd found talking far easier than he ever thought it could be. Until he'd gone and blown it.

He couldn't shake the image of her tearstained face, the pain in her eyes when he'd broken her trust. He'd done that. He'd thought he was doing right by her, and instead he'd caused her pain.

"What if I hurt her?"

Again. What if he hurt her again? The question came out gruff and low, but Kit heard it, and he...laughed.

"Then you un-hurt her, man." Kit slapped a hand on his back. "You make it right, and you do better."

Nash turned to his friend. "What if, for her, it really was all fake?"

Kit arched his brows. "Then you make it real."

"She has a life in Chicago," Nash said.

"Then offer her one here."

Nash scrubbed a hand over his face. "Are you going to counter everything I say?"

"If you keep on saying stupid stuff, I will." Kit snickered. "I could do this all night, man."

Nash gave a grunt of acknowledgement. He was being stubborn. Finding excuses not to talk to her, not to spill his guts. Because the moment he did, it would be out there.

And he could get hurt.

He shut his eyes tight with a groan. He was being a coward. He didn't want to hurt her any more than he already had—and he was terrified that she'd break his heart in turn.

Kit's tone turned serious. "Nash, you're my best friend and I want you to be happy."

"Thanks," Nash muttered.

But Kit wasn't done. "So get your moping butt out of this church hall and go get your woman."

Nash looked over in surprise.

Kit nodded toward the door. "Life's too short for any other option."

There was a sadness in Kit's smile that made Nash's heart hurt. His best friend had lost so much and in spite of his skepticism, Nash knew Kit missed being in love.

Because love was a gift.

And you didn't just turn your back on it because you were scared.

Nash couldn't do anything but nod at his best friend, adrenaline pumping through his veins. Life was too short to waste another minute without Emma. And time was ticking before her flight. He couldn't afford to waste a second being scared of what ifs, not when she was here now.

Not when he still had a chance to make her see just how much she meant to him. "You're right, Kit."

"Of course I'm right," Kit called out from behind him

as he weaved his way through the dancing to reach his sister. He made an excuse and kissed her cheek. She was glowing with happiness as she winked and told him to go get his girl.

Again.

This time he'd find Emma and he wouldn't let her go until she knew exactly how he felt.

E mma had fallen asleep.

Her eyes puffy from crying, she woke up as light began to seep into the living room. She sat up quickly, her mind racing to make sense of the fact that, while still stretched out on the living room couch, she'd been covered with a blanket and had her bedroom pillow laid beneath her head.

The smell of coffee had her waking up even further and she blinked at the room around her, her gaze falling to the coffee table.

It was covered in flowers. Beautiful, colorful, wild flowers.

Her lips parted and her heart started racing as she reached for the card resting on the pile of blooms.

Emma was printed neatly on the outside, and her heart started to pound when she flicked it open and read:

Good morning, Beautiful. Coffee's ready, fresh donuts from the bakery are on the counter, and I am ready and waiting to have that talk whenever you are.

   — Nash

She blinked once. Twice. Was he serious? The alluring scent of coffee told her this was very real. Nash was awake and waiting for her.

She ran a hand over her face, moaning softly at how she must look after crying herself to sleep. Nerves held her hostage for a moment. What did he want to say? What did *she* want to say?

A small part of her contemplated lying back down and throwing the covers over her head.

But wild flowers and sweet notes.

Her heart wouldn't let her do anything but throw aside the cover and burst into motion, splashing water on her face and tying her hair up to keep the tangled mess out of her face. She didn't bother changing out of the wrinkled dress she'd slept in.

She couldn't believe she'd fallen asleep. And now he expected her to have *the talk*, and she was no closer to knowing what she wanted to say than she had been when she'd fled the reception last night. She'd fallen asleep before making any real decisions about anything.

But she was keenly aware that Nash was waiting for her, so she didn't let herself stop to think. She grabbed a coffee, and in spite of the fact her stomach was growling with hunger, she left the donut, figuring she was too nervous to eat. With her fingers wrapped around the hot mug, she sought him out.

She knew where he'd be. The back porch overlooking the range had become their place. It was where they'd spent a few relaxing evenings, and where they'd shared several meals together.

Sure enough…

Her heart skipped a beat at the sight of him leaning back against the low railing that surrounded the porch. He was sipping a coffee, and while she was certain he heard her, he didn't turn around right away. She had a moment to take stock, and she realized with a start that he was still wearing his formal clothes from the night before too. The shirt was unbuttoned at the collar and he'd ditched his fancy shoes, but there was no mistaking the groomsmen outfit.

Which meant…what?

Confusion and hope now warred with trepidation as she walked over to him.

"Morning," she murmured when she reached his side.

He turned, and the look on his face left her breathless. There was more emotion in his gaze than she could even begin to name. "Morning, beautiful."

Heat crept into her cheeks. She'd seen her reflection in the bathroom mirror. She was hardly looking her best, and yet his gaze made her feel like she was gorgeous…to him, at least.

She cleared her throat. "Sorry I left the reception early. Well, before it even really started."

"I understand." His gaze moved over her. "Are you feeling better?"

She looked out across the beautiful land, watching as a hawk swooped low.

Was she feeling better?

She answered honestly. "I'm not sure." Blinking rapidly, she forced a smile. "How was the rest of the night?"

He tilted his head to the side. "Casey and Ryan had the time of their lives, so it was a success, I'd say."

Her smile felt more genuine hearing that. "I'm glad. Were you…" She eyed his attire. "Were you up all night?"

His mouth hitched up on one side in a rueful grin. "I left early to talk to you, but you were asleep when I got here. I didn't want to wake you."

Her heart clenched in her chest at the tenderness in his gaze. "And you didn't go to bed yourself?"

He shrugged. "I couldn't sleep."

He'd been waiting. For her. For *hours*. And all so he could say whatever it was he wanted to say.

She tried to keep her emotions in check but her heart was already racing with fear and hope. She took a deep breath. "You said you needed to talk to me?"

He nodded, turning to face her and setting down his coffee on the rail before doing the same with hers. "I wanted to ask you a couple questions."

She smoothed her clammy palms over her wrinkled dress. Her heart felt like it was trying to escape from her chest. "Okay."

His gaze fixed on her with such piercing intensity, she couldn't move if she wanted to. His voice was gentle, but firm. "You have to promise you'll be honest. You're not allowed to say you're fine. I don't want you to spare anyone's feelings or worry about anyone but yourself. I just want the truth, plain and simple."

Fear shot through her at that. Her mouth went dry but she gave a firm nod. Honesty she could do. That was what she wanted between them, even if it ended in heartache.

He rested a hand on the railing beside them and his Adam's apple bobbed as he swallowed. "Emma, do you want to go back to Chicago?"

Her mind went blank. Staring into his deep blue eyes, so gorgeous, so earnest and sincere, her mind refused to work.

She answered slowly. "I should."

His brows came down in that stern expression she knew so well. "But do you *want* to?"

She swallowed, her heart thudding so hard it was a wonder it hadn't scared off the birds in the tree overhead. She couldn't think when he looked at her like this, but she could *feel*. Her heart was working overtime even if her mind refused to function.

She tore her gaze away from his, taking in the land that spread so far and wide it made her feel free and untethered. This place made her soul want to sprout wings and soar. Here, staring out at this view, the world and her future seemed limitless and ripe with possibility.

The image of her coming home to this house every night, sitting to eat dinner beside Nash, waking up in the morning and sharing breakfast together before she left for work. She pictured a classroom filled with sweet country kids like Corbin and Chloe, family barbecues on the weekends and heart-warming festivals.

Sweet country kids.

Hadn't Principal Toulouse practically offered her a job? She could take it. She could honestly have a life here.

Emma loved her family and the benefits of being in a city, but she'd never felt such a sense of belonging than she did when she was here on this land or when she was part of the community in town.

Her heart pounded even harder as questions started to brew in the back of her mind. But what about Nash? What would that mean for them? For her sisters? For his father?

"Emma?" His low voice wrapped around her,

reminding her to stick to their agreement and be one hundred percent honest.

Did she want to go back to Chicago?

The answer was clear. She turned back to him with a sigh. "No. I don't want to go back. I like it here. Very much."

A muscle worked in his jaw, and his nostrils flared like he was battling emotions, but his voice was even when he said, "You know you don't have to sell then."

"No, I don't." She winced. "Although I'm not sure how my sisters will feel about that."

She couldn't even bring herself to think of Lizzy's reaction if she chose to stay. But then there was Dahlia who was so eager to sell, not to mention the others and their individual concerns and desires.

The thought of all six of them weighed on her.

"It's not like they're going without," Nash said. "The ranch makes enough of a profit that they'll get their share."

"Only a supplement," she said. "That's what the lawyer said. They'll make more if we sell."

"This ranch makes good money every year," he insisted. "And it could make more with the right management and more involved owners to make the necessary upgrades."

The confidence in his tone made her wonder. Those questions were back in full force, because...

What would her staying mean for him? For his family?

If this land had so much earning potential then urging her not to sell wasn't in his family's best interests. So...

What did that mean? Her pulse was loud in her ears. She had no idea, and was afraid to guess. Terrified to get her hopes up.

"If you want to keep it, you should," Nash continued. "Your father wanted every one of his daughters to agree before selling and I don't think any of your sisters have a right to sign until they've actually been here and seen this place for themselves. That's what you should be fighting for, Em."

Em. Her lips twitched with a small smile. She liked the way he'd shortened her name. Normally only Lizzy and her parents did that. There was a familiarity about it that made her heart warm.

"You could stay here." His gaze fixed on her again, and she felt a shift in him. A new intensity that made her light-headed with expectation. "You could stay and you could take that job at the elementary school."

Her breath caught as those idyllic images raced through her mind again.

Nash reached out for her, trailing a hand down her arm before lightly playing with her fingers. He gave her a small, rueful smile. "You could date yourself a cowboy."

"A cowboy." She could barely breathe as she dropped her gaze to watch his strong fingers softly run over hers. "And who would I be dating?"

"Me, of course." His lips curved up in a crooked smile that made her heart melt.

She shook her head, pulling back her hand. Her heart was aching. One blow and it would break. Fear and hope were torturing her. She wanted to believe he meant it, but she was so scared of being wrong...again.

"Nash, I'm not doing any more of this fake dating thing. My heart can't take it. Besides, I deserve the real deal."

His voice was a low growl. "My heart can't take it either."

She froze, her mind racing to decipher that as emotions ricocheted in her chest like a pinball.

"My turn to be honest." He swallowed visibly before taking her hand in his again, this time squeezing firmly. With his other hand, he touched her cheek—lightly, like she was some fragile treasure. "Truth is, I liked you from the start, I was just too shy or scared to make it something real. But it *was* real."

It was real. The words had her chest expanding to where she thought she might explode.

"This whole time," he continued. "I didn't think I wanted a wife, a family, any of that stuff. The ranch, what I do here, it's always been enough for me. But now..." He shook his head and the open emotion, the vulnerability there had her reeling.

She squeezed his hand, moving forward to press her other hand to his heart. "Now?" she prompted, her voice breathy and high with anticipation.

"Now I just want to be yours, Em. Plain and simple."

Joy burst inside of her like starlight. A smile spread over her face even as tears stung her eyes. "Do you mean it? Do you really mean it?"

He tugged on her hand, pulling her even closer until her body pressed against his and she could feel the rumble of his low voice when he answered. "I've never been more serious in my life."

A breathy laugh punched out of her and she lost the battle with tears as she gazed up at this man who'd so quickly become the center of her world.

He stroked a thumb over her cheek, wiping away her tears. "If you'll have me, Em, I will love you and look after you." He stilled, his brows drawing down as he leaned in with a new urgency. "I need you to know, this land doesn't ever have to belong to a Donahue. I don't want your land. I just want you."

Her lips had parted and she wasn't sure she could speak through all the emotions that were filling her heart and flooding her veins. Her mind had caught on one word in that gorgeous speech of his.

"You love me?" she whispered.

He arched a brow in an adorably uncertain expression. "Is it too soon to say that?"

A laugh bubbled up inside her—sheer happiness that couldn't be contained. "Not if you mean it."

He smiled. "I do. I'm falling in love with you. You make it impossible not to."

Her grin widened at the sincerity in his tone, at the sure and confident way he said it—like a promise.

Like a vow.

She didn't have to think. Her heart was speaking loud and clear. "I'm falling in love with you, too."

He drew in a relieved breath, his chest expanding and his eyes dancing with happiness like she's just made his year. "Hey, Em?"

"Yes?"

He leaned down so close she could feel his breath against her cheek. "I'd really like to kiss you now."

She let out a breathy giggle as she launched herself up onto tiptoes so she could press her lips to his. He groaned, his arms wrapping around her waist and lifting her off her feet as he kissed her with a passion that stole her breath.

And in the moment, as their lips danced to their own melody and made the rest of the world fade away, she knew without a doubt that this was it. This was her home.

Here at this ranch. Here in Aspire.

Here...with Nash.

35

W as it possible to die of happiness?

Nash was starting to suspect it might be. He couldn't stop grinning, which was strange enough. But this feeling in his chest every time he caught sight of Emma was making him wonder if he ought to see a cardiologist.

Nearly twelve hours had passed and his heart was still as full as it had been. Spotting Emma in the distance talking to Myrtle and the other pigs had it expanding within his ribcage all over again.

"You were a married man," Cody said to Kit as they worked in the stables behind Nash. "How long before he loses that goofy grin?"

Kit laughed. "Don't ask me, bro. You know my deal with Natalie was..." He huffed and shook his head. "Ask JJ."

"I don't think so. My marriage lasted all of five seconds. I know even less about love than Kit does." JJ's low voice came from the back doorway.

Nash hadn't even heard him show up. Not a surprise.

To say he'd been distracted ever since he and Emma had officially become a couple was the understatement of the century.

Normally, talk of marriage would have put him on edge, but right now it only made his goofy smile broaden. "You guys do know I haven't proposed to Emma yet, right?"

"Yet!" Kit shouted the word with triumph as if he'd personally gotten the two of them together. He stabbed a finger in JJ's direction. "Told you he's already thinking marriage."

"Good. Although, take your time." JJ cringed when Nash whirled around to study him. "I met and married in less than six weeks. I was signing divorce papers ten months later." He clicked his tongue and looked to the dirt. "Look, I think Emma is an amazing fit for you, I just…" He shrugged.

"Emma is the best," Cody agreed.

Nash grinned, grateful for the support.

"Don't listen to me." JJ waved his hand through the air. "You know your heart."

"No, I appreciate where you're coming from, man. Thanks for caring enough to be honest."

JJ grinned. "Not to get all sappy on ya, but I love you, man. I just want you to be happy."

"Thanks." Nash nodded, knowing how much the sentiment would have cost a mountain man like JJ.

"And besides, I need time to organize my date and take that pretty lady out. Can't be doing that when she's got a ring on her finger now, can I?" JJ winked, but Nash still felt his insides rumble in protest.

Pointing a finger at his worker, he gave him a silent *don't you dare.*

JJ laughed and wiggled his eyebrows. "She won that auction fair and square."

"She'll be giving that prize to some other lucky lady."

JJ shook his head. "Only if she wants to."

Kit and Cody had joined in on the laughter and Nash spun away from them, glancing back up to the house and noting Emma's blonde hair blowing in the wind. "Hey, do you guys mind if I cut out early—"

"Go." JJ was already shooing him out the door.

"It's just, we've got that send-off dinner for Casey tonight—"

"Get out of here," Kit called. "Take the whole week off to celebrate with your girl."

"We've got it handled around here," Cody said.

Nash tipped his hat, already backpedaling toward the house. It had only been a couple hours since they'd had lunch together, but he was dying to see her again. And hold her, and kiss her, and hear her laugh...

Oh yeah, he was definitely a goner. And he couldn't wait to let the world know. He caught up with her at the fence where she was talking to the pigs, wrapping his arms around her waist and nuzzling her neck.

"What does Myrtle have to say about you staying?" he teased.

She laughed. "She had her reservations at first. But once I promised to keep the food coming, she came around."

"And the others?"

"Oh, they're all for it," she said quickly.

He laughed. "Good. I'm glad we're all in agreement."

She twisted to face him, wrapping her arms around his neck. "So, dinner tonight..."

"If you don't want to go—"

"Oh no, I do. I want to see Casey and Ryan before they leave on their honeymoon. And I barely got a chance to talk to your cousins from out of town. It'll be nice to meet them now, knowing it's not all a sham."

He nodded, dropping a kiss on her nose. "If it's all right with you, I was kinda hoping to come clean."

She grinned. "Me and my conscience would love that."

He grabbed one of her hands and twined their fingers together. "I'd like to tell them you're staying, too. But I know you still have a lot to work through so—"

"Tell them." Her confidence as she said it had joy flooding through him.

"Yeah?"

She nodded. With a sigh, she squeezed his hand. "I told Mom and Dad about an hour ago. They're surprised, of course, but they understand where I'm coming from and really want me to be happy. They want to meet you, too." She shot him a nervous grin that made his insides jitter.

"Want to meet the man who's stealing their daughter away, huh?" He tried to make light of it, but the joke came off a little lame.

Her nose wrinkled. "Think we could arrange a little Zoom call sometime soon?"

"For you? Anything." He kissed her smile, then pulled back, sad to see it fading so quickly.

"To be honest, they sounded kind of...off. I'm not sure what's going on, but maybe they're more upset about my move here than they wanted to let on." She bit her lip and frowned. "I kind of chickened out and wrapped up the call. Maybe they just need time to process my unexpected news, you know? They promised not to say anything to Lizzy. I still haven't been able to get a hold of her, but I sent her a text to let her know I won't be coming back on Tuesday." She winced. "I told her I'd explain why I'm staying when she calls me back."

He saw the worry in the tightness around her eyes and reached a hand up to smooth her furrowed brow. If he could, he would handle all of Emma's problems for her, but she'd never allow that. "She'll call. And when she does, she'll understand."

Emma smiled. "You sound awfully certain of that."

He squeezed her hand. "She loves you and wants you to be happy."

"You're right." Emma nodded.

"What about the rest of your sisters?"

She heaved a sigh. "I haven't told them yet that I've changed my mind. But the way I figure it, I've got time." Her expression turned stubborn. "If they couldn't be bothered to help sort out this inheritance, then they can't second guess any of my decisions."

Pride had him grinning down at her again. "Good for you, sweetheart."

He loved the pink blush that spread across her cheeks whenever he called her *sweetheart*.

Glancing back up at him, she grinned. "It's time I focus on what I want. And if they don't want the same thing, then we'll just have to come up with a compromise." She nodded. "And I think you're right that they shouldn't be able to sign anything until they've been here to see the place in person. They owe it to themselves and to Frank's legacy."

He squeezed her hand in agreement and together they walked back toward the house to get ready for dinner. It wasn't until they were in the truck and heading to his parents' house that she surprised him with the fact that she'd already called the elementary school principal to arrange an interview.

"You'll get it. Abigail's only making you interview to follow the process. I bet she'll offer you the job before you even leave her office."

"It's funny," she said as they walked into the Donahue's house hand in hand. "It's like the whole time I've been here, little things have been calling to me. This place owned my heart before I even got here. It's just been waiting for me to show up."

He wrapped an arm around her waist and dropped a kiss on top of her head. "I'm sure glad you did." He smiled down at her. "The moment I let myself admit that I was head over heels in love with you, what I had to do next was obvious."

"So it's fate, then," she said.

Fate. He let the word roll around in his head as they walked into the crazy chaos that was the entire extended Donahue clan.

A few weeks ago he might have laughed at the idea of fate, but watching Emma be embraced by his family—watching them light up with joy when she announced that she was staying here in Aspire and that they were now a true committed couple—it was hard not to feel like this moment was meant to be.

Nash stood on the sidelines as Emma was rushed by his mother and sister and a bunch of other overjoyed family members who wanted to pester her with questions about their relationship.

He heard his mother ask her when she knew it was true love and just barely held back a groan.

He supposed he should be glad he wasn't the one in the hot seat.

"So, Emma is staying then, huh?" His dad was at his side, watching the emotional lovefest right alongside him.

Nash stiffened. This was the only conversation he'd been dreading tonight, but he wasn't about to put it off any longer. He turned to face his father with a scowl—

"Now, now." Patrick held up a hand to stop him. "Before you start in on how wrong I was, I want..." He cleared his throat. "I need to apologize."

Nash's eyes widened in surprise.

His father looked away with a huff. "I had to confess all to your mother this morning and got myself an earful. She was so ashamed of me, just the way you were." He shook his head, looking uncharacteristically abashed. "I'm not proud of the conclusions I jumped to, and quite honestly, the fact that I suspected you would do such a thing...the fact that I would approve of it..." He winced. "Well, it got me thinking about my priorities and how far I've gone off track. I just get so focused and I..." He cut his hand through the air and winced again.

"Dad—"

"No, son." Patrick shook his head. "I don't need anyone making excuses for me. I've gotten too obsessed with my ambitions, and I'm not proud of that. I plan on apologizing to Emma tonight, just as soon as I can get her away from her fan club."

Nash chuckled at the appropriate term for the crowd surrounding her.

"But I owe you an apology, too." Patrick stuck a hand out. "I'm sorry, son. You've always made me proud, and the way you protected Emma and have kept her best interests in mind rather than your own..." His father cleared his throat. "Well, you made me proud."

Nash felt a tightness in his own throat and looked

away to take a deep breath. "Thanks, Dad. That means a lot."

"Now…" Patrick's tone lightened. "Let's talk about all the ways we can help Miss O'Sullivan get that ranch as productive and profitable as possible." His father smiled. "For her, and for her sisters."

Nash nodded. "I'd appreciate the help, Dad."

"And then, when we're done with that…" His father's voice was light with mischief. "Then we'll talk about just how soon I can expect a grandbaby—"

"Dad," he groaned. "I met her less than two weeks ago."

"When you know, you know." His father laughed, catching his wife's eye and giving her a smile that was reserved just for his lady love.

Nash watched the exchange and knew in his heart that Emma and him had something similar.

He did know, and he couldn't deny it.

The thought of marrying Emma didn't scare him in the least. He watched his gorgeous girlfriend light up with laughter at something his sister said, and he knew.

One day, this woman would be his wife. She'd be his wife, his partner, his best friend, and—God willing—the mother of his children.

And nothing had ever sounded so right.

36

E mma was still pinching herself the next day.

She woke up late, but this time she wasn't over-tired from a lack of sleep or a night fitfully dozing on the couch. Nope. She'd just stayed up way too late with her boyfriend discussing her future here in Aspire.

Her boyfriend.

She grinned at her reflection in the mirror as she brushed her teeth.

Boyfriend. She let herself revel in the word. She wasn't sure she'd ever get used to it. Well, she probably would eventually, since they were already making long-term plans together.

She dropped the hand holding her toothbrush with a sappy sigh.

But even if she got used to having Nash as her partner, she hoped she never took this for granted. Finding love with such a kind, thoughtful, steadfast man felt like winning the lottery after so many crushes on guys who took her for granted.

She rushed out of the bedroom, eager to see him again,

although she was sure he'd been up and working for hours already.

Sure enough, she found a new bouquet of fresh wild-flowers on the kitchen table. She grinned and rushed forward at the glimpse of another note.

Sorry I kept you up so late. Is it crazy that I miss you already? So happy you're here and not on your way to the airport. I love you, sweetheart.

Emma clutched the note to her chest, her heart so full she thought she might burst. She'd found herself a cowboy who left her love notes and flowers. A laugh escaped as she realized she was actually grateful to every guy who hadn't returned her feelings or who had taken her for granted, because if that hadn't happened she might not have met Nash.

The Lord knew best. He always had a way of making good shine out of the dark times.

If Frank hadn't passed away and left his daughters this place, Emma may never have found her true home.

The thought of her decision to stay and Nash's mention of her flight were the only thoughts that could mar her morning, and she found herself stewing over the fact that Lizzy still hadn't returned her messages or her texts about not flying back to Chicago.

Either Lizzy had fallen into the same communication hole as Sierra and April or she was giving Emma the silent treatment for not coming back when she'd promised she would.

Nerves scurried through her and she got busy making

breakfast to try and distract herself, or maybe fortify herself for the call ahead. One way or another, she was speaking to her sister today.

"Morning, beautiful." Nash's voice gave her a start and she spun around just in time to be snatched up in her new boyfriend's arms.

"Morning," she said, her lips still pressed to his in a lingering kiss that had more sizzle than the bacon frying on the stove. She nodded toward the pan. "I hope you're hungry because I'm making breakfast for two."

"Sounds great to me," he said, all smiles as he opened the bread box and pulled out a few slices to toast.

He'd been smiling a lot these past two days, a fact that Emma loved. She'd been grinning a ton too, but she was a naturally smiley person. To see Nash so unabashedly happy made her insides light up with joy.

"You still feeling good about your decision this morning?" Nash asked as they loaded their plates with bacon and eggs, then took them out to sit in the sunshine.

"Of course," she said quickly.

Maybe a little too quickly because Nash arched his brows in a silent question.

She rolled her eyes. He couldn't possibly doubt that she was happy about staying—they'd spent hours laughing and talking and dreaming up all the new adventures she'd have this summer in Aspire.

"I'm not having second thoughts," she said, because clearly he needed to hear it. "It's just..." She sighed. "I'm not looking forward to telling Lizzy about my new plan. I need to give notice to my school, too, and that's leaving me feeling bittersweet."

He nodded, reaching across the table to squeeze her hand. "I know there's a lot going into this. It's only natural that there will be some drawbacks to moving. If you have second thoughts, I hope you know you can talk to me about them."

She smiled. "I know. And it's definitely not second thoughts." She set down her fork as she took a deep breath, trying to find the words to explain. "I woke up feeling completely at peace with my decision, and so excited for my future—" Her cheeks warmed and she shot him a shy smile. "Our future."

She was rewarded with a grin that made her knees weak.

"But," she added slowly. "I don't love the idea of disappointing people I care about."

"That's understandable." He tucked into his breakfast, taking a mammoth forkful.

She hitched her lips to the side as she buttered her toast and thought about the calls to come. "But at the same time," she finally continued. "I can't keep living my life for other people. I have to pursue my own dreams, and build a life I want."

He leaned forward, his hand covering hers again. "Have I mentioned how honored I am that you're choosing to build that life with me?"

She laughed, flipping her hand over to hold his. "Once or twice," she teased. Truthfully, he'd made at least a dozen comments to that effect.

"I suppose I can't put this off much longer," she said when they were clearing their plates. "I'd better call Lizzy again, see if I can get a hold of her."

JJ walked in through the mudroom. "Hey, you guys know who's pulling up out front? I don't recognize the car."

Which was strange for Aspire, Emma knew that much.

Nash frowned. "Maybe it's the lawyer coming to check on your progress with the signatures," he offered.

"Maybe." Emma wasn't convinced though. She'd been emailing with Mr. Billman regularly to keep him updated. She'd even emailed him the day before to see if there was something he could do to try and get April to return her messages. She'd hoped maybe if he acted as a go between, the youngest O'Sullivan sister might be more likely to talk.

JJ rested a hand on his hip. "I was thinking of taking Marlon out to the northern paddocks. I didn't get a chance to check the fenceline last week, unless there's something else you'd like me to do? Or a different horse you'd like me to take?" JJ asked Nash.

"Yeah, take Marlon, he needs the exercise." Nash pointed to JJ's belt. "You didn't have to walk all the way up to the house, you should have just radioed to ask."

"I did. Someone wasn't answering their radio." JJ grinned.

Nash gave a guilty swallow and looked behind him. The radio sat unattended next to the toaster.

JJ chuckled and headed for the door. "I'll catch you lovebirds later. Emma, still looking forward to our date sometime."

"Keep dreaming," Nash growled, following him to make sure he left the homestead.

Emma walked away with a giggle, heading for the window by the front door. She pulled back the curtain just in time to see a car stop by the front steps and the back door fly open.

The first thing Emma noticed were the expensive sandals stepping out of the vehicle. The shine on those straps would last all of two seconds with the summer dust swirling over everything.

And then her sister's face appeared, pale and overwhelmed, looking around like she'd just stepped onto a different planet.

"Lizzy!" Emma gasped so loudly, Nash came running.

"What's wrong?"

Emma was already throwing open the door as a stranger—a taxi driver she assumed—opened the trunk and pulled out Lizzy's luggage. Her sister had frozen for a moment, staring at Emma with wide eyes before bursting into tears.

"Lizzy? What's the matter? What are you doing here?"

She'd barely gotten the words out before Lizzy was tackling her in a hug, noisy sobs wracking her taller frame.

"Em?" Nash's voice was wary behind her. "Is everything okay?"

She awkwardly turned to glance at him with wide eyes as if to say 'I have no idea.'

Lizzy lifted her head, her wide eyes huge. Tears always made her green eyes so vibrant. "Who's this?"

"Um, Lizzy this is Nash." Emma gestured to Nash. "Nash, this is my sister Lizzy."

Lizzy stared. "This is him? The guy? The fake one?"

Emma shook her head. This was so not how she planned on telling her sister about her and Nash's new relationship. "Uh, yeah, I need to update you on that."

Lizzy's chin bunched, her mouth forming a wonky line as new tears descended.

"Lizzy, sweetie, you're scaring me. What are you doing here? What's wrong?"

"Oh Emmy," she sobbed, covering her mouth and muffling her words. "My life is over."

Emma held her close, aware of Nash as he moved

behind her, placing a hand on her shoulder in support. "What is? What happened?"

"The wedding is off," Lizzy wailed. "It's over! It's totally over."

Emma's jaw dropped, and luckily Nash had a lot of experience as a big brother because he instantly stepped into the role. He gently wrapped an arm around Lizzy and led her inside, his voice low and soothing as he told her it would all be okay, that she should make herself comfortable…

It was all the things Emma should have been saying, but she was too shocked.

It was over?

She didn't understand.

By the time she found her voice, Nash had Lizzy settled on the couch with a glass of water, a box of tissues and a bowl of chocolates that she wondered where on earth he'd been hiding.

"I'll go pay the driver and make some tea," he said as he left them on their own.

Lizzy snatched a tissue out of the box and dabbed her face, before delicately blowing her nose. Emma sat on the coffee table, worry eating her alive as she tried to wrap her head around this heartbreaking news.

"So that's him, huh?" Lizzy sounded drained and dazed. She glanced at Emma. "He seems nice."

"He is nice." Emma smiled. "But I want to hear about you. What's happened? Why is the wedding off?"

Lizzy sighed and rubbed her forehead with quivering fingers.

Emma blinked, her lips parting when she noticed the serious lack of ridiculously large diamond on Lizzy's ring finger.

Wow. This wasn't just some drama queen moment. The wedding was seriously off if Lizzy wasn't even wearing her engagement ring anymore.

She was about to ask where it was, but Lizzy started muttering, "I'm not ready to talk about it. I just...I couldn't stay there, you know? Sarah was at her boyfriend's and you'd sent that message saying you were staying here for a little while longer and...." Lizzy's eyes welled up again. "I... I... I just had to get away," she squeaked, her words falling apart as a fresh wave of tears took her out.

"Aw, sweetie." Emma rubbed her arms, up and down, just the way Mom did when they were upset.

Nash walked quietly into the room, placing down a steaming cup of tea.

Emma gave him a grateful smile and he replied with a worried frown before easing back out of the room.

"I'm glad you came here," Emma said quickly. "This is your home too, you know."

Lizzy sniffed, and Emma bit her lip to keep from spilling all her news, including the fact that she was planning on staying for good. There'd be time enough for all that after Lizzy calmed down.

"Nash made you some tea." Emma picked up the cup and held it out to her sister.

Lizzy just stared at the steam, like she didn't know how to drink tea anymore.

"Okay. You don't want it? That's okay. Um, what can I do to make you feel better?"

"I don't know," Lizzy blubbered. "I don't know anything anymore."

Emma's insides writhed with confusion. She was desperate to find out what went down in Chicago. How could Lizzy go from happily planning her wedding to sitting on this couch in tears?

As much as she wanted to pepper her sister with questions, she knew now was not the time.

"How about I go get a room ready for you, okay?" Emma said, brushing a hand over Lizzy's blonde hair which had always been so much smoother and more manageable than hers. "For now, why don't you lie down in my room, hmm?"

Lizzy nodded with another sniff, tears streaming down her cheeks.

Lizzy's whole life had always been smoother than hers. Everything had seemed to come so easily, which meant any life crisis felt monumentally bigger. This break up must be killing her.

She wasn't used to disappointment, let alone heartbreak.

When Lizzy was settled in Emma's room, half asleep the moment her head hit the pillow, Emma went back to the kitchen to find Nash waiting for her with a concerned frown. "Is she all right?"

"She will be," Emma said with more confidence than she felt. "At least, I hope she will be. She's never faced anything this big before, but she's strong, you know? She can bounce back. I just wish I knew what happened."

Nash reached out and pulled her into his arms, holding her so close she could hear the steady beat of his heart. "Let me know what I can do to help."

She nodded. "Thanks. I didn't tell her about us yet. Or...this." She made a broad sweeping gesture to encompass the house and the whole town.

"There's time," he said as he dropped a kiss on top of her head. "We have all the time in the world."

The words wrapped around her and made her smile. "For now, I just want her to know she has a home here. This place is hers too, obviously. It's all of ours."

She heard his murmured assent, a low rumble through his chest.

"We'll take care of her. Together." With a low laugh he added, "Heck, she'll have half the town wanting to set her up with bachelors and the other half force feeding her chicken soup if word spreads that everyone's favorite kindergarten teacher has a sister in need."

Emma laughed at the image. "That right there is why I love this town." She smiled as she remembered one of the first things he'd said to her about this place. "Neighbors helping neighbors."

He rubbed her back and kissed her head one more time.

"Thanks for being so great with her before," Emma said. "I appreciate that, and I'm sure Lizzy did too."

"What are big brothers for?" he teased. "She might not know it yet, but she's my family, just like you are."

"I'm your family, huh?" she said with a laugh as she tipped her head back to look at him.

"Oh sweetheart, you're not just my family." He took one of her hands in his and held it over his heart. "You're my heart. You're my home…" He kissed her lightly on the lips. "And you are the love of my life."

EPILOGUE

The night sky was vast and expansive, not a cloud in sight, allowing the moon to soak the land with its pale glow. Stars twinkled above them and Nash gazed up with a contented smile.

He didn't think he'd ever felt this at peace, sitting on a wooden lounger, which he'd dragged onto the lawn at Emma's request.

"Let's sit out under the stars. I know it's late, but I don't care. I'm just not ready to say goodnight to you yet."

He wasn't about to argue with that. Yeah, he'd feel it when he had to get up at the crack of dawn tomorrow, but Emma wanted snuggle time. It'd be the perfect way to end a busy day.

He'd settled down on it and Emma had climbed between his legs, nestling her back against his chest so he could wrap his arms around her.

He lightly played with the ends of her hair, and his heart filled to overflowing when she let out a dreamy sigh.

"I could stay here all night," she said.

He chuckled, loving the romantic idea. Kissing the side

of her head, he leaned his cheek against hers and softly asked, "How was your day? I didn't get to hear the rest of it? Did the interview go well?"

Emma swiveled her head to grin up at him. Her smooth skin glowed in the moonlight and all he could see was an angel.

"It went really well. Abigail offered me the job on the spot. Just like you said she would."

Nash's heart trilled. "And you accepted?"

"Of course," she said. "Easiest decision in the world. You are now snuggling with Aspire Elementary School's new kindergarten teacher."

His chest rumbled with a laugh. "Well, Aspire is one blessed town, then."

Emma kissed the tip of his chin. "You always say the sweetest things."

"You make it easy to."

She lifted her arm and brushed her fingers along his neck. "I'll head back to Chicago in a couple weeks to pack up all my stuff."

He couldn't help a small frown, hating the idea of her leaving, even just for a couple days. "Do you want me to come with you?"

"I'd love that, but I need you here to keep an eye on Lizzy. I doubt she'll come with me. Even though she probably should, I'm pretty sure she's set on hibernating in that room for the unforeseeable future."

Nash frowned. It'd been over a week since she'd arrived and other than the first day, she'd been locked up in her room, flipping through fashion magazines and crying into endless cups of peach iced-tea.

It was really worrying Emma and her parents.

"I understand it, after what she's been through," Nash murmured, trying to make his girlfriend feel better.

"She can't stay in there forever." Emma shook her head.

"I know, but she'll surface when she's ready. Broken hearts take time to heal. I saw it with Kit. When Natalie first left he stopped functioning for a while. If it wasn't for the twins, he would have shut down completely. He was devastated."

"Poor man."

"He got there. Look at him now."

Emma laughed. "The best flirt in town."

Nash chuckled and squeezed her close, relieved she hadn't fallen for the charms of Kit Swanson. Many women had, but not his Emma.

Thank you, Lord.

A comfortable silence settled over them, interrupted only by the hoot of a great horned owl. Its haunting melody brought a familiar comfort to Nash and had his mind wandering from the past to the future.

Camping out in the backyard with Kit, feeling like kings at the age of seven as they unearthed their smuggled candy and ate late into the night. Fresh images appeared in his mind at the thought of his own kids pitching a tent on the lawn, excitedly preparing for a night of what felt like total freedom.

His kids.

Emma's kids.

His heart beat with the thrill of what was to come and he picked up Emma's hand, running his thumb over the spot where an engagement ring would one day sit.

"What are you thinking, cowboy?" Emma's voice had a teasing lilt that made him smile.

"I'm picturing a diamond on this finger of yours." He lifted her hand to his lips and kissed her ring finger.

Emma let out a dreamy sigh. "I'm going to love that, but we can't while Lizzy is dealing with a broken engagement. That just seems cruel. Plus, we've only known each other such a short time."

"I know. And I've been warned not to rush into something." JJ's words whistled over him. "Our relationship is still so new and fresh, but Em, I know. I know you're meant to be mine forever. You're the first woman I've ever met that hasn't made me want to run for the hills over the idea of marriage."

Emma giggled, and he absorbed the sweet sound like he was tasting chocolate for the first time. He'd never tire of her.

"I was a fool to ever try and fake anything with you. I was just scared, I guess, and I didn't want to tie you here when your life was in Chicago. I thought that was what you wanted, and I didn't want to stand in your way."

"Thank you," Emma whispered.

"For what? Being a fool?"

"No." Her laughter was breathy as she shifted in his arms so she could gaze up at him in the moonlight. "Thank you for being everything I've ever wanted. Thank you for falling in love with me."

"You made it so easy."

Her lips curled with a smile that made his heart sing. She gently played with the collar of his shirt, resting her head against his shoulder. "All my life, I've always wanted to feel this way. To be loved and have someone... the right someone... love me in return. And now I've found you."

She looked up at him again and he cupped her cheek,

running his thumb over her smooth skin. "It was like God was saving us up for each other."

Emma's smile grew to that sunshine brilliance he adored so much. "I like that. I like that a lot."

She leaned in and he met her lips with a kiss that felt so familiar yet still held the excitement of a shiny new toy. He deepened it for a moment before pulling away and brushing the tip of his nose against hers.

"The timing may not be right just yet," he whispered. "But know this, Emma O'Sullivan, I'm going to ask you to marry me one day."

"And I'm going to say yes." Wrapping her hand around his neck, she pulled him down for another kiss.

The owl hooted from the nearby tree, like he was watching them and approved of the match. And he should.

Because Nash knew without a doubt in his mind that Emma was born to be his.

Thank you so much for reading PRETEND TO BE MY COWBOY!
I hope you've loved entering the world of Aspire and falling in love with Nash and Emma.

Find out what happens to the next O'Sullivan Sister, Lizzy, when she discovers her true purpose in the last place she expects to…
GUCCI GIRLS DON'T DATE COWBOYS is releasing February 14, 2022.

While you're waiting, you can sign up for my newsletter

to find out why Lizzy left Connor, and which cowboy is going to win her heart in an exclusive, bonus introduction to: *Gucci Girls Don't Date Cowboys.*

Please note: This is not a preview or teaser. This is bonus content that you will not be able to get anywhere else.

SIGN UP LINK:
https://www.
subscribepage.com/sophiaquinn_newsletter_exclusive

ACKNOWLEDGMENTS

Dear reader,

Thank you so much for reading my debut novel. It has been such a thrill to work on. I've fallen hard for the characters in Aspire and I can't wait to share more stories with you over the coming months.

If you enjoyed the book, I'd like to encourage you to leave a review on Amazon and/or Goodreads. Reviews and ratings help to validate the book. They also assist other readers in making a choice over whether to purchase or not. You honest review is a huge help to everyone.

And speaking of help, no book is complete without a team of people, so I'd like to thank Deborah for a cover that ticked all the boxes, Maggie for her words that brought the book to life, Melissa for her vision and editing skills, my eagle-eye proofreaders who caught those extra mistakes I'd missed and my amazing reviewers who have helped promote the book and left reviews that made my heart all warm and tingly.

Thank you for your support. Here's to many more sweet small town romance novels!

And just before I go, I can't write any book without acknowledging my ultimate inspiration. To my heavenly father, for fueling my dreams and inspiring me every day. I love you.

xo,
Sophia

ABOUT THE AUTHOR

Sophia Quinn is the pen-name of writing buddies Maggie Dallen and Melissa Pearl Guyan (Forever Love Publishing Ltd). Between them, they have been writing romance for 10 years and have published over 200 novels. They are having so much fun writing sweet small-town romance together and have a large collection of stories they are looking forward to producing. Get ready for idyllic small towns, characters you can fall in love with and romance that will capture your heart.

www.foreverlovepublishing.com/sophia-quinn/

26858996R00207